RITUAL

RITUAL

palm south university book 5

kandi steiner

Ritual picks up right where *Legacy* left off. As this book is
part of a series, you will need to read the other books
in the series before beginning this one:

Rush, PSU #1 (http://amzn.to/2vQcj7G)
Anchor, PSU #2 (http://amzn.to/2vLkDXN)
Pledge, PSU #3 (http://amzn.to/2vQ1m5R)
Legacy, PSU #4 (https://amzn.to/2yQDsML)

Welcome back to PSU... ;)
Tweet as you read using #PalmSouth and
join the Facebook discussion group here
(https://www.facebook.com/
groups/712042985606913/).

EPISODE 1

Jess

"FUCK OFF, KADE."

A laugh bubbles out of him, and I flick my right foot up to my ass long enough to snatch the heel off it and hold it up over my head in a threat to squash him like a bug.

Kade holds up his hands, eyes bulging out of his head. "Jess, come on," he says, but that motherfucker is still smirking. "Look, I've apologized. I've all but groveled at your feet, for Christ's sake. I *know* I was an asshole."

"It's not about you being an asshole," I seethe, still holding my weapon of choice ready to strike. "It's that you wasted my time."

"I'm an idiot."

"You act like that's news to me."

He softens, that stupid smirk still on his face as he takes a step closer to me. I cock an eyebrow in warning, holding the shoe up a little higher, but he reaches for it, gently lowering it until it's between us and no longer a threat.

"Look, I really am sorry," he says, more sincerely. "I asked for your help and then I blew you off. I can't help it, I'm a stupid boy."

I scoff.

"But I'm serious now. And I want another chance."

Inside me, there's a bear growling and tearing trees to shreds. On the outside, I'm cool as a cucumber. Kade is a junior who I met last semester when he rushed Alpha Sigma. He's close friends with Kip, Skyler's boyfriend, which made him part of our group pretty fast.

When I first met him, I was annoyed with everything he was.

The more he talked to me and flashed his corny pickup lines, the more that annoyance turned to something between curiosity and the urge to bang him.

And when he made a proposition that I should hang out with him this summer, teach him how to have better game and how to be better in bed, in exchange for getting to drive his car and have guaranteed sex anytime I wanted it? Well, I thought it was the most ridiculous idea I'd ever heard of.

And yet, I'd agreed — for no other reason than I was bored and needed a distraction from Jarrett and the heartbreak that was forever lingering in his absence.

It had seemed like a good idea.

Until this twat rag blew me off and made *me* look like the idiot.

"Well, good for you," I snap, tugging my heel back on and crossing my arms. "But I don't give second chances. Now, if you'll excuse me, I have a recruitment to run."

Before I can shut the door in his face, Kade blocks it with his hands.

And then, the motherfucker falls to his knees.

"Oh, *please*, Jess," he says, so loudly that his voice echoes off the walls in the Kappa Kappa Beta house foyer. "Please, give me another chance. There's nothing I want more than to rub your body down and learn your kinky ways."

My eyes bulge, and I kick my heel right into the middle of his chest until he tumbles backward onto the house porch. I slam the door shut behind us, fuming.

"There are *potential new members* in there, you asshat."

He's still flat on his back, holding up his hands in surrender.

And I hate myself a little, because in that moment, he looks a little like he did the first night I threw him down on his bed and rode him until he moaned my name.

"Get up," I said, pretending to be disgusted. "You look like a fool."

"Only a fool for you."

I roll my eyes, sighing with as much dramatic flare as I can manage when he's standing again. "Why should I give you another chance? This whole..." I wave my hand at him. "*Training* thing was your idea in the first place, and then you bail. What are you even looking for? What's the motive here?"

"I already told you," he says, stepping into me. "I know I flaked this summer. There was..." He swallows, looking down Greek Row as if it were a hall of ghosts. "I had some family stuff to handle, and I wasn't in my right state of mind. Okay?"

He looks like a puppy that's just been kicked, and I hate that I care.

"But I mean it this time. I have zero game, and I need your help. Plus," he says, smirking as he steps more into me. His hand creeps up my arm, tucking a strand of my hair behind one ear. "After our first round, you can't tell me you don't want more, too."

Heat snakes up my neck from where his fingers brush the sensitive skin, and my eyes flutter before I shove him back with two hands.

"I can get hot sex from anyone I want," I remind him.

"I know that."

"Then you also know that you're wasting your time."

"Jess," he says, seemingly exhausted now. "Come on. I'm sorry. I have now *literally* groveled at your feet." He swallows. "I need this."

I narrow my eyes, annoyance mixing with the ridiculous attraction I have for this kid and making me want to slap myself. When I first agreed to this *insane* proposition at our formal last semester, it was because I was in a dire state. I was still heartbroken over Jarrett, and — if I were being completely honest — I was fascinated by the thought of being in power over this young buck. I would be his teacher, his Dom, his sexual sensei.

Above all, he would be a distraction from Jarrett.

And after our first romp in the sack to gauge just what kind of lessons would be needed, I discovered that bulge I'd seen in his swim trunks at Spring Break was just the tip — and not of the iceberg.

But now, I was busy with recruitment. And when it was over, I'd be busy with my last semester of college. Plus, this little fucker had *played* me. It was all his idea, for me to help him with his game, teach him how to flirt and date and fuck like a pro — and then he'd bailed. After one round, he flaked.

Still, I can't deny the way my body is heated at the sight of his tattoos peeking out from under his tight t-shirt — tattoos that I know spread across his chest and abdomen and down the length of his muscular back. It should be illegal for a kid this young to be this ripped, but even if it was, I have a feeling Kade would break the law.

I appraise him, and before the words are out of my mouth, I wonder if I'm conceding because I want to, because I feel bad for him, or because I'm annoyed and need him off my porch so I can get back to recruiting the best damn rush class our sorority has ever seen.

"*Fine,*" I grit, but before Kade can thrust his fist all the way into the air, I wrap my hand around it and hold it firmly. "But you *will* follow through with your part of the deal this time."

He raises an eyebrow.

"The car," I remind him. "I want your keys. Now."

"I don't have them on me."

"Then I guess we're done here." I turn to head back inside, but Kade rounds me quickly, holding up his hands.

"Wait, wait, wait," he says, fishing his keys from his pocket. He holds them out to me with a cringe. "Please, don't wreck it."

I smile wickedly, snatching the keys from his grasp before I press up on my toes. "Oh, sweetheart. The only thing I plan on wrecking is you."

I thread my hands into his hair, tugging with enough force to make him suck in a breath through his teeth before my mouth covers his. I kiss him like I hate him, and I know I'll fuck him the same way later.

"Don't touch your dick until the next time I see you," I whisper against his mouth before I bite his bottom lip. "Don't masturbate, don't edge, don't even hold it any longer than you have to to piss. Understand me?"

Kade swallows, and I don't miss the twitch of his already-growing erection in his basketball shorts. "There she is," he whispers on a grin.

I grin back, leaning in like I'm going to kiss him again, but then I shove him away and maneuver around him, pushing through the front door of the Kappa Kappa Beta house and shutting it again before he can say a word.

You want to play, Kade Brewer?

Fine.

Let's play.

Bear

FAMILY.

That one word can mean so many things.

It can mean a house on a hill with two parents who adore you, and an older sibling who cares for you, and grandparents and aunts and uncles who gather near for holidays. It can mean someone to lean on — always — no matter what you're going through. It can mean safety, and comfort, and support.

Family can also mean a mother addicted to drugs and gambling, and an older brother who follows in her footsteps. It can mean the parents of your best friend taking you in as their own, like my little brother and Mac. Like me and Skyler.

It can mean never really feeling like you had a family at all, and so you build one at the college you go to, surrounding yourself with fraternity brothers and sorority girls and making your own dysfunctional unit.

Or it can mean a baby, one of your own.

One never born.

One you never knew existed — not before it was too late to have a say in whether it stayed that way or not.

It's the Saturday before fall semester, and I should be happy. It's my senior year, my fraternity is *finally* off suspension, I'm in the best shape I've ever been in, and I've got the hottest, smartest, kindest girl I've ever known wrapped around me in my bed. Skyler is here, too, sitting in the bean bag on my floor with her feet propped up on my desk as she relays her summer to us. She and Becca have become friends — my two favorite girls — and yet, still, there's a hollowness inside me.

Because down Greek Row, there's a girl who carried my child inside her.

A girl who never let that child be born.

"I will say this," Skyler says, letting her legs drop to the floor as she sinks even lower into the bean bag. "I am *so* glad rush is over. I usually love Bid Day, but I was exhausted today."

"Maybe you're getting old," Becca offers

"I am. I most certainly am."

"And you're still considering running for president?" Becca asks

Skyler frowns, a strand of her long, brown hair falling into her face. "As crazy as it sounds, I am. I know Erin and I went through a lot of shit last year, and I wasn't sure if I'd ever want to have anything to do with the presidency after that. But... I love KKB. That's my family. And to lead them for a year? That would be an honor."

I listen to them talk in a sort of numb daze, broken up time to time only by them saying Erin's name. Every time I hear the two syllables, a zing of something hot and uncomfortable assaults my chest.

"You okay, babe?" Becca asks me quietly when Skyler pulls out her phone. I bet money she's texting Kip. With him being at school in California, they're committed to the long-distance relationship thing — and I am not envious of the work that goes with that.

"I'm good," I assure her, rubbing her back before I press a kiss to the sunshine yellow bandana tied around her hair and covering her forehead. "Just going to run to the bathroom real quick."

"Okay," she says, smiling at me, but I see the worry etched in her eyes.

When I slip out from under the covers, Skyler whistles.

"Hot *damn*, Bear," she says, eyeing me from head to toe. "I didn't think it was possible for you to get more beastly than you already were. What the hell have you been eating?"

"He eats like The Rock now," Becca answers for me. "I swear, I counted one morning, and the man had *eight* whole wheat pancakes. And a half a pound of turkey bacon."

Skyler whines. "Not fair. If I ate like that, I'd have an ass the size of Texas."

"Ain't nothing wrong with that," Becca says, smacking her own ass.

When I don't so much as chuckle, Skyler eyes me warily, but I avoid her eyes.

"He's also been working out like a mad man," Becca continues, but I snuff out her next sentence with the gentle *snick* of the bathroom door closing, reveling in the time alone.

After I piss, I wash my hands and dry them before splaying them on the bathroom counter. My eyes find those of my reflection, and I hold my own gaze, searching for the man I used to be in the mirror. But he's not there, he's not *anywhere* — not anymore.

They say there are moments in your life that change everything. I could look back and name a few in mine — when Mom first asked me for money, and when she and my older brother bailed on life, leaving behind my nephews and my little brother, Clayton. I could even peg my breakup with Shawna as one that changed me, and the night I saw Erin raped definitely fell into that category, too.

But finding out I had fathered a child with her, one that she never told me about, one that she aborted — it didn't just change me.

It fucked me all the way up.

I search my dead eyes for a sign of humanity, of someone still capable of feeling, but come up short. Becca is the only person I've been able to be even close to myself with over the summer, but even she can't break through entirely.

I can't discern what I feel. It's like a never-ending tornado, one that has lifted everything in my life up into the air — me included — and is just tossing me around, dropping me and picking me back up again, not sure where it wants to leave everything when it finally dissipates.

In the past few months, I've cycled through everything from anger and guilt, to crushing depression and horrifically sad understanding. I want to hate Erin, but I also want to run to her. I want to shake her and demand answers, but I also want to hug her and tell her there's no need, that I already understand.

And in the process of these cycles, of this tornado, I've lost myself completely.

I sigh, scrubbing my hands over my face before I shove through the door and back into my bedroom. Skyler is gone, and Becca sits on my bed in one of my t-shirts, her legs tucked under her.

For a long while, she just stares at me, her eyes speaking to mine without a single word being said.

Then, she leans back, pulls her knees up to her chest, and slowly, seductively, she lets them fall open, revealing that she doesn't have a pair of panties on under that shirt.

"I know we've been taking it slow," she whispers, and I see her throat constrict as she swallows. "But I feel how lost you are right now, Clinton. And I want you to find yourself in me."

My eyes trail her slight curves visible even in the loose fabric of my t-shirt, and when my gaze settles on the wet heat between her legs, I will myself to feel something — anything. Because that's my M.O. If I have something to run from, I find solace in fucking, and working out, and drinking myself into oblivion.

But the desire I yearn to feel for Becca is subdued, suffocated by the vision of another girl I'd been inside of — one I'd "lost myself" in when I was running from something.

Erin Xander.

Still, I can't walk out on Becca — not with her vulnerability on full display like this. So, I shove my own fears and anxieties out, ignoring the anger and the desire for answers I'll never get to questions I should never, ever ask.

In the end, it was Erin's body, and it was her choice.

I find as much resolve from that fact as I can, and in two strides, I'm standing over Becca, sliding my hands up her shins, over her knees, along the warm, smooth skin of her inner thighs. And for the first time since we started dating, I slide my palm over her clit, my fingers dipping between her wet lips.

She shivers, hands fisting in my shirt and holding onto me for dear life as her eyes flutter shut. She lets her head fall back when I press my fingers inside her, slowly, tentatively, and I will myself to be present. I will my dick to stand at attention, will my brain to focus on the beautiful woman giving herself to me.

But everything feels dead.

Lifeless.

Empty.

"I want tonight to be about you," I say with a groan, escaping her hands just before they dip below the band of my sweatpants. She pouts for only a moment before I'm on my knees, tugging her ass to the edge of the bed. "Let me discover you."

At that, her eyes heat with desire again, and she smirks, letting me have my way with her.

And I do.

I take my time, testing out what makes her writhe. Is it when I flick my tongue over her clit, or when I roll it hot and flat along her seam? Is it when my fingers just barely enter her, or when they curl deep inside? Does she like it when I bite her and grip her hard and give her bruises, or does she want me slow and soft and romantic, does she want care and concern?

I find the answers to every single one of my questions, but I do so with a sort of distant, numb version of myself — as if I have a clone, and I'm in a room miles away controlling him.

I asked Becca to take it slow because I'd been hurt before. Because I felt so much for her. Because I knew she was special, and I didn't want to fuck it all up by moving fast.

I'd waited so long to touch her this way.

And yet, I feel nothing.

Becca's nails dig into my flesh. Her body writhes in my sheets. Her cries are heard through the entire Omega Chi house before she grabs one of my pillows and bites down hard to subdue them.

She comes with her hands in my hair and my name on her lips.

And still, I am numb.

Cassie

THE EXCITEMENT THAT COURSES through my veins on the first day of a new semester is a neon flashing sign for how big of a nerd I am.

Fortunately, I've gotten pretty good at hiding my geeked-out joy, though if anyone looked close enough, I'm sure they'd see it.

I'm sure they'd see my hands shaking a little as I unpack my new notebook and fresh pack of Le Pens, ordering them in color on my desk, ready to mark up the syllabus once the professor hands it out. They'd see my smile — not overly obnoxious or visibly excited, but permanent in its place. They'd see that my new, short hair is perfectly styled and that I had this outfit laid out a week in advance. They'd see the foot hanging where my legs are crossed under my desk, swinging slightly, and the cool, calm collectiveness I'm faking as I open my laptop — just in case I need to take notes there, too.

It's junior year, and I'm not messing around.

I'm finally out of all of the general education classes, and *firmly* in the core curriculum that will get me my bio med degree. This isn't even the prerequisites we're talking about. I'm *done* with biology I and II, with organic chemistry, with my first labs. I'm officially in the classes that *really* matter, the ones where I don't just like getting As, but where I will *need* them if I have any prayer of getting into the medical schools on my dream list.

This is it. The big leagues.

And I'm ready.

I uncap the deep blue Le Pen first, writing *Genetics* in perfectly neat handwriting at the top of my notebook, and feeling a zip of excitement run through my veins just as a familiar voice speaks my name.

"Cassie?"

All the joy fades instantly when I look up and find Grayson standing in front of my desk, something between a smile and a cringe on his face.

"Hi," he says when I don't respond.

"What the hell are you doing here?"

I can't help the bitterness in my voice when I finally speak, and a few students around us cast us weary glances as Grayson cocks a brow.

"Same as you, I'd expect." He holds up his notebook with a black pen hooked in the spiral ring.

I narrow my eyes. "You're a music major. Why are you in *Genetics*?"

What was left of his smile slides off his face like a runny egg. His eyes harden — eyes the color of a deep sapphire.

Eyes I used to long for, to lose hours in.

To lose *myself* in.

"Yeah, well, let's just say I *was* a music major, but my father decided that wasn't an option anymore."

My heart squeezes with something close to sympathy before my head snuffs it out with a firm boot heel. "Okay. That still doesn't explain how you've met the pre-reqs for this class."

"I took a lot last semester and over the summer. You would know that if you were still speaking to me."

My jaw clenches. "Why in God's name would I *ever* talk to you again?" I shake my head, throwing my hands up. "I don't know why I'm talking to you now!"

More people turn to look at us, and I blush, ignoring him as I turn my attention back to my pen and notebook.

"Cassie, I'm sorry—"

"Just leave me alone, Grayson."

He stands there for a long while, and I ignore him dutifully until he finally concedes and takes a seat somewhere behind me.

And from that moment on, my focus is shot.

It's impossible not to think about the fact that I'm in the same room, the same class, the same fucking *lab* with my ex-boyfriend who cheated on me and made a fool of me, and almost cost me my relationship with the one man who truly loves me. No matter how I try, every part of my mind and body is unpleasantly aware of my proximity to that danger.

I sit there with my jaw clenched, my brain a whir of angry nonsense as I try to listen to the professor warn us that we're in for a challenging semester. I take notes, mark up my syllabus, and add important dates to my calendar on my laptop, all while trying to pretend I don't care that Grayson is a few seats behind me.

When the professor dismisses us, I bolt out of that room like it's on fire, not giving Grayson the chance to even attempt to talk to me again. It's not until I'm a hundred yards away from the science building and nearly to the student union that I take a calming breath, releasing the tension in my chest.

As soon as I do, I'm lifted from behind and spun around in a frenzied circle.

I scream, swatting at the arms around me until I'm dropped back to the Earth. When I turn and find a sexy, lazily smiling Adam, I shove him hard in the chest.

"Asshole! You scared the living hell out of me!"

He chuckles, wrapping me in a warm hug and kissing my nose as I pout. "I'm sorry, babe. I just couldn't resist. I haven't seen you since this morning. I missed you."

"You saw me three hours ago," I say, but already I'm smiling and leaning into his chest with a sigh. I wrap my arms around his waist and rest my head under his.

"Three hours is too long." He pulls back, grabbing my hand as we continue making our way toward the student union. "How was class?"

Anxiety rips through me — and this time, not from having Grayson in the same room with me, but with the decision of whether or not I should tell *Adam* that he was in the same room with me. I glance at him from the corner of my eyes, swallowing.

"It was fine."

"*Fine*?" he asks with a smirk. "You were practically bouncing like a little kid about to ride a carousel when I dropped you off in front of the science building. How come you're not smiling like a loon now?"

I blow out a breath. "It's an advanced Genetics class, Adam, not a carnival. Excuse me if I'm not excited about the massive amount of lab work I'll have this semester."

I inwardly cringe at the way I snapped at him, but he just stops walking, pulling me to a halt, too, and framing my face with his hands.

"Hey, I'm sorry," he says — even though it's *me* who should be apologizing. His brown eyes search mine. "Are you okay? Did something happen?"

I sigh, shaking my head and leaning my forehead against his. "I'm just a little stressed with the new work-load, I think."

It's a lie. A blatant lie. And I can't figure out why I'm making it. I should just tell him what happened, tell him

Grayson is in my class and it freaked me out to see him after everything.

But Adam and I are *finally* happy. We're finally together — *really* together. We've spent the whole summer falling in love and getting even closer than we ever were before. And for the first time since we met, there's no one and nothing between us.

And I don't want to ruin it.

Adam kisses my forehead, pulling me in for a long hug with his chin balanced on the crown of my head. "That's understandable, Red."

I pinch his side and he makes an *oaf!* sound before chucking and hugging me tighter.

"How about we grab lunch, I'll walk you to your next class, and then when you're done we can go get Moon Pie pizza and hide away in my bed for the rest of the night?"

I pull back and peer up at him. "I thought we were going to work out after class?"

He shrugs, a smirk on his too-hot-for-his-own-good face. "We can work extra hard tomorrow. Tonight, I want to hold my beautiful, amazing, smart, incredible girlfriend and make all her stress go away." He leans in, grabbing my ass as he whispers in my ear. "And I know *many* ways to do it."

I shove him away with a roll of my eyes, pretending to be annoyed, but as soon as he's away from me I'm grabbing his hand and holding it tight. I lean up to kiss his cheek. "You're perfect."

"That's you, baby girl. Now," he says, opening the door to the boisterous student union. "What's for lunch?"

Jess

"ALRIGHT, LADIES," ERIN SAYS, highlighting something on her clipboard before smiling at the group of our sorority sisters gathered in her bedroom. "I think that's it for today. Thank you for meeting with me. I think it's important that we're all on the same page heading into our first Sunday Chapter of the semester tomorrow — *especially* since we'll have the most fantastic group of new members this sorority has ever seen, thanks to J-Love."

I smile and pretend like I'm blushing, waving off the little round of applause from the other executive board members.

"Oh, stop. You're too kind."

"Don't play modest," Ashlei teases. "We all know you're not."

I toss one of Erin's pillows at her, and then everyone is dismissed.

Ashlei kisses both me and Erin on the cheek before being one of the first to bolt out of the room. It's Saturday, which is about the only day she and her sexy, suit-wearing CEO can get in some hump time nowadays, and she doesn't play coy when she lets us know that's *exactly* where she's heading. But I hang around until everyone else is gone and it's just me and Erin.

"Great first meeting, Prez," I say, reaching into her secret stash of snacks in her bedside table drawer. I crack open a bag of white cheddar popcorn and shove a handful in my mouth. "On a scale of one to ten, how ready are you for this semester to be over?"

She smiles, still jotting something down in her planner. "You know I love being president, and I'm in no rush to graduate, either. But, I'll admit," she says with a sigh, finally looking at me. "It's been a rough few months, and I'm not excited to be back in the full swing of things."

I frown, wiping my hands together to dust off the cheese powder before I hop off her bed. I lean against the foot of it right in front of where she's seated in her desk chair. "How are you, Ex?" I ask. "I mean, really."

Erin sighs, capping her highlighter and shutting her planner. "I'm okay. I actually have group therapy in about an hour, so I need to get ready for that."

"Group therapy?" I ask. "I know you were seeing a therapist over the summer, but I didn't realize it was a group thing."

"This is part of my overall recovery plan," she explains. "Something my therapist recommended. It's been good," she adds quickly, and I don't miss something curious in her eyes as she smiles. "Strange... but good."

I smile in return, but my heart aches for my best friend. She hasn't been herself in what feels like at least a year, and I hardly noticed because I'd been caught up in my own shit. I was caught up in Jarrett, in Greg, in Kade. I had no idea what Erin had been through, or why she hadn't told any of us, but I was glad she was getting help.

"You know you can talk to me," I say, barely above a whisper. "I love you, and I would never judge."

"I know," she says, and she stands, wrapping me in a hug that surprises me. I wrap my arms around her hesitantly while she squeezes me tight. "And I will. One day."

When she releases me, she hangs her hands on her hips, eyes on her closet. "Welp. Time to figure out what the hell to wear."

"To therapy?" I smirk, pushing myself off the bed to stand. "I'm sure what you have on is fine, Ex."

"Well, I might go to dinner after, so I just want to be prepared for both."

I cock a brow. "Dinner? With who?"

Her eyes widen as she finds me, but she shrugs quickly. "Just some kids from therapy."

She doesn't elaborate, and I take it as a cue that she doesn't want me prying, so I drop it, but not before giving her a look that I know lets *her* know that I know.

Something.

I just don't know *what* I know.

"Alright," I say, still eyeing her. "Well, I'll see you at Chapter tomorrow. Love you."

She makes a kissy face, dipping into her closet as I let myself out.

Skyler is nowhere to be found when I make it to our room down the hall, so I put on some music while I get ready. I take my time, brushing my teeth and applying my makeup with care before slicking my long hair back into a fierce, high ponytail. I dig out one of my favorite little black dresses, slipping it on over my head — but only after layering up my new, hot pink lingerie set — complete with a garter belt and stockings.

When I'm dressed, I slip into my high heels and make my way downstairs, a wicked grin on my face as I fire Kade's car to life. It's a short walk down Greek Row to the Alpha Sigma house, but I want to remind him that I'm the one with the power in our little arrangement.

Plus, high heels and long walks are not friends.

I haven't talked to Kade since he showed up on the Kappa Kappa Beta front porch during rush week. Now that recruitment is over and the first week of classes is under my belt, I'm ready to deal with him.

And he may think he's ready, but he's nowhere *near*.

I park my car in the Alpha Sigma parking lot, ignoring the blatant stares and gaping mouths as I strut my ass through the yard, shoving the front door open without knocking.

I know the code, obviously, because I'm fucking J-Love.

Adam is in the living room with a group of his brothers, and they all stop talking when they see me. But I don't acknowledge a single one, keeping my eyes locked on the hallway as I make my way toward it.

Every open door I pass is quickly filled with heads leaning out to watch me walk by, and I smirk at the power I feel rushing through my veins. When I make it to Kade's room, I stand in the doorway, popping my weight onto one hip.

He's on his bed, with two other brothers in the room with him. One is in the bean bag on his floor, and the other is sitting backward in Kade's desk chair, all of their eyes locked on the television screen.

On some stupid video game, to be more exact.

At first, none of them look up, but the one in the bean bag glances toward the door. He looks back to the television, then does a double-take, and his jaw drops as he hits the leg of the kid sitting on the chair.

"What the fuck, you're both going to die," Kade says, still hammering away at the remote control in his hands. He scowls. "What are you losers gaping at?"

Then, he turns and sees me, and all the blood drains from his face.

Carnage ensues on the television screen with the three of them watching me, and I smirk like the devil I am.

"Out," I say simply to the two brothers with their jaws on the floor.

They jump up without question, averting their eyes from me the best they can as they make their way past me and into the hall. As soon as they're gone, I shut the door behind me and turn to face Kade.

He swallows.

"So," I say, walking toward him with my hips swaying slowly and purposefully. His eyes drink in every inch of me, and when I'm right in front of where he's sitting on the edge of his bed, I stop, just out of his reach. "Have you been a good boy?"

His eyes grow hungrier and hungrier, his erection already so hard and strong that his basketball shorts look like a fucking tent.

I reach out and forcefully grab his chin, tugging it up until his eyes are on mine. "Answer me."

"Define good," he rasps out, already panting.

"Did you listen to my instructions when you left the Kappa Kappa Beta house?"

He gives me a look of confusion, and I'm so annoyed I roll my eyes and debate dropping the whole thing.

But, truth be told, I'm turned on, too.

And I'm just getting started.

I release his chin, trailing the long fingernail of my pointer finger down his chest, his abs, running it along his hard shaft as he inhales a stiff breath. "I told you not to touch your dick until I saw you," I remind him, then I grasp his cock hard and squeeze, and he groans, head falling back. "Did you listen?"

"Um..."

I squeeze again, this time in a way that I know probably hurts as much as it makes him feel good.

He winces, but his hips buck against the touch, anyway. "I... I..."

"Don't lie to me."

I stroke him softer, rolling my hand from the tip down to the base, all with the fabric still separating us.

He looks at me again. "I didn't listen."

I cluck my tongue. "Bad boy. I'll have to punish you for that."

To be clear, I have *no* idea where this dominatrix side of me has come from. All I know is that I woke up with the urge to hurt Kade after him blowing me off this summer and then making a show of himself at the KKB house during rush.

But I also woke up with the urge to turn him on, too.

And I guess when you combine the two, you get this.

"On your knees," I say.

He cocks a brow, smirking. "You're joking."

"Now," I say, this time grabbing a fistful of his hair and shoving him down to the ground.

He drops the remote control he still had in his hands, doing as I said, and when he's on his knees looking up at me, the power that rushes through me is so addicting I want to bottle it up and get drunk on it forever.

With one hand on the foot of his bed steadying me, I lift my left leg, pressing my high heel into his chest until his back is against the bed. His eyes greedily take in the view my dress is offering him, and I smirk.

"I hope you're hungry," I state, and then I yank my dress up to my hips, place my high heel on the bed behind his head, and lunge forward until my pussy is hovering over his sweet mouth.

He groans, hands reaching out for my thighs and running the length of them as he appreciates my pink lingerie.

The one-piece is crotchless, my pussy framed by the garter belt, and when his finger grazes my clit, my eyes flutter at the contact.

I reach out, fisting my hand in his hair again until his mouth is on the very clit he just brushed.

The rush of heat is instant, the same way it had been our first night in bed together. Kade brings out a power-hungry side of me, one that's controlling and bossy and hellbent on getting an orgasm the way *she* wants it. It's a new and exciting side of myself, one I want to explore more.

And even though he needs help in the flirting and dating and game side of things, I have to give it to him: Kade is a fucking *magician* when it comes to pussy worship.

His tongue is fast and focused, flicking my clit with just the right force to have my orgasm building. When he slides his fingers inside me to help push me to the edge, I lean into the touch, basically riding his damn hand as he continues pleasuring me.

It doesn't take me long to come, and as soon as the orgasm rocks through me and my legs give out from the weight of my body, I pull Kade to stand and shove him back onto his bed.

"Get naked. Now."

I've never seen a man strip faster than he does in that moment, and I stay standing on the edge of the bed, leaning over him when he's fully naked and grabbing his erection in my hands. It's slick with pre-cum, and I run my thumb over the slick tip, coating him with his arousal.

"Fuck," he moans out, writhing in his sheets.

"How badly do you want me to suck your dick right now, Kade?"

"Oh, God," he cries out, eyes shooting open as he finds me. "So fucking bad."

"Yeah?" I ask, and I bend at the waist, taking just the tip of him inside my mouth. I swirl my tongue around his tip, slide it along the length of his base, and cup his balls just as I take him all the way inside my mouth.

He's already close to coming — I can tell from the way his balls hang, tight and high, and the way his legs flex as he tries to catch the orgasm.

So, I suck faster, using my hand in rhythm with my mouth, and Kade flexes and pushes farther inside me, nearly making me gag when he shoves in deep.

"Oh fuck," he moans. "I'm going to come."

And as soon as he says the magic words, I pull off.

Kade's eyes shoot open again, this time in confusion and shock, his body trembling as he reaches for me when I'm already standing and two feet away.

"Wait, no, no, I was so close."

"Were you?" I asked, wiping the corners of my lips innocently. "Aw, that's too bad."

Kade's mouth drops, but before he can say another word, I rush him, straddling him and sitting right down on his cock when my mouth covers his.

His entire body trembles, and I ride him fast and hard, mimicking the pace I'd had with my mouth just moments before. I bite his neck, suck on his ear, nearly draw blood from his bottom lip. It's rough and nasty and hot as *fuck*.

And when his hands tighten around my hips, a guttural groan ripping from his throat, I push myself off of him, breaking every spot of contact all at once.

Kade shakes violently from head to toe, and when I'm standing at the edge of the bed again, I have a glorious view of him ejaculating all over his abs without so much as touching his dick.

"Jesus Christ," he cries out, leaning up on his elbows and assessing the mess he's made on himself. He looks up at me with wild, confused eyes. "What... the fuck... was that?"

I smirk, walking over and pressing my mouth tenderly to his in a long, sweet kiss.

"*That* was payback," I whisper. "The real lessons haven't even started."

He whimpers, reaching out for me but I pull away before he can get a grip.

Then, I tug down my dress until it's covering my hips again, and I don't give him so much as another look when I swing his bedroom door open.

"Don't touch your dick until I see you again."

And with that, I strut my ass out of that house like the goddamn Queen I am.

Bear

INTRAMURAL FOOTBALL IS JUST about the only thing keeping me alive.

Once school started, I found that the hole I'd slid into over the summer was deeper than I realized. I couldn't focus in class — which I really need to do, considering I'm in my cornerstone courses now that I'm a senior — and even with most of my nights spent exploring Becca, the hole continued to grow, and I fell in deeper.

It wasn't until the first IM football game with my Omega Chi brothers that a small spark of my old self came back to life.

Now, it's the only thing I look forward to.

The Alpha Sigma quarterback hikes the ball, and I slam into the offensive lineman across from me, overpowering him in seconds and sliding past him. I growl, thighs burning as I run as fast as I can, and I launch for the quarterback, taking him down before he has the chance to throw the ball.

It's my seventh sack of the game.

Cheers break out from the crowd of Greek students watching the game from the sidelines, and I'm almost positive I hear Skyler screaming above all the noise. I don't celebrate, though — in fact, I remain stoic all game as if I'm not even playing at all.

Because the biggest part of me is still numb, no matter how I try to bring it back to life with the things I used to love.

By the time the game is over, we've outscored the A Sigs by seventeen and clenched our second win of the season. I shake hands with the other players and immediately strip out of my helmet and jersey, desperate to get my pads off.

Every muscle is aching. I know I'll need an ice bath and I'll still be paying for it tomorrow, but that pain reminds me that I'm still here.

I'm still breathing.

I'm still alive.

I've barely peeled my pads off when Skyler is on my back, her legs wrapped around me and fist in the air.

"My best friend is a fucking BEAST!" she screams, chanting my name until a small crowd joins in.

I muster the best smile I have, tickling her sides until she falls off me and lands on the ground, hanging her hands on her hips.

She nudges me playfully with a wide smile. "You murdered them today."

"Just doing my job," I said on a shrug.

"Well, you're doing it well. I don't think anyone can overpower you now that you've beefed up to twice your original size — which was already ghastly, by the way." She squeezes my biceps, but when I don't smile, her eyes grow sad. "Hey, I know you already know this, but... you can talk to me. If something is going on."

"It's not."

She frowns. "It's just... you don't seem like yourself since we came back to school. I know I was busy with Kip and his dad over the summer, so I'm sorry if I wasn't—"

"You don't need to apologize, I'm fine," I clip, shoving my shit into my gym bag with more force than necessary. I don't know why I'm pissed that she's asking if I'm okay when, *clearly*, I am not, but for some reason, it fires me up. "I gotta run."

"Bear..."

"I'll see you around."

I don't look at her again, don't let her get another word in before I sling my bag over my shoulder and start the walk across campus to the Omega Chi house. Most of the guys drove, and a few of them offer me rides, but I decline, looking forward to the alone time.

When I pull my phone out of my bag, there's a few missed texts from Becca wishing me luck on the game. She's at work, and her last text asks if I want her to come over after. I don't answer, switching instead to the missed text from my little brother.

Clayton: Call me when you get this.

My stomach drops. Clayton is still living with Mac and his family in Pittsburgh, and though I'm happy he can be with his friends, and I know from my time spent with them that there's no better place for him to be than at Mac's, it still hurts to be so far from him and know he has no one in *our* family.

I dial his number from my favorites list and plug my headphones into the phone jack, popping the buds in my ears just as he answers.

"Hey," he answers, and I can tell by the sound in his voice that my stomach lurching wasn't for nothing.

Something is wrong.

"Hey, Little Bro. Sorry I didn't call sooner, was at an IM game."

"You clobber them?"

"Naturally," I answer. "What's going on?"

I get straight to the point, and Clayton sighs on the other end before I hear what sounds like a door closing and then the faint sounds of him being outside.

"Mom messaged me."

My heart stops, along with my feet, and I stand frozen for what feels like an hour in the middle of the sidewalk trail that leads around our circular-shaped campus before I find the will to speak.

"What the fuck do you mean, she *messaged* you?"

My mother had disappeared the fall semester of my sophomore year — immediately after I'd given her two-thousand dollars, thanks to Skyler's help — and she'd taken my older brother, Carleton, with her. Other than them occasionally checking in with Carleton's wife and two sons, none of us had heard from them. *I* had seen his kids more than he had, and I'd given up on ever seeing Mom again. Hell, I'd lost every ounce of care I had left for her when I realized what she'd done to Clayton.

How could she just leave him there? He was alone, staying on Mac's couch until his parents really took my brother in and made a new home for him.

What kind of mother could leave her teenage son like that, without so much as a phone call every now and then to check in?

"I mean, she messaged me. She's on Facebook now, I guess... she made a new profile."

"What the fuck did she say?" I ask, and already I'd pulled over to one of the benches near the reflection pond, plopping down and pulling up Facebook on my phone. I search her name, gulping when her profile comes up and I realize she sent me a friend request, too.

"She just said, 'Hey, son. It's Mom. How are you?'" Clayton answers, and then he pauses a moment. "I just got the message late last night, around three in the morning or so. I didn't know what to say, so I didn't respond. I wanted to talk to you first."

"Jesus Christ," I mutter, swiping through the few photos she'd uploaded. One is of her on a beach, the other is in front of some old, run-down house. She's somehow even thinner than the last time I saw her, and she's cut all her hair off.

My heart breaks at the sight of her frail form, of her sad, drugged-out eyes.

But then it hardens right back up, remembering what she'd done.

"Don't message her back," I say finally, grabbing my bag as I close Facebook and resume my walk again. "Not until I figure out where she is and what her intentions are."

"Okay," he says, not arguing, but I can hear the disappointment in his voice.

"I know you miss her," I say on a sigh, eyes rolling up to the sky and fists clenching at my sides. I want so badly to hurt my own mother, and I know what a twisted, fucked-up thing that is, but I want her to know this pain we've felt as her kids. "Just let me figure out a few things first, and then you can talk to her if you want. Okay?"

"Yeah," he says. A pause. "I do miss her, but I think I miss who I thought she was. You know? Not who she really is."

I inhale a stiff breath, blowing it out as calmly as I can as I scrub a hand down my face. Clayton is around the same age I was when I realized who my mother truly is, and I remember how badly it killed me.

I hate that it's doing the same to him.

"Hey, we have each other, right?" I remind him. "What else do we need?"

"Not a damn thing."

"That's right."

I change the subject to football, asking how his season is going so far. He's a sophomore and already on the varsity team, a wide receiver with stats more impressive than I ever had when I played in school.

After a while, we end the call, and I walk the rest of the way to the house in a fuming silence. As soon as I get back to the Omega Chi house, I lock myself in my room, text Becca that I'll see her later in the week, and then run a shower so hot my skin is a bright red when I finally emerge.

I might as well have steam wafting off my skin with the anger still sourcing through me, and I can't get my thoughts straight to figure out what I want to do next.

Before I realize what I'm doing, I have my phone in my hand, Erin's name on my screen, and a text message written in the box below it.

Me: Are you free? Really need someone right now.

I stare at the words, eyes welling with tears that burn as I try to figure out why the hell *she* was the one I thought of, why *she* was the name I typed, why *she* was the one I wanted to talk to.

None of it matters, not anymore.

Not since I realized everything I thought we had between us was a lie.

The truth is I can never lean on her.

She's the last person I can trust.

I delete the text, swiping at the one tear that managed to slip free from my eye before it has the chance to roll down my cheek.

Then, without a plan or a single fucking clue as to what I want to say, I open my laptop, pull up Facebook, and message the woman who gave me life.

Cassie

"AND... I JUST FEEL..." Adam grunts, straining himself up and planting a kiss on my lips before he lowers back down to the ground, his hands behind his head. "A lot... of pressure... you know?"

Another lift. Another kiss.

Sit-ups are my favorite.

"That makes sense," I tell him, holding his feet firmly down to give him support as he lifts again. The sun has just set over campus, and on top of the parking garage where we like to be masochists with our workouts, there's a spectacular view of the pink and purple sky, and the lights flickering on all across town.

I also don't mind the view of his glistening abs, still tan from our days in the sun this summer, flexing and releasing each time he does another sit-up and gives me a kiss.

"You're the first person to ever be president for a second term in Alpha Sig," I remind him. "Anyone would feel pressure."

"I just... think I need... to do something... *different*," he continues, and I chuckle at him trying to speak through the effort.

"Like what?"

He lifts once more, grabbing my face this time and holding me to his mouth for a long, hot kiss that sends a jolt through me before he lets me go. He smiles, tracing my bottom lip before his eyes find mine. "One hundred. Your turn."

"I'm *not* doing a hundred."

"You're doing fifty. Now, come on, switch."

He grabs my breasts and squeezes them through my sports bra before I swat him away and lie back, not ready for my torture.

"Wipe that look off your face, you know you love it," he says.

"I do *not* love it," I argue, doing my first sit-up and kissing him before I lower back down. The first few are easy, but when I get to the tenth, my abdomen fires up in protest. "I'm doing it because I'm a biology major and a future doctor and I need to learn how to put nutrition and fitness in the forefront of my priority list. That doesn't mean I have to *like* it, though."

Adam smiles, kissing my nose on the next sit-up. "You're cute when you're complaining about a workout."

I flip him off, but continue the reps as he starts in on his ideas for his second year as A Sig president. Now that we're a couple of weeks into the school year, I'm in my routine, feeling solid for the first time since I got to Palm South University. Maybe it's because I'm finally in my cornerstone classes, or maybe it's because Adam and I are together, *finally*, without anyone or anything in-between us.

It's crazy what feeling settled in your love life can do for the rest of your life.

"And I was thinking," Adam continues when I'm on my fortieth rep. "Instead of doing the concert like I've done the last two years, what if I changed it up a bit?"

I frown. "That concert... got you... on the map again," I remind him. "It took Alpha Sigma from..." I groan, wrenching myself up and kissing him reluctantly before I lower again. "Nothing... to the talk of Greek Row."

"I know, and I think that's just it. It's served its purpose, you know? But I want to keep things fresh and exciting." He grins, kissing me before I go down for my last three reps. "What do you think about karaoke?"

"Karaoke?" I echo, finishing my last reps and enjoying the long, sweet kiss that follows the end of my torture before I lean back on my hands, sweating, panting. "As in, poor quality instrumental music from a speaker with an amateur singing the words on a monitor in front of them?"

"Exactly. Except, better."

I chuckle. "Okay. I'm listening."

"Picture this," he says, excitement rolling off him. "We set up a huge stage, just like we normally do for the concert, and there's a band set up — drums, guitars, bass, backup singers, all that. Then, each fraternity and sorority gets to compete for the trophy by pulling out their best karaoke skills. We'll encourage them to not only bring out their best singers, but to also go for the entertainment factor — humor, dancing, all of it. Can you imagine how fun that would be?"

I tilt my head, cocking one eyebrow. "Honestly, my sisters *do* love karaoke."

"Who doesn't?"

"You said there'd be a band? So, instead of instrumental, it's a real band?"

"Exactly. I already talked to a local band who does weddings and stuff. They said they can give me a giant list of songs they know for the fraternities and sororities to choose from. And we'll do the lights up just like we do for the concert, and the fog and confetti and all that. It'll *feel* like a real show."

"That's really cool," I muse, smiling.

"And, we'll make more for our charity this way, too. We can charge an entry fee for the fraternities and sororities to enter, and charge a low-ticket price, get prizes donated for the winners — first, second, and third place." He's so excited that he's breathing as hard as he was when we got to the top of the parking garage after running up the stairs. "And if it goes off the way I have it planned, I feel like it would become a new tradition, kind of like the Greek Week games where we all compete."

I lean forward, grabbing his face in mine and kissing him hard. "How did I get such a smart, sexy boyfriend?"

"Well, it wasn't exactly easy."

I snort, but before I can sass back, he's pulling me in closer, wrapping me up in his arms, his love, kissing me like it's the first and the last time at once.

"What about you?" he asks, popping up to stand before he reaches his hand down to help me up, too. "How has the new school year been for you so far? Anything new and exciting in the land of KKB?"

He grabs my shoulder as I grab his, and we both pull up the opposite foot to our butts, stretching our quads.

"We got a great group of new members," I say, frowning. "And the pressure is on from my G-Big to take a Little."

"Ex?"

I nod. "I didn't take one last year, mostly because I just didn't feel ready to, you know? And I guess I do feel ready this year, but... I don't know." I struggle to find the explanation. "It's my junior year, you know? I have a ton of schoolwork, and I don't know if I..." My stomach drops as the root of my concern hits me. "I don't know if I'd be a good Big."

We switch legs, and Adam squeezes my shoulder where he holds me. "Cassie, you're an amazing friend, an amazing sister, a *phenomenal* kisser — er, I mean, girlfriend."

I smirk.

"And I *know* you'd be an amazing Big — but only if you want to be one. Don't feel like you have to just because it's the norm. Take a Little if you want to continue your family line and pass down some traditions, if you want to mentor one of the new girls and help her find her footing in the sorority the way Sky helped you."

I smile. "I really do think I'd like that. I don't know what I would have done without Skyler, maybe dropped out of KKB altogether."

"Well, then, maybe that's your answer. But sleep on it, okay? You have time to think."

I nod, and we finish stretching in a comfortable silence.

"What about school? Your classes as hard as you thought they'd be?" Adam asks as we cross the top of the garage to start making our way back down.

My throat tightens, a jolt of nerves flittering through me at the thought of the past two weeks. Classes have been fine, for the most part. I prepared over the summer, and I've always been one of those students who excelled pretty easily. I'm not intimidated by my cornerstone classes.

But I *am* freaked out about having class with Grayson.

He hasn't tried to talk to me again since that first day, but I feel his energy every time I'm in that classroom with him. It makes my skin crawl.

And as ashamed as I am to admit it to myself, it also makes me sad.

I can't place why, and I never give myself time to think on it before I push him out of my mind and focus on the professor.

But I still have yet to tell Adam about it, and I don't know if I even need to.

Why would it matter? It's just a class together, and I don't even talk to Grayson or anything. It's not like I'm doing anything *wrong*.

Adam glances behind him on our way down the stairs when I don't answer for a while, and I shake my head, smiling.

"Sorry, just tired. Yeah, school is fine. I feel like me staying here over the summer to get ahead was smart."

"You're the smartest girl I know," he says, and when we reach the bottom of the stairs, he grabs my wrist and tugs me into him.

His mouth is on mine in the next instant, his hands in my hair, running through it softly before he tugs it at the end.

"You got homework tonight?" he husks.

"Nothing that can't wait."

"Good," he says, smiling at my shortness of breath as he slips his tongue inside my mouth, swirling and teasing. "Because I think we have some anatomy to study."

"Mmm," I muse, running my hands down his back to hook into the back band of his shorts. "I *do* still need some help in a certain area, come to think of it."

Adam frowns. "And that is?"

I lick my lips, leaning up on my tiptoes to whisper in his ear. "Blow jobs."

A shiver runs through him, and he groans, looking up to the sky as if he needs a god to save him from me. "Jesus Christ, woman. I've got an instant boner and we have to walk all the way across campus."

"Guess you better walk behind me, then," I say, turning and leaning my ass into his hard on.

He groans again, smacking my ass and tucking his erection into the band of his shorts before we start our walk — both of us a little quicker than necessary now that we know what waits for us when we get back to the A Sig house.

Yeah, I think. *No sense in bringing up Grayson.*

We're happy — *finally* — and there's nothing to tell, really. It's just a class together, nothing to concern him over.

For now, I'll keep it to myself.

What's the harm in that?

EPISODE 2

Ashlei

THE WOOD FLOOR OF the studio is cool under my bare feet, and I wiggle my toes, reveling in the feel of it as I close my eyes and listen to the music. It's a slow, exotic song, filled with heat and energy, and slowly, my hips begin to sway to the beat.

On my next breath, I lift my arms over my head, rolling them in time with my hips before I trail them down, gliding my fingertips over my body, the song sinking in deeper and deeper.

When my eyes open, I see the center pole four feet in front of me, and I lick my lips, still moving in time with the music as I strut toward it. My right hand reaches out, wrapping around the chrome, and I swing, lifting my feet off the ground and letting the momentum send me spinning.

Everything is lost in moments like these, when I'm in the studio, the music loud, just me and my body dancing and making art. My feet barely hit the floor before I grip the pole in my armpit and lean back, legs tucked before extending into chopper, and then I'm hooking my outside leg and letting the rest of my body hang.

The skin on my inside thigh burns to life, but it's a comforting pain, one that I know from experience will go away the longer I practice. I use my legs and arms to make shapes as the pole spins, and then I swing my inside leg around, hooking it over the pole before my right leg extends.

Leg hang after leg hang, shape after shape, I feel my way through the song. I alternate between tricks in the air to low flow and floor work, and by the time the last beats of the sexy song fade away, I'm dripping in sweat, chest heaving, abdomen contracting and releasing where I lie on my back on the floor.

From the corner of the room, Karen, the studio owner and my own personal torturer — er, trainer — applauds.

"Fantastic work, Ashlei," she says, leaning over and extending a hand to help me up. When I'm on my feet again, she smiles wider. "Truly. I'm amazed at the progress you've made since you first came to our studio."

"All thanks to you," I pant.

She shakes her head. "No way. This is all *you*. You worked hard over the summer. Hard to believe you're the same girl who stumbled her way through basic spins and sits the first time you walked through those doors on Valentine's Day."

I smile, thanking her before she winks and makes her way over to the desk to welcome the girls showing up for her next class.

Karen is nothing like my previous pole studio owner.

She's kind, and caring, and driven and smart. At five-foot-eight, she's almost all beautiful legs and strong, toned arms. I watch her with appreciation as she checks girls in, her wide smile bright against her dark brown skin. Her long, black hair is in a hundred tiny braids and piled into a gorgeous bun on top of her head, all of it contained by a bright headband.

It's as if the yellows and oranges in that headband are her aura, her energy, that bright, sunshine vibe she always gives off.

My muscles are deliciously sore as I throw her a wave over my shoulder on my way out, smiling and thinking about everything she said about my progress. It feels good, the reward slowly showing from all the hard work I've been putting in.

And that smile doubles when I push through the doors that lead onto the sunny downtown street, and I see Brandon's pearl white Acura NSX parked on the curb.

The driver side door opens as soon as I'm on the sidewalk, and he steps out, looking dapper as ever in a custom beige suit, tailored to fit every muscle. His eyes are shielded behind dark square sunglasses, but he takes them off as he rounds the car, opening the passenger side for me with a grin.

"Your chariot, Miss."

I shake my head, handing him my gym bag when he reaches for it before I plant a long, warm kiss on his lips. He wraps his arms around me, inhaling at the contact as if it were his first breath all day.

"Hi, baby," I whisper.

"Hi," he says back, kissing my nose before he releases me. "I missed you."

"Clearly. I don't remember asking you to pick me up," I point out. "*Or* making plans at all today."

"Yeah... about that... get in, let's talk."

I cock a brow, sliding into the passenger seat before he gently shuts the door behind me. He walks around the back, tossing my bag in the small trunk before he's in the driver seat next to me, roaring the engine to life.

"Do you have pole tomorrow?" he asks, checking his side mirror before he pulls onto the road.

"No, I need a rest day."

"And it's Sunday, so you wouldn't have class, right?"

My suspicion rises. "No... but I *do* have Chapter at six."

"Chapter..." he muses, side-eyeing me with a grin. "Damn sorority."

I smack his arm playfully.

"Do you think you could skip it, just this once?"

"Probably not without a death threat from Ex," I say seriously. "But... what are you proposing?"

We pull up to a red light, and Brandon bites his lip before turning to me. "The Bahamas."

"The Bahamas?!"

"The Exumas, technically."

"The *Exumas*," I repeat, sounding like a freaking parrot at this point. "You're proposing we go to the Exumas tonight," I clarify. "As in... the place where you swim with pigs."

"I was thinking more like the place where I fuck you on my yacht and drink fruity cocktails out of coconuts with you on the beach," he says on a smirk, and the light turns green, making him turn back to the road with a shrug. "But if you'd rather swim with pigs..."

I laugh, shaking my head at the ridiculousness of it. I'm tempted to say *We can't just go to the fucking Bahamas, Brandon,* but I know that's a lie.

He has a yacht.

And more money than he knows how to spend.

Technically, we *can* go to the Bahamas.

I'm quiet for a long while, and Brandon glances at me from the corner of his eye before pulling into a random restaurant parking lot. It's a Mexican diner, not even open yet, since it's only ten in the morning. When he's parked, he turns to me, grabbing my hands and pulling them into his lap.

"Look, we've both been busy this summer — you with your exec position in the sorority, and pole... me with this national client we're in the bidding war for... *both* of us working hard at *Okay, Cool* after everything that went down in the spring with Kim… and now, school is back in session, it's the last semester before you graduate, we're both hard at work, and I just…"

He smooths his dark thumbs over my wrists, his eyes that are usually so intense, soft and vulnerable now.

"This might be our last chance to spend some real, quality time together before life gets even crazier than it already is."

My heart melts into a puddle right there on the floorboard of his expensive ass car, and I lean over the console, kissing him long and hard.

"Let's go to the Bahamas," I whisper between kisses. "You're right. Everything else can wait."

He sighs, wrapping his arms around me until he's pulling me into his lap. I squeal and laugh, but then my next breath is stolen by the erection growing in his slacks.

"This would be a lot easier on the yacht," I say, rubbing the seam of my leggings against his hard-on.

"Maybe," he says, sucking on my bottom lip and releasing it with a pop. His lips trail down my neck as my head rolls back. "But these windows are tinted, and you're sexy when you say I'm right."

I bark out a laugh that's stolen with another kiss, knowing tinted windows or not, if anyone walks by, they'll know what's going on in here. I have yet to be fucked by Mr. Church without screaming out his name a time or two.

"How long has it been since you fucked me?" I ask, slipping my hand between us and gripping his cock hard.

He groans, flexing into my fist through the fabric of his slacks. "Too long."

It's only been a week, but I agree with the sentiment, and both of us lose our ability to go slow and take our time with foreplay. Instead, I lift up on my knees just enough to unfasten the button on his slacks and slide the zipper down, then I'm yanking down on his pants and briefs together. He lifts his hips to help me, and as soon as his shaft is free, I turn into a trapeze artist.

"What the hell are you doing?" Brandon asks with a smirk when I start flipping upside down. I pause long enough to peel off my leggings, and then I'm ass up, face down, with my pussy in his face and my arms straddling his thighs.

I don't have to answer his question with words. Instead, I take the tip of him in my mouth, slowly at first, just enough to swirl my tongue and get him wet. He groans, palming my ass cheeks with both hands before smacking them hard.

I yelp, taking him all the way in my throat, and then I'm rewarded with a lash of his tongue on my clit.

It's not easy, balancing on my forearms in what is practically a yoga inversion with my legs straddled around his face, but Brandon holds onto my thighs and ass, taking his share of the weight and making it easier for me to focus on getting him off.

It's been a year now since I met this man, since he stole my breath away in the elevator at *Okay, Cool* and then I spent months trying to avoid him, trying not to give in to his devilish stare and sexy confidence.

But I was a goner from the first time I laid eyes on him, since the first time he laid eyes on *me*.

And I was a fool to ever think otherwise.

"God*damn*, Ashlei," he groans, flexing his hips until his cock bulges in my throat. I do everything to keep from gagging, letting him hold himself there for a long time before he withdraws. Then, he's assaulting my pussy with his tongue, his fingers, burying his face between my thighs.

My legs shiver and quake around him, and when he circles my clit time and time again with his tongue, working it in rhythm with his fingers inside me, I have to take a break from sucking his dick. I have to just hold myself up and let everything else go as an explosion of fire and stars invade my vision, all the blood rushing to where his tongue drives me to climax.

I rock my hips against his mouth, and his free hand grabs my ass and pulls me into him, letting me know he can take it. Each new wave of my orgasm hits harder than the last, and I ride his face until I'm spent, until I'm nothing but a mess of shallow breath and trembling muscles.

When I'm done, Brandon hits a button that sends his seat back a little farther. Then, he leans it back and flips me over in a complicated tangle of limbs until he's on top of me and I'm half bent over the console, half bent over his seat.

Without a chance to catch my breath, he slides inside me from behind, stealing my next breath with the raw sensation of being filled after just climaxing so fucking hard.

I cry out his name, holding onto the leather seats for dear life as he pounds into me hard, harder, over and over, punishing and claiming.

And when he's ready to come, he pulls out of me and flips me back over, climbing up the seat to empty inside my mouth.

I swallow every drop.

Skyler

"NO, NO, NO," **KIP** groans, shaking his head on the screen of my laptop. "You're supposed to take the clothes *off* — not put them *on*."

I chuckle, zipping up my black dress pants and fastening the button at the top before I shove one arm through the long-sleeve, white, button-up top. I lean forward once both arms are in, pushing my cleavage together.

"Take one last look, baby," I tease, biting my lip. "Because in about two minutes, I'll look like a cocktail waiter and your sex drive will die right along with my pride."

Kip chuckles, but his eyes are on my chest with a longing sigh on his lips. "Please don't button up that top."

"But I have to go to work."

"You should come here, instead."

I smile. "To California? Sure, I'll hop the next flight."

"Great. See you soon!"

Kip jokes like he's going to hang up our video chat, but of course he doesn't, and then we're both smiling and staring at each other through the screen, wishing we could touch from across the country.

As horrible as the summer was with his father passing away, I hadn't realized until the new semester started how spoiled we had been. Even after his father had passed, we'd spent time with his mom, in his hometown, falling more in love every single day — while also dealing with the fall-out from the tournament. It didn't take long for the reporters to put the pieces together and realize Kip was the same guy from the bonfire photo that had been leaked of me, and needless to say, we were the juiciest story the poker world had seen in a while — especially once I disappeared off the scene.

In those short months of summer, Kip had become my person. We'd spend nearly every day together, every night in each other's arms, and now we had thousands of miles between us.

And there was just no way around it.

It hurt.

Kip was finally at his dream school — UCLA — chasing his dream of becoming a script writer. And as much as I knew he was where he needed to be, and I was where *I* needed to be at PSU, I hated that those two schools were not in the same zip code.

Or even the same state.

There was only so much a text or a phone call or even a video chat could do.

I stand, shrugging the dress shirt on and start buttoning it from the bottom up. "What are you going to do tonight?"

"Dream about you stripping out of that outfit."

I roll my eyes.

"Alpha Sigma is having a little party to kick off Greek Week," he says after he gets his rise out of me. "Rick and I are going to head that way after our Character Creation class."

"I still can't believe you managed to find not only a fraternity brother with the same major, but then he ends up as your roommate, too."

Kip chuckles. "It's not so weird here, babe. Everyone wants to work in movies or TV or music." He shrugs, a dreamy smile on those perfect lips I love to taste. "That's why I wanted to be here. It feels like home."

My heart rips somehow with a gentle pang of longing, as if his words hurt just as much as they made me proud of him. I still remember our first date, when he opened up to me about his dreams of writing scripts, and now, he's on his way to doing just that.

"What's wrong, Ella Mae," he asks, leaning forward. The movement allows me to see the *Singing in the Rain* movie poster hanging above his bed behind him. "You seem distant tonight."

I sigh, flopping down in the office chair at my desk as I struggle with the red bow tie around my neck. "I don't know. I guess I've just been feeling a little... lost. Now that I'm not playing poker professionally, I feel like one of my limbs has been cut off."

"You still *could* play, you know," he reminds me.

I nod, but fall quiet, because we both know *not* continuing to play was the best move for me. Kip and I made quite the scene in Vegas last year, and really — I've accomplished what I wanted to. Mom and Dad are set up financially, my tuition and *then* some is paid, and I have a solid savings stashed up for when I graduate. Plus — I got the guy.

What more do I need?

Poker has served its purpose for me, and now I want to dive deeper and find out what I want to do with the rest of my life.

But I'm already a senior, and I'm just now thinking about my career after college.

To say I'm behind is an understatement.

"Do you want to talk about it?" Kip asks. "I know you started taking some entrepreneurship and business classes this semester, but we haven't talked about how they're going. Do you like them? Do you feel like they fit you?"

Anxiety flares in my chest, as it often does when I try to find out where I fit in. It's been like that my entire life.

The only place I've really been able to find my footing is in Kappa Kappa Beta and the Greek community at Palm South.

Once I graduate, all that will be gone, too.

I shake my head, forcing a smile. "Not right now. I don't really have much to say yet since it's only been a few weeks. Besides," I say, waggling my eyebrows as I pull on the slick, black vest and button it up, standing back with my arms wide. "This sexy thing has a shift to work on the casino boat."

Kip smiles, too, but his blue eyes shine with worry. "I wish I was there to hold you in my arms right now."

My smile falls at that. "Me, too."

A long moment stretches between us, and finally Kip sighs, his smile genuine again. "They're all going to love you. I can't wait to hear how much you make in tips."

"It's going to be keeping my mouth shut when they do something stupid that will be hard."

He barks out a laugh at that. "Nah, don't hold back. School 'em. Maybe they'll tip you more if you give them advice and they win."

I point at him in a *touché* gesture, and then lean forward, blowing him one more kiss. He catches it, holds it, and then throws it up to the sky — something we've done every time we can since his dad passed away. It's a little reminder to keep him in our hearts, and also to live each day to the fullest.

"I'll text you after my shift," I say, knowing that even though it'll be late here, the night will just be getting started in California. "Have fun at the party, but tell Rick to fight the girls off you for me."

"You're the only girl for me and everyone here knows it."

I smile at that, giving him one last longing look before I close the screen on my laptop. Then, I look in the floor-length mirror in the room I share with Jess, adjusting the ridiculous bow tie and sighing at the way the work uniform hides all of my best features. I look like I'm wearing a large potato bag painted black, white, and red.

But as much as I don't have the desire to play poker *professionally*, I can't deny the rush flowing through me at the thought of being around *other* players. I'll be dealing blackjack most of the night, and if I have my charm turned up to a hundred, I'll also be walking out with a pocket full of cash in tips.

It isn't the Friday night I'm used to. I *should* be getting ready to go to a party with Jess and Lei, preparing myself to take shots instead of to take chips. But something tells me this casino boat is where I need to be, that even though I'm not playing poker for money, I'm not quite done with it yet, either.

With a strange, unfamiliar feeling floating in my stomach, I push all my anxious thoughts down and cover my lips in matte red lipstick for good measure. Then, I head to work.

I think of Kip the entire drive.

Adam

"AND FOR HALLOWEEN, THE sandbar party was a success last year," I say, tapping through the lists of things in my notebook that I wanted to discuss with Jeremy. He sits on my bed, looking bored, tossing my baseball up into the air over and over again while I ramble away. "I think we should do it again. But maybe bigger this time." I pause. "Do you think we could get a DJ out there?"

Jeremy tosses the ball up. "Everyone plays music on their boats," he pointed out. "I think it'd be too much noise."

"But if the DJ was in the *middle*," I pointed out. "It'd be an attraction, something to draw people onto the island more so than just into the boats."

"True." He snatches the ball from the air and sits up. "But first, I think you need to remain focused on this karaoke thing."

"It's pretty much handled," I say, waving him off. That fresh energy I get from making a list, a plan, a new goal rushes through me, and I smile, jotting down more ideas.

"I'm serious, man," he says. "The event is a couple weeks away and there's still so much we haven't nailed down. We need an emcee. We need monitors. We still haven't received the entry fee from half of the fraternities and sororities who've entered. Plus, we haven't talked at all about day-of fundraising tactics."

Jeremy continues on, but my phone buzzes on my desk with a reminder that Cassie's class ends in fifteen minutes, and already, I'm closing up my notebook and packing my bag to go meet her.

"… the food and the…" He stops. "Are you listening to me?"

"Yeah," I answer easily. "I gotta go, but don't worry, okay?" I slap him on the shoulder as I swing my backpack onto mine. "I've got this under control."

Jeremy stops me before I can turn, his hand landing hard on my forearm. "I'm serious, Adam. This is your second year as president — something no one in this fraternity has done before. And I'm just saying, I'm not the only one who notices that you're a little distracted."

I frown. "Distracted?"

"With Cassie."

At that, my expression hardens. "What does she have to do with anything?"

"I'm just saying," he says with his palms out. "You two have always been dancing around each other. This is your first time being *together*, and, well… let's just say it's very apparent that she's the first priority for you right now."

My defenses spike, and I point a finger at my closest fraternity brother, narrowing my gaze. "I've been present for everything. I've been running Chapter, coming up with new ideas for the semester, already planning for Rush that isn't even until the spring, and I literally brainstormed and made this entire karaoke fundraising event come together in just weeks." I shake my head. "I can be happy with Cassie and still get shit done. If anything, she's motivated me to do even *more*."

Jeremy folds his arms over his chest. "You've been here, yes, but you haven't been present. You're always on your phone — texting her, calling her, whatever. You spend more time with her than you do with your brothers. It doesn't matter that you're here making *plans*," he says. "What matters is that you're *here* — really and truly here. When was the last time you played video games in the main room? Stayed for a party instead of hiding out in your room with Cassie? Attended an IM game to just be with your brothers instead of watching it with her and then leaving immediately after to go on a date?"

The more he shoots at me, the more my shoulders slump, guilt sinking in. I haven't even noticed I've been doing any of those things, but as he lists them off, my defenses crumble.

Because he's right.

"I love Cassie," he says when I don't respond. "You know that. I've wanted you two together for years. But... just remember that we're your brothers, and as our president, we need your time, too. *Especially* right now, changing up a concert that's been working to try something new. This was your idea, brother," he says, standing. "So, lean into it and help us pull it off successfully."

I sigh, chest tight with shame. I can always depend on Jeremy to give it to me straight, but I hate what I'm hearing from him in this moment.

"I hear you," I say, gripping his shoulder in one hand as I level my gaze with his. "Thank you for helping me see what I couldn't. I promise, I'm here, and I'll *be* here more. Don't worry about the karaoke event this weekend," I assure him. "I've got this."

Jeremy's lips press together, and he nods once. We exchange a unique handshake we've had since freshman year, and he claps me on the back as we head out of my bedroom.

When we make it to the main room, a bunch of our brothers are gathered on the couches and beanbags, watching two seniors battle it out in a game of Madden on the big screen. They welcome Jeremy easily, scooting over on the couch to make more room for him and handing him a beer out of the ice chest at the edge of the coffee table.

Then there are eyes on me.

"Heading out, Pres?" Kade asks, drinking a beer with his eyes still on the screen. He rushed last spring, in Kip's class, and already he's been showing leadership potential.

Before I can answer, one of my brothers says, "Of course he is. Time to go pick up Cassie from class, right?"

There's a snicker from my other brothers, one I wouldn't have even noticed had Jeremy not just had the conversation with me that he had. Before, I would have laughed it off, said something to the effect of *you bet your ass*. But now, I watch them exchange knowing looks, feeling like an outsider in the family I spent the last year building.

"I'll be back after lunch," I say.

"Yeah. See ya," Kade replies.

And then the attention is back on the game, and I'm invisible.

My mind is spinning the entire walk across campus to the Science Building, and I chase each thought, holding onto it by the tail before it wriggles free and another comes into view.

I love Cassie. I love spending time with her. But have I really been so wrapped up in her this semester that I've been neglecting my brothers?

I know the answer solely from the interaction I just had with them in the house. If Jeremy hadn't pulled my head out of my ass, I'm not sure I would have seen it *even then*.

The truth is I *like* being lost in Cassie. I like that she's my entire world.

But if I'm going to be president, and if Alpha Sigma is as important to me as it always has been, I need to find the balance.

The more I think on it, the more I can't wait to talk to Cassie about it all. She's my best friend, and I know she'll have exactly the right words to say.

When I see her red hair bounce out of the front doors from where I'm sitting on one of the benches fifty yards or so from the building, I smile, my heart already fluttering with relief just from seeing her.

But then my eyes land on the person walking out of the building with her.

The person I hate more than anyone in the world.

Grayson fucking Anderson is walking next to Cassie — so close their arms brush a little as the crowd moves around them.

My heart stops in my throat as I watch them come to a stop in the sea of students leaving the building. Cassie stands with her arms crossed over her books tucked into her chest, and Grayson is talking animatedly, his hands moving, sincerity on his face as he says whatever it is he's saying.

Cassie listens, chewing her lip, and when he's done, she says something in response. I have no idea what it is, but I know he smiles after she's said it, and that alone sends a rip current of anger rushing through me.

I stand, snatching my backpack off the bench and throwing it on my shoulders, determined to march my ass over there and shove Grayson away from her. I want to remind him that he's not welcome to talk to her — *ever* — but before I can move, he salutes her, and she offers him a small wave, and then he turns and walks in the opposite direction.

I pause, watching Cassie as she watches him leave, an unreadable expression in her eyes. After a moment, a big breath leaves her chest, and she turns, searching for something.

For me.

I know that's what her eyes are scanning for, that *she* knows I'm out here somewhere, walking toward her or waiting for her to make her way toward me. I know she's wondering where we'll go for lunch before I walk her to her next class.

But for the first time, I don't want her to find me.

Something indescribable sears through my spine like a hot wire, and I know if I talk to her right now, I'll blow. I don't have the details. I have no idea why Grayson was with her, or what they were talking about, but I know if she walks over to me and I ask her how class was and all she says is *fine* and then pretends like nothing happened and we go to lunch — I won't be able to let it go.

So I don't give her the chance.

With my backpack on my shoulder, I fall into the sea of students and make my way back toward Greek Row, pulling out my phone to send her a text.

Me: Got caught up with A Sig stuff. Text you later.

I shove my phone back in my pocket, ignoring the response buzz that comes through less than sixty seconds later, and keep my head down the rest of my walk.

Why the fuck was she with Grayson? He's a Music major — there's literally no reason for him to be in that building. And why was Cassie talking to him, *listening* to him? I don't care if he was apologizing for what he did to her, or talking about the fucking weather. She *hates* him.

Doesn't she?

Shouldn't she?

It doesn't make sense to me why she would give him even two minutes of her time.

And the worst part is that whatever she said brought a relieved smile to his face, and they'd waved goodbye to each other like they were friends.

Friends.

Just the thought of it sends another chill of rage through me, and I shake my head, letting out an audible, frustrated growl that earns me a few weary glances from the students walking around me.

I need to get back to the house, and I need to get my mind on literally *anything* else.

I'll talk to Cassie about this later, when I've cooled down, when I can be rational.

As I storm through campus, I know I'm lying to myself.

Because rationality doesn't exist in me.

Not when it comes to that motherfucker and my girl.

Cassie

I PACK MY BOOKS and laptop up with more aggression than necessary at the end of Genetics, grumbling to myself as I shove everything in my bag. I've been doing great in this class so far, and effectively avoiding Grayson.

Until today.

Because the professor just assigned us as lab partners.

I inhale a stiff, hot breath and blow it out like a dragon before slugging my bag onto my shoulder. I don't make it two steps from my desk when Grayson jogs down the steps in the classroom to catch up with me.

"So, lab partners," he says on a grin, waggling his brows at me. "Talk about some fucked-up fate, huh?"

"I'm putting in a request for someone else," I growl out, locking eyes on his. "Right now."

"Wait!" He rounds to stand in front of me, reaching out for my arms to grab me and pull me to the side. I rip away from his touch, but let him guide me out of the path of the other students. "Don't do that."

"We can't be lab partners, Grayson."

"Why not?"

"Oh, do I need to remind you? Well, let's see…" I tap my chin, ready to pop off *every* thing he's ever done wrong, but he holds up his hands in surrender before I do.

"You don't have to remind me that I hurt you," he says, sighing. "I just… What about forgiveness?"

I laugh, shaking my head and trying to push past him, but he steps in my way again.

"I'm serious. Look, I hurt you. I fucked you over and you *deserve* to hate me — now and forever."

"Gee, thanks for the permission," I reply flatly.

"I didn't mean to hurt you. I didn't *want* to hurt you." Grayson shoves a hand back over his hair, trailing the length of it before hooking his hand on the back of his neck. His eyes flick back and forth somewhere in the distance. "I was lost. I was fucked up and I acted out and hurt the one person who was there for me. I just... I didn't know what to do. My parents were on me to pick another major, and threatening to pull any and all financial support if I didn't. I was in denial, playing shows, focusing on my music career, all the while knowing it was about to end for good."

Do not feel sorry for him. Do not.

"I don't have enough excuses to make you truly forgive me. And you never have to. But I'm asking you to give me a shot at being your friend."

"My friend," I echo.

"Yes." He sighs, stepping a little closer and lowering his voice. "I know how badly it hurts you to lose people in your life. I remember what you told me about Paris. I remember how badly it hurt you to pick me over Adam when I was being a selfish little boy with you."

That last confession surprises me, because I never thought I'd hear the day when Grayson admitted he was wrong about asking me to choose between him and Adam.

"I don't want to hurt you even more than I already have by disappearing from your life. We had a great friendship, Cassie. And I miss it. Don't you?"

My throat is tight and sticky with the question, and softly, quietly, somewhere deep within me, I hear a distant *yes*.

I shake my head, shoving past him and over to the professor.

"Professor Drumm, sir," I start. "I'm sorry to bother you. But about the lab partner assignment..."

"No changes," he says without looking up at me from his laptop. "It takes a long time for us to pair students, and we do so with careful intent." He glances at me briefly, then over the top of his glasses. "If you've got a problem, figure it out. You'll have to work with a lot of people you don't like when you're a doctor, Ms. McBee."

My next breath is subdued by a smile I force so hard my cheek hurts, and I nod, thanking him before grinding my teeth and bolting out of the classroom.

Grayson is right on my heels.

"Just give me a chance," he pleads. "If I pull anything that makes you uncomfortable, you have permission to deck me in the face."

He holds the doors open for us to exit the science building, and then falls in step next to me.

"We have to be lab partners," he says, pulling me to a stop. "You heard Drumm. There's no getting out of this. So, we can either make an attempt to be friends, or we can both be miserable for the rest of the semester. I know which option sounds better to me," he says with a shrug. "What about you?"

I chew my lip, watching his sincere blue eyes like they're a snake that's been beside me in the grass all this time. I'm equal parts terrified, and sure I'll die from a venomous bite as I am surprised he hasn't struck me down yet. Something close to trust niggles at me from the inside, but it's against a strong warning from every cell in my being.

He's right. I *do* hate losing people. I hate it more than anything.

And as much as what he did hurt me, it killed me more to have someone I loved, someone I gave myself to completely, just disappear from my life overnight.

What if we *could* be friends?

Am I crazy for thinking it's possible?

"We can attempt to be friend*ly*," I decide on, which makes Grayson instantly smile and do a small fist bump by his side. "But I'm not making any promises that I'll be okay with it. I'll try. That's all I can give."

"That's enough," he says. Then, he stands straight and salutes me. "See you Thursday, partner."

I offer a small wave, chest tight even after he's gone. Then, I scan the yard for Adam. Now that Grayson and I are lab partners, it's time to tell Adam what's going on.

I don't find him after a long moment of searching, and I frown as a text comes through my phone saying he got caught up with Alpha Sigma stuff.

He's been stressed out, and I know he has a lot going on with the Alpha Sigma karaoke event coming up *and* the Halloween bash not too far after.

Maybe I should wait until things settle down a little bit.

Maybe by then, I'll know if Grayson is true to his word or not.

With a deep and uncertain sigh, I reply to Adam's text to let him know I'll see him later, and then I make my way to the Student Union to have lunch alone.

Erin

I NEVER EAT THE donuts or drink the coffee at group therapy.

I don't know why I choose this exact moment to notice that, but as the usual group files in, I stare at the donuts, the various colors of sugar and sugar substitutes, the tiny, individual cups of creamer, the simple red stirrers, and the steaming, black liquid as it flows from the pot and into a Styrofoam cup that's then carried away and I wonder — why do I never get any?

Part of it is vanity, I suppose, because I gave up coffee for fear of stunting my growth and yellowing my teeth, and donuts, well, that one is pretty obvious. I work hard enough to keep my thighs cellulite-free and my hips fitting into a size six, that even thinking about how many miles I'd need to run to work off a donut stresses me out.

But deep down, I think I know it's because that seemingly innocent table spread of caffeine and sugar is a watering hole.

And in my eyes — a trap.

When I come to group, I walk straight to the same chair I've sat in every week, sit down quietly, place my large purse in my lap, and cross my legs.

Then, I wait.

I watch as other members talk to each other while making their perfect cocktail of coffee and sugar and cream, and I smile politely if someone catches me looking — but I never join them.

And yet, I always take my time to get dressed up for session. I change into a different outfit so I'm fresh, redo my makeup and hair if need be, and I always look like I'm ready to go out to dinner after.

Maybe it's because sometimes, I hope I will be.

My vision is blurred and out of focus with my mind buzzing, until a dark shadow crosses between me and the coffee table. It's just a blur of black and gray that whooshes by, but I blink, waking from my daze, and my gaze follows the shadow.

Of course, when my vision focuses once more, I realize the shadow is a human. A boy — around my age, I guess — with olive skin. He's dressed in dark, skinny jeans and a black, long-sleeve shirt that makes *me* sweat thinking about the fact that it's September in South Florida. Those sleeves are crossed over a broad chest, and he stretches out his long legs next, crossing them at the ankles and sinking down into his chair. His face is hidden by the bill of a gray ball cap, pulled down over his eyes, just the hint of stubble on his chin visible to the room.

I've been coming to group therapy all summer, and I haven't seen him before. Everyone *else* in the room I know very well — at least, well *enough*.

There's Cyndi — with an *i*, which she'll remind you nearly every session — a white, middle-aged redhead who has an obsession with the color green and has been plagued with guilt since she backed out of her driveway and accidentally ran over her thirteen-year-old cat. There's Jonathan, the father who put his gambling addiction before his children, and they now want nothing to do with him. There's Kendall, the kleptomaniac — which I smiled at the first time I heard it, because it somehow sounded cute, the combination of her name and her affliction.

There's Sam, the man cheated on by his wife before she divorced him, and Clarence, the quiet old man who always smiles when someone's talking and barely ever says a word about himself. Harper is my favorite, mostly because she always sits next to me and leans in to offer her commentary on everyone's *problems*.

I could go on and on, but the point is that I know everyone in this group.

Except for the new shadow.

I wait for myself to feel something about him, about his newness, but all I can think is that he's very tall, very lean, and very sad.

The last fact is as obvious as the color of his shirt.

I'm still watching him when our group leader, Jackie, clicks the top of her pen and holds the notebook in her lap by the serial binding, her usual cue that we're about to begin. With one last, curious look at our new addition, I turn my attention fully to her, and straighten my back, meeting her smile with my own.

"Hello, everyone," she sings in her calm, soothing voice. "Welcome to group."

There's a murmur of *hellos* from the group — from everyone except our new shadow.

"So, before we get started, I want everyone to get comfortable in your chair, and then I want you to close your eyes."

I want to *roll* my eyes, but I close them as she instructs, reminding myself to remain open to the energy she's trying to give off. That's what my *personal* therapist always says. She knows how I've felt in the past about group therapy, about therapy *in general*, and she always reminds me that I'm on the road to healing, and if I snub my nose at everything I pass on this road, I'll just end up right back where I started.

Once our eyes are closed, Jackie leads us through a breathing exercise, reading off some calming mantras as we tune into our breaths. The more we breathe, the more she speaks in her soothing tone, the more I relax and drift into the open space she wants us to be in.

But suddenly, I feel like someone's watching me.

I creak one eye open, and then the next, glancing around the group at all the other members who have their eyes closed. Jackie is still speaking, and I frown, not knowing what made me feel uneasy and snapped me out of the moment.

Until I lock eyes with the shadow.

He's still in the same pose — long legs outstretched, arms folded across his chest — and his eyes aren't closed like Jackie instructed.

They're wide open, and completely zeroed in on me.

I blink at the boldness of them, of *him* — his gaze and his demeanor. His eyes are a bright, Caribbean water blue — almost see through, almost green, almost gray. They're light and playful as they take me in, and just as Jackie signals for everyone to open their eyes, he smiles at me.

Just a tiny curl of his lips, but it does something to my stomach that I *do not* like.

"Alright," Jackie says, and I tear my eyes from the shadow and back to her. "Who would like to start?"

The group takes turns sharing, then — tentative hands raising before something good or bad from the week is divulged. Jonathan had a phone call with his daughter, though it was short and he could tell she didn't want to talk to him. He felt like it was a step in the right direction, but was seeking advice on how to bridge that conversation gap between them. Kendall had a breakthrough when she was shopping with her sister and resisted the urge to steal a pair of earrings.

It goes like this for nearly an hour, and I listen to everyone speak, nodding in empathy and offering words of encouragement when it feels right. I really do like being in the group, for as much of a fit I threw about going in the first place. I might not be the most talkative, but I do like helping others when I can, and I like feeling like I'm not alone in my struggle to move past all my own shit.

"Erin, what about you?" Jackie asks toward the end of session. "Anything going on with you this week?"

I take a deep breath, adjusting my legs to cross the opposite way as I balance my notebook in my lap. "Well, school is back in session," I remind her and the group. "And sorority life, too. So... it's been interesting, adjusting to having classes and responsibilities again. But it feels good. I'm redoing a wing of our sorority house and helping some of the other sororities plan their philanthropy events. Being president keeps me busy, and I've found when I'm busy, I don't have time to dwell on everything that makes me sad."

"But it's okay to be sad sometimes," Jackie gently reminds me.

I nod. "I know. Trust me, I still go there. But... I don't take out my sadness on the people I love anymore. At least, I'm trying not to. There are still some bridges I'm trying to mend but..." I scratch the back of my neck, thinking of Skyler.

Of Clinton.

"Well, all things in time, I suppose," I finish.

Jackie smiles. "That's exactly right. And what are you working on this week?"

My heart squeezes. "Writing letters. I'm trying to write letters to the people I know I hurt... not necessarily to send, but just to figure out my feelings."

"What happened to you?"

The question is loud and abrupt, and all heads swing to the shadow, who's looking at me with his fierce eyes again.

I swallow. "Sorry?"

"What'd you do? Who'd you hurt? What happened to you to make you come here?"

Jackie smiles apologetically at me, and then she addresses the shadow in a soft tone. "We actually don't encourage questions like that here," she says. "We prefer to let our guests speak about whatever it is that they're comfortable with."

He keeps his eyes on me when he speaks. "That doesn't really make sense, does it? Isn't the whole point of therapy to talk about your shit and work through it?"

"I *have* talked about my shit," I say to him, folding my hands over my notebook. "You weren't here. Sorry you missed the show."

"So, tell me now."

"I don't feel like talking about it today."

"Why not?"

My heart picks up its pace, but this stranger isn't backing down. He just cocks his head, like he's trying to figure me out, like I'm a puzzle to be solved.

"Why don't you tell us about you, instead?" Jackie offers, noting the flush of my cheeks at all the attention.

The shadow smiles then, shrugging before he turns to Jackie. "Okay. I'm Gavin Lindberg. I'm a graduate student at Palm South. And I'm here because I got drunk and slammed my car into a tree with my little sister in the passenger seat. I killed her."

He says the words with conviction, with punctuation, as if each word is a fist he's throwing into our jaws. I feel each punch, and when he's done, he looks at me again.

"I had an abortion that I didn't tell anyone about, and when I finally healed from that, I was gang-raped by a guy I was seeing and three of his fraternity brothers," I say, not backing down from his gaze. "Then, I became the villain, and I hurt everyone I love most."

The room goes completely silent, and my heart beats so loud in my ears I wonder if they can all hear it, too.

Gavin smiles, and so softly under his breath that I almost don't hear him, he says, "There she is."

Jackie wraps up our session a few minutes later with another breathing exercise, and as soon as we're dismissed, various members join in little groups to chat and finish up the last of the donuts. I'm just throwing my purse over my shoulder when I feel body heat behind me.

When I turn, I'm met with those piercing blue eyes up close and personal.

I wait for him to speak, but for the longest time, he just looks at me, his eyes trailing over me from head to toe. It's not in a way that creeps me out, oddly — not like he's checking me out or assessing my size.

Just like he's *seeing* me, like he's taking the time to look at the girl I hide from everyone else.

When his eyes finally trail up to mine again, he slides his hands into the pockets of his dark jeans, and that same crooked grin finds his lips.

"Thanks for sharing," he says.

And then he brushes past me and walks out the door without another word to anyone else.

Ashlei

WALKING BACK INTO *Okay, Cool* feels a lot like coming home.

I greet everyone on my way in, taking a little more time to chat with MyKayla at the front desk. She catches me up on her online dating ventures, while I fill her in on how Kappa Kappa Beta recruitment was and how classes have been so far. Then, I make my way to my new, *permanent* cube, and I sit down in the chair with my chest swelling as I adjust my little keyboard.

This is *mine*.

I feel it deep in my soul, that earned possession. Now that everyone knows about me and Mr. Church, I'm free from having to hide anything about myself. And with my internship being over, I've fully transitioned into a full-time paid position.

Ashlei Daniels, Account Manager at *Okay, Cool*.

My heart flutters a little with the feel of it. After my internship ended, I offered to extend over the summer, and of course, Brandon okayed it. And in the middle of July, my manager offered me the full-time position.

It wasn't that I was shocked at the offer, but more so that it had come not from Brandon, but from my manager and her team. *They* wanted me here, and not because I gave great blow jobs.

Because I'd *earned* my spot.

Another smile finds my lips as I log into my computer, going through the flurry of emails that came in while I was gone. I took four weeks off between my internship and my first day in my new position, mostly to be there for Jess during recruitment, and to get through syllabus week before work got crazy.

And then, there was the weekend in the Bahamas with Brandon.

I bite my lip as last weekend flashes through my mind — days spent on the boat and exploring the island, nights spent wrapped in the sheets. My skin is still bronzed from the island sun, the tan line left from my swimsuit top visible around my neck, and I run my finger over it with my cheeks flushing.

It had been absolutely perfect, wasting away a few days with him before we both got back to reality. I could still close my eyes and see his eyes dancing in the candlelight over our private dinners served on the yacht, could hear his laughter as I swam with the pigs and one nipped at the strings of my bikini, untying the bottoms, could still feel his warm hands framing my face as he swept his lips over mine on the beach, the moon high and full above us, waves crashing gently at our feet.

I sigh, feeling warmth spread through my chest like that island sunshine.

I've known Brandon for a full year now, and somehow, he still manages to surprise me.

He's still on my mind after I have lunch with MyKayla, so before my first team meeting, I slip into his office, hellbent on sneaking a kiss or two.

That plan is throttled, however, when I walk in and find two, long, tan and toned legs with red-bottom stilettos strapped to the feet hanging from the edge of his desk.

I stop in the doorway, following the line of those legs up to the body attached to them. The girl sitting on the corner of his desk — the desk he'd bent me over too many times to count — is younger than me, by the looks of it, with long, bleach-blonde hair and lips painted the same bright red as the bottom of her Louboutins. She's wearing a chic, black pencil skirt with a crisp, white button-up top that cuffs at her elbows. She has her arms wrapped around a binder, and her eyes on my boyfriend as she laughs.

As he laughs with her.

I'm not sure how long I stand there — it must only be a fraction of a second, though it feels like hours. And when the laughter subsides, Brandon finds me in the doorway, and his smile somehow stretches even wider.

"Well, if it isn't our brand-new account manager," he says, standing and fastening the button of his blazer. He turns his attention back to the girl. "Sophie, this is Ashlei Daniels. She started as an intern, too, and today is her first day as a full-time employee."

Sophie turns her wide, sparkling, honey eyes to me, then.

We're practically twins.

"Wow, so *you're* the famous Ashlei Daniels," she says, genuinely.

She stands then, and I take a breath that doesn't burn quite as badly now that her legs aren't dangling off Brandon's desk anymore.

"Sophie Miller," she says, extending her hand for mine. I shake it with the best smile I can muster. "I've heard a lot about you already."

"Have you, now?" I ask, quirking a brow at Brandon.

"You have a great reputation here," she explains. "I've only been here two weeks and already I've heard your name referenced a million times. It's nice to finally put a face to the name."

The longer she talks, the more I realize I can't figure her out. At first, she seemed bubbly and sweet, but something about the firmness of her handshake, the way her eyes linger on mine, the confidence in the way she holds her shoulders back, in her smile…

It puts me on edge.

It's like she already owns this place and everyone who works here, too.

"That's sweet," I say when our hands release. "It's nice to meet you."

"Sophie is already making a name for *herself*, too," Brandon says, circling his desk to join us on the other side of it. "Two weeks in and she's already brought in a new client."

Brandon smiles at Sophie, and she beams under his gaze like a prized peacock.

I narrow my eyes.

I don't know why jealousy is flaring hot and bird-like in my chest, but it is, and I hate that I feel threatened by this girl just as much as I hate that I had no idea who she was before this very moment.

Why hadn't Brandon mentioned her to me?

Then again, why *would* he?

I've been off work for three weeks. I've repeatedly told him *not* to talk about work around me because it was my break, my time off, my vacation.

Now, I'm back.

And apparently, there's a new girl in town.

Sophie waves him off, blushing — and I swear to God, my fists curl at my sides at the sight of those stupid red cheeks.

"You're too kind, Mr. Church," she says, tucking a strand of hair behind her ear as she peeks up at him through her lashes.

Yes, *peeks up at him*, like a shy little girl.

"I'll get these reports on your desk by the end of the day," she says, patting the binder in her hands. Then, she turns to me, and there's a glint of something in her eyes when she smiles. "It was *so* nice to meet you, Ashlei. I look forward to working together."

I smile, too. "Yes, you too, Sophie."

With one last little wave of her fingers, she's gone, and Brandon pulls me into his arms for a kiss that distracts me long enough to forget why my chest was tight in the first place.

Why did I just feel threatened by a freaking *intern*?

I shake my head at myself, wrapping my arms around Brandon's neck with a sigh. "Hi," I say.

"Hey, you. How's the first day back going?"

"It's busy," I admit. "Took all morning just to catch up on emails and get my calendar in order. I'm about to walk into my first meeting, but I wanted to see you first."

"I'm glad you stopped by," he says, releasing me and putting a work-appropriate distance between us. "We still on for dinner tonight?"

"You bet your sweet ass, we are."

He chuckles. "Good luck at your first meeting, babe."

My heart flutters at the pet name, and he leans in to kiss my cheek before rounding his desk to get back to work. I'm almost to the door of his office when I turn again, watching him, something pulling at a string tied around my chest.

He stops typing, looking at me with a frown. "Everything okay?"

There's a question looming inside that aching chest of mine, but I can't quite figure out what it is. All I *do* know is that it was born from jealousy.

And that that jealousy is unfounded.

So, I force a breath and smile, shaking my head. "Just taking one last look at my hot boyfriend."

Brandon rolls his eyes, balling up a piece of notebook paper on his desk and throwing it at me. I catch it and toss it up in the air before pretending to slam-dunk it in the waste bin by his door.

"See you tonight, cheese ball."

"Tonight," I echo.

And I ignore what's left of that burning question as I make my way down the hall to my meeting.

Skyler

MY BEST FRIEND IS out of orbit.

I've been suspicious of it since the summer, when he all but ignored me. And once we got back to school for fall semester, I knew it was true. He's too quiet, too broody, too shut off. He's not cracking jokes or cracking beers, and both are tell-tale signs that he's not okay.

Which is exactly why I'm flopped on the bean bag in Clinton's room while his legs hang off his bed above me, both of our eyes fixed on his television screen. We're both silent, save for the clicking of buttons as we play some stupid video game that I only marginally understand.

But that silence is about to be broken, because I'm tired of pretending like everything is fine.

"So," I say as our characters traipse through the mystical woods of another world in search of our next mission. "How are classes going so far?"

Clinton grunts in lieu of an answer.

"That good, huh?"

No answer.

"You been spending a lot of time with Becca?"

Again, he doesn't answer, and when I glance at him, he just shrugs.

"How's Baby Bear?" I ask, referring to his little brother.

"Seems good."

I sigh, pausing the game before I pop up off the bean bag and sit on the bed next to him. He scowls at the screen, trying to restart the game on his own controller, but since I'm the one who paused it, the play remains frozen.

"Bear, can we stop? Please?"

"Stop playing?"

I narrow my eyes. "Yes. The video game *and* whatever game it is you've been playing since last semester." I relax my glare on a sigh, reaching over to squeeze his forearm — which is so buff from all his working out that I can barely squeeze it at all. "Something is going on. Talk to me."

Bear drops his shoulder and the controller at that, a long exhale leaving his giant chest as he scrubs his hands over his face. When his hands fall, he stares at the paused television screen, opening his mouth before he closes it again.

"My mom is back."

I blanch, because that was the absolute *last* thing I was expecting him to say. "Back? As in..."

"As in, she messaged Clayton on Facebook a couple weeks ago, and I told him not to answer until I talked to her."

"And did you?"

He nods, just once, barely visible.

I swallow. "What did she say?"

"I asked her what the hell she was doing messaging Clayton, and told her if she was looking for more money to piss the fuck off."

"Fair," I say, but I reach for his hand, squeezing it in my own because I know this kind of callousness doesn't come from my best friend unless he was really, really hurt.

"She said she just wanted to talk, to catch up. She's back in Pittsburgh."

"Shit..."

"I told her to stay away from Clayton. At least, until I can see her and make sure she's clean."

"What'd she say to that?"

Bear finally looks at me then. "She booked me a plane ticket home."

At that, my jaw hinges open. "She... like, she *paid* for it?"

He nods. "I'm going the weekend before Halloween."

A long silence passes between us, and I watch him, searching his eyes for some sort of clue as to what he feels about all of it.

"Want me to go with you?"

He shakes his head immediately. "I need to do this on my own."

"Okay," I whisper. "So... this just happened a couple weeks ago?"

He nods.

"Then... what's been going on before this? You haven't been yourself all summer, all fall semester."

Clinton's jaw ticks, but before he can answer me, his eyes shift to something behind me, and he stands.

I turn, finding my Big standing in the frame of his bedroom door.

Erin is completely put together, as she always is, with a Lily Pulitzer dress and matching bow in her hair. But aside from her perfect makeup and outfit, there's something off about her, too. There has been ever since she betrayed me at Spring Break last year.

But whereas I've felt a calling to find out what's wrong with Bear, I haven't felt anything toward Erin.

Other than the urge to stay away from her.

Her big, brown eyes are locked on Bear, and when I look up at him, he's staring right back at her. Erin's hands are folded in front of her, and she picks at her nails, but Bear just stands stoic, unflinching, his jaw still hard set from our conversation.

I finally clear my throat, addressing Erin. "Uh... what's up?"

Erin blinks, as if I've woken her from a daze, and then her eyes find mine. "I was hoping I could talk to you."

She says the words to me, but her eyes move to Bear's again, and I can't help but feel whatever weird tension is going on between them. I know they were friends before last semester, but I also know that Bear lit her ass up after what she did to me and Kip. I had no idea if they'd ever worked through it.

Judging by the way they're acting now, I'd say it's a big fat *nope*.

"Um, sure," I answer, standing. I turn, giving Bear a big hug and assuring him I'll text later before I make my way to where Erin is.

She and Bear don't exchange a single word.

When we're out of the Omega Chi house and on Greek Row, Erin takes a deep breath, like she'd been stuck on an exhale the entire time we were inside.

"Thank you for talking to me," she starts.

I nod, and for a few steps we're both quiet, other than the clicking of her kitten heels and my sandals on the sidewalk.

"I know things aren't going to get better overnight," she says after a while. "Between us. I know I royally screwed up. I betrayed you, asked you to do something... *horrid*," she whispers, shaking her head. "And then I went full-on crazy and you were in the line of fire."

My nose flares, but I tell myself to listen, to be open to what she has to say.

"But," she continues. "I've been going to therapy for months now, and something I'm really trying to do is make amends with the people I've hurt."

Her expression morphs then, her brows folding together as she casts a glance back at the Omega Chi house. Then, she lets out a long sigh.

"Last semester, when I apologized, it wasn't sincere. I know that now, looking back. I tried to blame you, too — to make it somehow partly your fault that I did what I did to you."

She stops walking, waiting for me to face her, and it's such an interesting sight to behold — this perfectly put-together girl falling apart on Greek Row on a sunny, South Florida day.

"I am so sorry, Sky. Truly," she whispers, her bottom lip quivering. "I'm sorry I asked you to lure Kip in for me, that I manipulated you with the presidency, that I turned on you in front of everyone we know." She chokes on a sob, shaking her head and covering her mouth. "I am truly ashamed. I was in a very, very dark place, but that does not excuse what I did to you. And I hope we can start over, from this moment on. And I don't expect you to forgive me, but I hope one day we can have a friendship again."

My heart breaks at the sight of two tears streaming simultaneously down each of her cheeks, and I sigh, reaching out for her. In the next instant, she's in my arms, holding me so tightly I chuckle.

"I already forgave you," I tell her. "But I appreciate the genuine apology." I pull back then, looking her in the eyes. "And I'm sorry I've been avoiding you. I just... I guess part of me wondered if that version of you I saw last semester was still hanging around. I was a little scared."

"That's fair," she says, sniffing. She pulls a tissue from her purse and wipes daintily at her nose. "That version of me was an absolute monster."

"And who are you now?"

She laughs at that, shaking her head as she folds the tissue. "Figuring that out."

I smile, squeezing her arm. "You said you were in a dark place... what happened?"

"Oh, boy," she says, blowing out a breath and looking around Greek Row. Then, she loops her arm through mine, steering me toward the house once more. "There's a lot more to the story of everything that happened last semester, and before that. But... I can't tell you. Not yet, okay? I'm just... I'm not there yet." She looks at me with a glossy smile. "But I will be. One day. Hopefully soon."

I cover her hand that's looped through my arm, smiling back. "Whenever you're ready."

"Right now, I was kind of thinking... margaritas?"

I nudge her. "Oh, now you're just trying to butter me up."

"Is it working?"

"Add in some chips and guac, and I'll be as buttered as a biscuit."

We both laugh, and just like that, the past is the past.

At least, for now.

Adam

THE LAST TWO WEEKS have been hell.

After seeing Cassie with Grayson, I completely lost it. I found myself in one of my old habits — numbing. And I knew it was wrong. I knew it wasn't healthy. But there was literally nothing I could do to stop it.

I *still* can't.

For the last couple of weeks, I've thrown myself into everything Alpha Sigma. I've spent more time with my brothers, worked on our plans for the semester and next, and more than anything, dedicated time and effort to getting everything in order for tonight's event.

The Alpha Sigma Karaoke Showdown.

Jeremy had me worried, after our conversation a couple weeks ago, that I'd made a terrible decision in changing up the event. After all, he was right — the concert *had* been successful for two years. It was part of what got our fraternity on the map again. And as soon as it had a reputation, I get the big idea to go and change it up.

But now, halfway through the event and having already raised more than double what we did with the concert funds last year, I know I've made the right choice.

And still, I feel numb.

It doesn't matter that the event has gone over without a hitch, that every fraternity and sorority showed up to participate and compete, that the crowd is *packed* with students from all over campus, here for the entertainment and the opportunity to help determine the winners.

It's exactly as I imagined it.

Except that in my mind, I always saw Cassie right by my side through it all.

And since that day, I've been avoiding her.

It's not that I don't want to be with her. It's the exact opposite, really. But, the first few times we hung out after I saw her with Grayson, I tried several different ways to get her to bring up that she'd talked to him. I asked about her classes, asked if anything strange had happened, asked if there was anything going on that she needed to talk about. I literally asked her in every single way I could without coming right out with it.

And she hadn't said a word.

She still hasn't told me that she spoke to him. For all she knows, I'm still oblivious to the fact that she's talked to him at all since she found out he cheated on her at her semi-formal last year.

I've tried to understand, tried to give her space, tried to put my anger at bay by throwing myself into other things.

But one thing remains ominously true.

She's hiding something from me, and now, I no longer trust her.

Every day, when that thought crosses my mind, a sharp pain like a knife to the gut passes through me. It happens again as I make my way across the large lawn where we're hosting the concert during intermission. She's standing with some of her sisters and my brothers, smiling and blushing and watching me walk toward her.

And I feel nothing but betrayal.

"There he is!" Kade says from where he's standing in the crowd. He rushes over to me, launching himself high into the air and forcing me to catch him whether I want to or not. When he's cradled in my arms — the beast of a guy

— he rubs his knuckles against my skull. "El Presidente, putting on the best damn show this school has seen."

I chuckle, dropping him to the ground to the tune of light applause and other brothers joining in on his sentiments.

It's a moment that should fill me with pride, but instead, I only feel dread. Because the moment Kade is out of my arms, Cassie's in them.

"You're doing amazing!" she squeals, hugging me hard before she presses up on her toes to give me a kiss. Her soft green eyes are bright and wide under the hanging lights spanning the massive length of the yard — a last-minute touch I'd added to make it feel like a backyard barbecue — and her hair is smooth and straight, angling at her chin in a way that makes me stare at her lips.

"Thanks, babe," I say, but I immediately release her.

I don't miss the way she frowns up at me, but luckily I don't have to answer for my actions. Jess is next in line to congratulate me.

"Not bad for an Alpha Sigma shindig," she says, cocking one brow.

"Is there a compliment hidden somewhere in there?"

Kade shakes his head, clapping me on the shoulder. "Trust me, coming from this one?" He points a thumb at Jess. "That *is* a compliment. A high one."

She narrows her gaze at him, but then smiles, poking him hard in the ribs until he releases his hand on my shoulder and throws his arm around hers, instead. She crosses her arms like she's annoyed, but I don't miss the way she leans into him.

I have no idea what the fuck those two are.

They've been doing something close to seeing each other, and something equally as close to being mortal enemies, ever since the end of spring semester. But I've given up on trying to figure them out — especially since I have my own fish to fry.

After a few more notes of congrats, conversation moves away from me, everyone falling back into what they were discussing before I showed up. One of the students we hired to walk around with red plastic cups of beer on fancy serving platters walks past us, and I snag a beer from them, draining half of it in one swallow.

"Need some booze for those nerves, huh?" Cassie teases, threading her arms around me and looking up at me with her gorgeous eyes again. I usually love them, the way they always seem to find me, to light me on fire, to fill me up from the inside.

Now, I just wonder what else they're hiding.

"Something like that," I murmur.

"Everything is perfect," she says, looking around at the packed yard. It's the same place we had the concert in prior years, but we've completely transformed it this time around. The lights strung high above us, criss-crossing the space between the fake plants on either side, make it feel like a private, exclusive event. We found clever ways to weave the casual in with the fancy, the backyard family feels with the black-tie event vibes. Music plays from the stage, where the next groups of karaoke singers are getting set up, and without a doubt, I know that everyone is having a blast. "It's everything you wanted it to be and more."

She's right.

And yet, I'm counting down the minutes until it's over, until I can be alone again.

I sigh, chugging the last of my beer before trading it in for another. Cassie takes it away before I can drink too much.

"Hey," she says on a giggle, raising one eyebrow. "Maybe save the celebrating for *after* the event? You still have to get up there and emcee."

"I'm fine," I say, snatching the beer back from her. I don't mean to, but in the attempt, half of it splashes onto her shirt.

She gasps, stepping back from me, shocked at first, but then laughing. "Jerk," she says, shoving me playfully as she flicks the liquid off her hands. She even pegs me with a few droplets. "You're lucky you're cute. And that I happen to loooove you."

Cassie drags out the word *love*, long and sweet and adorable, coming in to cuddle me again regardless of the wetness of her shirt.

My jaw clenches, heart stopping altogether when I look down at her. "Do you?"

Her smile falls, brows tugging together. "Of course I do." Then, her eyes search mine, her arms tightening where they hold me. "Adam, what's going on? Are you okay?"

I can't help the smile that unleashes itself on my face, and it's an evil one — one accented by a chesty, one-syllable laugh before I drain my beer again. I toss the red cup in the nearby trashcan, shaking my head as I peel Cassie off me.

"I better get back up there."

She grabs my hand and pulls me back. "Adam," she pleads. She doesn't say anything else, but her eyes say everything her mouth isn't.

Talk to me.

Don't push me away.

I love you.

What's wrong?

I swallow, ripping my hand free from her grasp and shaking off the bad mood as I make my way back to the stage. Then, I finish the show, announce a final donation to our philanthropy that blows everyone out of the water, and high-five my brothers after an event well-done.

And I text Cassie, telling her I need to stay back to clean up and to head out without me.

I feel like shit, like an absolute fucking asshole.

But I also feel validated.

I don't want to hurt her. It's the *last* thing I want. But the truth is, she's hurting me. She's had her chance to tell me about Grayson — multiple times — and she hasn't. And maybe I should just ask her about it, but if I'm being honest with myself, I don't think I should have to.

If we're together, if she's my person and I'm hers... shouldn't we be honest with each other, always? No matter what?

That's what's on repeat in my mind as I help my brothers wrap up the event, as we celebrate well into the next morning, as I lie in bed hungover the next afternoon, with my eyes on the ceiling and the girl who's driven me crazy for years the only thing on my mind.

And the truth of what I'm feeling kills me.

Cassie can *say* she loves me all she wants to.

But until her actions line up with those words, I'm not sure I can believe them anymore.

Erin

I've started this letter and torn it up a thousand times, it seems. I don't think there are words to say what I need to say to you. I've tried and tried to find the right ones, but I always come up empty-handed.

I guess I should just start by saying that I am sorry.

But, God, that sounds so trite.

I want to roll my eyes at those words. They aren't enough. They don't do justice to how I really feel, to how much I care for you, to how badly it kills me to know that I hurt you.

They do nothing to explain what the choice I made did to me — long before you knew.

So, I'm going to try to explain. I know most of this won't make sense. Most of this won't

THE ALARM GOES OFF on my phone, a bright, cheerful jingle that signals it's time for me to leave to head to group therapy. I silence it, and then stare at yet another unfinished letter to Clinton. There's a pile of them in the waste bin next to my desk, and I crumple this one up into a ball and toss it in with the others.

The letter is still in my mind as I drive to therapy. The little church it's held in is off campus, just a short, ten-minute drive, but it's long enough to let me mull over the fact that I'm never going to be able to write out what I want to say to Clinton.

"You don't need to send the letters," my therapist had told me at our last session. *"Just write them to the people you've hurt, and say what you're too scared to say to them in person."*

I'd thought the exercise was annoying and cliché at first, but then... it had worked.

At least, sort of.

I'd written a letter to Skyler, and while I didn't give the letter to her, writing it helped me find the courage to talk to her. And now, we had finally taken a real, genuine step to putting everything that happened last semester behind us. I know we have a long way to go yet, but just having the conversation healed me in a way I couldn't fully understand.

Since then, I've written letters to my parents, to my unborn child, to my rapists, and to all of my closest friends — Jess, Lei, Cassie.

But I can't seem to write one for Bear.

If I could have anything in the world, it would be to have my friendship with Bear again. The way we used to be. Before he knew.

I'm still in a fog of thoughts when I make my way into therapy, and just like always, I bypass the donuts and the coffee and take my usual seat, pulling out a notebook and setting my purse in my lap.

And when I look up, Gavin Lindberg is staring at me.

The jolt of those electric blue eyes is enough to stop my next breath, and I stare back at him, unflinchingly, until Jackie asks everyone to find their seats and that we're about to begin. It's only at the sound of her voice that I finally blink, and with that blink, the rest of the room seems to come back to me in a whoosh.

I clear my throat, looking from him to Jackie, instead, and I keep my focus on her or whoever is speaking for the rest of group session. I'm not in the mood to talk today, so I just sit quietly and listen, and smile, and nod, and think.

And *not* look at Gavin Lindberg.

"Alright, that wraps us up for today," Jackie says after our breathing exercise. "Before you go, I want to leave you all with one last thought... this week, while you're going about your normal routine, I want you to ask yourself what you miss about what you perceive as *the old you*. If anything comes to mind, write it down. You don't have to do anything, not yet, I just want you to jot down anything that you used to do, or used to have, that you feel is lacking now."

I chew the inside of my cheek, already mentally noting a dozen things that I miss about the girl I used to be. I decide to write them down later, though — mostly because I'm already late to the Panhellenic meeting and I still need to set the house up for our KKB movie night.

As I'm packing my notebook into my purse, a shadow steps between me and the overhead fluorescent light, and I pause, letting my eyes slowly crawl up to Gavin's waiting face.

I hadn't noticed last week how tall he was, but as I stand, my eyes only coming to the base of his neck, I realize it. He's very tall. And very lean. And very... *dark*. It isn't just his hair or his clothes, but the way he stands, the hidden storm in his eyes, the lines in his face that somehow seem to hold more history than that of an old and tired man.

His skin is a golden brown, almost olive, like he's from the Mediterranean, and since he's not wearing a hat this week, I can see that his hair is a deep, rustic brown. It's short, but a little untidy, with ends sticking up here and there. And just like last week, he's dressed in dark, distressed jeans and a black t-shirt that says *Thy Art is Murder* on it.

"Hi," he says when I shrug my purse over my shoulder.

I swallow. "Hi."

"I wanted to apologize."

"Oh," I say, sweeping my hair behind one ear and over my shoulder.

"Yeah. So... this is me. Apologizing."

"You're doing great."

"I'm really very good. At practically everything. It's a curse."

I smile, and a quiet moment passes between us, with him staring at me and me checking the time on my watch.

"Seriously," he says when I meet his gaze again, shoving his hands in his pockets like they'll betray him if he leaves them dangling free. "Last week... I was a bit prickly. I didn't want to be here, and I... I don't really know why I attacked you like I did, but I'm sorry."

"It's okay," I assure him. "Really. I didn't think it was an attack at all. And, I get it. I didn't want to be here the first few times I came, either."

"And now?"

At that, I sigh, shrugging a little as I look around the room at the fellow misfit toys. "Now, I worry less about what I want, and more about what I need."

When our eyes meet again, there's an understanding there — one unlike any I've ever felt before. It's the kind of universal tug at my heart, at my soul, that makes me feel like I'm tethered to a stranger. Like somehow, there's a piece of me in them, and a piece of them in me.

After a minute, Gavin nods, and then without another word, he brushes past me and toward the door.

I stand for a second, face screwing up in a bit of confusion at the abrupt exit. But when I shake my head and turn to head for the door myself, I nearly run into Gavin where he's stopped and turned around.

I manage to put the brakes on before I run straight into his chest, but we're still a little too close for two people who just met when he looks down the crooked bridge of his nose at me and asks, "Would you like to have dinner with me?"

My eyes shoot open wide.

"Next week," he says when I don't answer. "After group. We can go wherever you want, unless it's Italian or Indian food because I hate both."

I bite my lip against the laugh that comes from me then, because it's both unexpected and absolutely lovely. I forgot what it feels like, to laugh like that, to feel joy fizzing in your chest like champagne bubbles.

At the sight of my smile, the side of Gavin's lips tug up, too, until he's wearing a shy smirk that somehow fits him perfectly.

"Sure," I say.

I debate offering him my number, but I don't have the chance. As soon as I agree, his smile ticks up a bit more, and then he nods at me, turns, and rushes out the door.

And I stand there in his dust, still a little sad from earlier, a little confused from our interaction, and a little something else, too.

Though I can't quite put my finger on what.

EPISODE 3

Cassie

IF YOU WOULD HAVE told me ten months ago that I would be sitting next to Grayson Anderson, listening to him play a new song, *without* wanting to strangle him and spit in his eye — I would have told you you were crazy.

Almost a year later, and I can still close my eyes and see him outside of semi-formal last year, talking to Malik, admitting that he had been screwing some girl named Alexis while we'd been dating.

While I'd been falling in love with him.

While I'd been trusting him.

While I'd been thinking about giving myself to him fully.

And once I had, he'd apparently told that girl to kick rocks — but that didn't change the fact that all the time I was dedicating to him, he was giving to someone else.

He'd cheated on me. He'd broken my heart. And I'd sworn I'd never forgive him.

But here I am, sitting next to him on the bench outside the science building, listening to him strum on his guitar and watching strands of his long hair fall out of the bun at the nape of his neck, into his face.

For the first couple weeks of class, I dutifully ignored him. Unfortunately for *me*, we were assigned lab partners during week three — which made it impossible to ignore him any further, unless I wanted to fail Genetics.

And I don't fail *anything*.

Still, I wasn't keen on the idea, and only conceded after Professor Drumm said I didn't have a prayer in changing partners, anyway.

Grayson asked me for forgiveness. He asked me for friendship.

And damn it if that doesn't hit some super soft bruise inside me that I didn't even realize existed.

Something I learned from my older sister is that holding onto a grudge, or something that hurt you, is useless. Giving anyone or anything that power only strips you of it and holds you back.

So, when Grayson poured his heart out, trying to get me to understand that he was in a bad place, I listened. When he told me his parents were already on his ass to change his major back then, at the same time his music career was taking off, I could see the internal struggle he must have been facing. And when he promised me he never meant to hurt me, and that if he could take it all back, he would — I believed him.

I don't have to forgive him, and I told him that much. But he asked for a chance for a friendship, and because I don't know how to stay mad at people who hurt me, I'm giving him one.

Or at least, I'm trying.

"That was really good," I say when he finishes the last note of the song. "Are you going to record it?"

Grayson sweeps his hair back off his face, something of a grin on his lips. "No more recording for me. I just do it for fun."

It's the middle of October, which should mean boots and scarves and pumpkin-spiced lattes — but in South Florida, it just feels like Summer Part Two. It's fifteen minutes until noon and I'm already sweating, my thighs sticking to the bench we're sitting on.

"Why? Just because you changed your major doesn't mean you can't still focus on your music."

"It does when I'm already behind in credits, and science might as well be another language to me," he argues. Then, he nudges me where I sit beside him on the bench. "Unlike you, brainiac."

"So *that's* what happened here — you bribed the professor to be my lab partner so you could pass, huh?"

"Damn it, you caught me."

Something in my stomach twisted at that, because the last time I *caught him*, it'd nearly killed me.

Grayson must have noticed the shift in me, because he set his guitar to the side, crossing his ankle over the opposite knee. "I didn't notice when we were dating just how smart you are," he says. "But I was so far up my own ass, I guess, that I didn't really see much at all."

I nod, because though it didn't feel like it back then, I look back on the time we dated now and see just how wrapped up I was in him. It was always me going to his shows, his place, hanging with his friends. Sure, he came to sorority events after I begged him to, but for the most part, I was happy to lose myself in who he was and not talk about me at all.

With Adam, it's the complete opposite.

He always builds me up, asks me about my classes, about my *dreams*. It's not just the here and now that he's fascinated with, but who I want to be next year, or in five years, or for the rest of my life.

It's like he knows he's going to be there with me, and he's so sure in that fact that he's determined to find out where he fits in my picture so he can step into the role fully.

My heart pinches the more I think about him, because as confident as I was at the beginning of the semester about us, something has changed in the last few weeks.

And I have no idea what's going on with him.

"Yeah, up your ass and probably a few other girls', too," I shoot back at Grayson, arching a brow.

He throws his hands up over his heart like he's been struck. "Ouch. Okay, I deserved that."

"You deserve a whole hell of a lot more than a jab for what you did." I shake my head, crossing my legs as my eyes scan the sidewalks for Adam. "You're just lucky I'm too nice to hand out punishment."

"I lost you."

I blink, turning back to him and finding sincerity laced in his gray eyes.

"Trust me," he whispers. "That was the worst punishment of all."

I swallow, something low and familiar hitting me deep in my belly at the sight of his pain. For so long, that boy had been everything to me. I'd loved him. I'd touched him and let him touch me, too.

God, is it awful that I've sort of missed him?

It's not that I want to be with him — not at *all*. Adam is everything I've wanted since I first stepped foot on this campus, even if we did have to take the long way around to finally be together.

But I miss talking to Grayson, miss listening to him play, miss the connection we've always had so effortlessly.

And I *hate* losing people.

It's the worst feeling in the world, in my opinion. I'd felt it the hardest when I'd lost my childhood best friend, Paris, after she'd betrayed me my freshman year. And it'd reverberated through me when I'd walked away from Grayson in that courtyard, knowing I'd never forgive him, that what we'd had was lost.

But now here we are, *trying* to be friends when it all seemed so impossible even a short month ago.

Something about that fills me with hope.

My gut drops again at the more pressing matter on my conscience — which is that I know when I tell Adam that Grayson and I are rekindling a friendship, he will be less than thrilled. And if there's one scar I don't want to re-open, it's the one that's still fresh from watching Grayson and Adam at each other's throats for an entire semester.

Last time the roles had been reversed.

But I have a feeling it won't matter to Adam that he's the one who has me now.

He still won't want to share.

I wanted to tell him after the first day of class, when I realized Grayson was in the same one. But at the time, there was really nothing to tell. We went to a small campus. It wasn't *that* weird that I ended up in the same class with my ex.

But once we started talking, once he apologized and asked me if we could try to be friends, I knew I needed to tell Adam — and I planned to.

Except he's been so distant.

First, it was the concert, and I didn't want to upset him when he already had so much to focus on. He had been stressed out that night, and it seemed like he'd been that way ever since. We haven't hung out much, and when we have, he's always on his phone, talking to Jeremy about fraternity stuff or working on his outline for Alpha Sigma Chapter or planning his next big thing — the Halloween bash.

But distractions or not, I have to tell him, and soon — which is why I'm not hiding the fact that I'm sitting with Grayson now as I wait for Adam to come by and meet me for lunch, like he used to do every day after this class.

When my phone buzzes in my pocket, I don't have to check it to know it's him saying he won't make it.

He's had some sort of excuse like that for the past couple of weeks, ever since his concert.

I sigh, pulling my phone from my pocket long enough to tell him it's okay and we'll catch up later, but my chest is tight as I do so. Jeremy had let it slip to me that night of the concert that some of the brothers had been giving Adam a hard time about spending so much time with me and not dedicating enough time to the fraternity, and ever since then, he's pulled back, focusing more on them and less on me.

Which is *fine*, I remind myself, because we're together all the time.

I can spare him and let him do his thing as president.

But I can't help but feel like there's something else going on, something he won't tell me...

"You okay?" Grayson asks, nodding toward my death grip on my phone with the open text message still glaring back at me.

I shake my head, finishing my text and shooting it back to Adam before I tuck my phone away again. "I'm fine."

"Mm. *Fine.* That's lady talk for *nothing is okay and I'm two seconds away from burning this whole mother-fucking campus down.*"

I roll my eyes, but a soft smile finds my lips. "I really am fine."

"Didn't you say you're waiting on Adam?" he asks casually, picking up his guitar again. "What time is he coming by?"

"He's not," I say, checking my bitter tone as soon as I realize the way I said it. "Uh... he has a fraternity thing I forgot about. Got my days mixed up."

Grayson holds his guitar in his lap, balancing his arms on the top of it and watching me carefully. "Everything okay with you two?"

At that, I chuckle, pulling the strap of my backpack onto one shoulder and standing. "Not happening, Grayson."

"What?" he asks, feigning innocence.

"I know we're trying to be friends again, but you'll never be the one I lean on when there's something going on between me and Adam."

"So there *is* something."

I swallow, heart ticking up a notch at the realization that I let that slip.

"I'll see you Thursday at lab," I say instead of acknowledging his assessment, and I can tell in his eyes that he doesn't want me to go, that he wants to know more about everything I'm not saying, but I turn my back on him and start the walk toward the sorority house without another word.

When I get back to my room, Ashlei, Jess, and Skyler are piled in a fluff of blankets in the middle of the floor, their laptops in front of them. They all smile when I walk in, and Skyler scoots over, patting the space next to her.

"Grab your laptop and take a seat, Little," she says with waggling eyebrows. "It's time to plan our Halloween costumes."

Then, Jess hands me a flyer — one confirming what my own boyfriend hadn't even told me yet.

Alpha Sigma is hosting another Halloween party on the sandbar, and with a live DJ, fireworks show, and open bar sponsored by one of the local clubs, the neon orange flyer promises it will be even bigger and better than last year.

I somehow manage a smile despite the rollercoaster dip of my stomach, and I pull my laptop from my bag, plopping down next to my Big to surf costume ideas as she hands me the open bag of Doritos, taking one before she passes it.

But before I pull up Pinterest, I text Adam.

We need to talk.

THERE IS NO BETTER feeling than having Kade's face buried between my thighs.

My hands are tangled in his hair, grabbing and pulling as I arch off his bed and grind my pelvis against his mouth. He already had a solid foundation in going down, but thanks to my expert teaching, he now knows just how to suck my clit, just how to curl his fingers inside me and make me writhe with aching need.

I finally understand that old saying now.

Hard work pays off.

When he releases the pressure, withdrawing his finger and rubbing the seam of my lips while he kisses inside my knee, I peer up at him through heavy lids, my lips parted, chest heaving.

"No," I whine, trying to drag his head back down. "Don't stop."

Kade smirks, balancing on his elbow with his face still fully between my thighs. Only now, he's stroking me between my wet and swollen lips, his fingertips skating over my clit before they dive back down again.

And all the while, he's sitting there with his stupid smirk, watching the show.

"Someone's close," he muses.

Something between a curse and a moan rips through me when he flattens his palm, rubbing it over the length of me with just enough pressure to have my whole body tensing and releasing at once, making me shiver and shake at the touch. I'm so wet from his mouth and my own desire that his hot skin slicks over me easily, and the more he rubs me, the more I feel that pressure mounting in my core.

Until he stops.

My eyes shoot open at the loss of heat, of connection, the cool air from his ceiling fan wafting over me uncomfortably.

"Damn it, Kade," I say, but before I can even lift my head to properly curse at him, his mouth is on mine, still covered with my salty taste as he backs me into the bed even more somehow.

His hand rests tentatively over me again, cupping me in warmth, and I gasp into his mouth at the sensation.

"If you want to get off," he whispers, sucking my lip between his teeth and holding it there before releasing it with a pop. "You'll have to get there yourself."

I narrow my eyes. "Fuck you," I spit, but then his hand cups me harder, and he moves it just an inch — up and back down — his deep brown eyes firing to life as he watches my eyelids flutter with the touch.

"Fuck my hand, Jess," he whispers, kissing my neck seductively, sucking my earlobe between his teeth. His next whisper is right into the shell of my ear, and it evokes a tsunami of chills over me. "I want you to fuck my hand until you come all over it, and then I can lick my fingers clean."

My mouth parts with a gasp, and in the next second his own covers mine, and he's kissing me hard and demanding, his hand just sitting there between my legs, warm and waiting.

I reach down with my own hands, holding his to me harder, and flex my hips.

Just that one motion has me sucking in a hot, stiff breath, and Kade devours it hungrily, kissing me harder as I buck my hips again.

His hand is so warm, so wet, and I hold it firm between my legs, rocking my hips back and forth, humping his palm as my clit fires to life. I know before a full minute has passed that I could get off just like that, without him even being inside me, but when I'm humping him hard and fast and he surprises me, slipping his middle finger deep and quick inside me before pulling out again, I groan at the feeling of being full.

"More," I pant, writhing under his touch. "I want you to fuck me, Kade."

"Not until you come."

I whimper, but it's silenced as soon as he dives back inside me again — this time with two fingers slipping easily into my soaked hole.

"Jesus Christ," I curse, and then without warning, I flip him over with his hand still cupping me, until the back of his palm is laying on his thick, muscular thigh and I'm straddling his fingers — all the while staring longingly at his thick, perfect, untouched erection.

Just the sight of it standing at attention pulses a new wave of need through me, and Kade's eyes intensify, urging me on. I sit back down on his fingers, feeling them deeper now, and he curls them inside me as I ride his hand the way I want to ride his cock.

The heat from his thighs press into every angle of my inner thighs, his palm hot on my clit, and I lean forward, getting more pressure where I need it and still fucking his fingers. And then everything clinches and releases, hot and fast, a lightning bolt of an orgasm striking me as I cry out.

Kade's hand slaps hard over my mouth, so much that it stings, but I cry into his left palm as I ride his right one, knowing he's just trying to save me from alerting the entire fraternity that he's getting me off.

Not that I care right now.

When my body slows, muscles already sore and aching, he removes his palm from my mouth with a knowing grin on his.

But before I can slump and let my climax lull me under, he sits up, kissing me hard and grabbing my ass firmly in both hands before he smacks it hard and flips me over.

I don't get another breath before he's wrapped in a condom and thrusting inside me — deep and urgent, every thick and pulsing inch filling me in quick, swift thrusts.

Damn, he's a good student.

This motherfucker was helpless just a few months ago, and now he's a sex god — one perfectly tailored to meet my kinky needs.

Maybe this deal wasn't a bad idea, after all.

Kade wraps both fists in my long hair and yanks hard, exposing my throat and cutting off my oxygen enough that I can't even cry out in approval. I'm so fucking turned on I could come again, but I don't have the chance before he pounds his climax into me, pulsing into the condom with subdued groans and his hands still in my hair.

He slows to a complete stop when he's done, releasing my hair, but then his hands pet down my back — slowly, softly, making goosebumps explode over my sensitive skin. He's still inside me, thrusting slowly and purposefully, and already I feel him softening, but he won't stop. Instead, he bends over me, pulling my back flush to his chest as he thrusts as deep inside me as he can with his erection quickly losing steam.

His mouth finds my ear, sucking the lobe, and then he grabs my chin and tilts it until he can claim my mouth.

I hate this kiss.

It's too intimate, too soon after making me come, too

close to real feelings that I break it quickly and roll over on to my back, chuckling with a satisfied sigh and closing my eyes.

Kade drops down beside me, still panting, one hand resting on his chest and the other reaching over to rest on my knee.

"Jess?"

"Mm?" I ask, brushing my hair back from my face.

When I creak my eyelids open, he's there balanced above me, something unreadable in his dark eyes.

"I think you're hotter than I've ever fucking seen you right now."

His eyes sweep over me, and a blush shades my cheeks as I cover my face with my hands. It's seven o'clock in the morning and I haven't even brushed my hair, let alone put on a stitch of makeup. I was just horny when I woke up and couldn't wait.

Usually, I dress up in lingerie for this prick — mostly because I like to boss him around in the bed and make him feel like I'm his Dom.

But this morning, *he* took control.

And now, he's got my stomach riding on the wings of butterflies with his stupid, *too-nice-for-a-fuck-buddy* comment.

I shove him away playfully with a roll of my eyes. "Whatever."

Kade laughs, tucking his hands under his head with his gaze on the ceiling. "You should have seen your face, getting all goopy-eyed over that romantic comment."

"You wish."

"Deny it all you want, J-Love," he teases, glancing at me with an arched brow. "But you know damn well that was an A+ move."

I don't deny it, but I *definitely* don't confirm it, either. Kade waits for a moment before giving up with a chuckle, rolling over and grabbing his phone off his nightstand.

"I feel like a Skywalker, conquering the Force."

I snort, but Kade just sits there with that doofus smile, flipping through his texts.

"Might have to pull out all the tricks I've learned on some unsuspecting hottie at the Halloween party next week."

My stomach takes a deep dive off the bed, and my eyes shoot open, throat constricting. I attempt a swallow but come up empty, and then I'm pissed at my body for betraying me, for being affected by what he said when *clearly* we shouldn't be.

I can almost see it — my brain putting her hands on her hips, glaring at my body like *Bitch, what the hell is wrong with you?*

But even as I sit there and convince myself I shouldn't feel the way I do after Kade's little comment, the feeling only sinks in deeper, and I press a hand to my chest, forcing a swallow.

Wait — am I annoyed?

Am I...jealous?

I frown at the thought, because why the *hell* would I be jealous that Kade wants to hook up with some chick at the Halloween party next weekend? It's not like we're dating. It's not like we're even *close* to that. We had a deal — I teach him how to have some fucking game, and he gets me off and lets me drive his car.

Plain and simple.

Except when I turn and see his goofy smile on his face, and another girl's name on his phone screen, my chest tightens, body betraying me once more.

Maybe it's not so simple, after all.

Bear

SITTING IN MR. AND Mrs. Harrison's backyard in Franklin Park, it's all I can do to keep my mouth shut and drink my beer while everyone else around me talks and laughs like everything is just peachy keen.

It's a perfect fall day, the bright blue sky virtually cloudless and letting the sun warm us where we sit around the small bonfire Mac's dad built. It's just cool enough to need the fire, and a light sweater, but not so cold that we need to bundle up or that we can't be outside enjoying the evening. I can't help but compare it to the hot and humid October day I left behind in South Florida when I got on the plane that took me back home just a couple days go, and perhaps what guts me is I don't know which one feels like home.

Honestly, neither really does anymore.

I've spent the weekend with my little brother, watching him dominate at his home football game Friday night, and then eating our way around Pittsburgh all day yesterday. It was the closest I've felt to myself since the day Erin told me about our unborn child, but I woke this morning with the same numbness, the same dread swimming in my stomach.

Because we were going to see our mother for the first time in two years.

I'd reached out to her after Clayton told me she was online again, and she asked to see us both. She wanted to explain, wanted to spend time with us, show us how much she'd changed. And while everything inside me wanted to scream at her to go fuck herself all the way off, I knew what my little brother wanted more than anything in the world was a relationship with at least one of his parents.

And since our dad was a piece of shit who took off shortly after Clayton was born, this was the only option.

It's a full house, with Mac and his sister, Kia, their parents, my little brother, me, and — the guest of the day — my mother.

Christine Pennington looks better than I've ever seen her look. Her normally ashen skin is golden brown and healthy, her big brown eyes wide and full of life, her smile no longer the dead one that I'd become accustomed to growing up, but rather one that glows and fills her entire face. She looks nothing like the profile picture on her new Facebook account — the one she'd contacted both me and Clayton on. That woman was skinny and drugged out and sad. The one sitting across the fire from me with a glass of water is healthy and sober and happy.

Still, I don't trust her.

And I don't like the way Clayton so easily does.

"I can't believe you've been in Mexico this whole time," Clayton says after our mother finishes off a story about her and my older brother, Carleton, in Tijuana drinking margaritas the size of their face. He had asked to come today, too, but I'd refused.

One fucked-up family member at a time.

"It was quite a ride," Mom muses, thumbing the condensation off the side of her glass with a smile. "The beaches there, they're just incredible." Her eyes find mine then. "Of course, I'm sure it's nothing compared to the beaches in Florida, right, baby?"

My nostrils flare at the pet name, because she hasn't ever called me her *baby*. Even before she bailed on her family, we had a strained relationship at best. Because unlike my younger brother who saw her as an angel, and my older brother who followed in her footsteps, I saw her for exactly who she was.

A monster.

And I wanted nothing but to get as far away from her as I could.

I take a sip of my beer in lieu of answering, and an awkward silence passes over everyone before Kia steers the conversation toward how Clayton and Mac are both doing so well in football. My shoulders ease a little once it's no longer my mother talking, until she somehow finds a way to bring it all back to her.

"I wish I could have seen you play your freshman year last year," she says to Clayton, reaching over to thumb his cheek. I don't miss the way his eyes light up at the affection. "I bet you were a stud."

"He really was. Made me look bad," Mac comments, nudging his best friend. "But now, we're dominating. Going to take this team all the way to state."

"Well, I can't wait to watch it."

I scoff, crushing the can of beer I just drained and tossing it in the bag for recycling before reaching into the cooler for another.

Everyone is quiet, and Mom looks hurt where she watches me across the fire.

"What?" I ask, cracking the top on my next can. "Disappointed that I'm not playing into your bullshit the way everyone else is?"

"Clinton," Mrs. Harrison warns me, but her husband touches her arm gently, shaking his head to indicate it's not her place. And while I respect the shit out of her for stepping up and caring for my brother like he was her own, right now, it really *isn't* her place.

"I'm not… I wasn't trying to…" Mom stammers.

"You're not what?" I ask, tilting my head. "Spewing off a bunch of lies like you always do? Showing up after ditching your family for two years for some vacation in Mexico and expecting it to all be okay?"

She swallows.

"I was just saying that I'm happy I'll be able to see him play," she whispers.

"Bullshit," I whisper, sucking down half my beer.

"Come on, bro," Clayton begs from across the fire just as Kia excuses herself to the restroom.

"No," I yell, and I surprise myself at how much my voice booms. Everyone else seems shaken, too, their eyes locked on me as I point across the fire at my brother. "Don't let her fool you. Don't let her get in your head with her lies. I've lived through enough of them to tell you that they only get better with age."

"I'm not lying," Mom says defensively, holding her chin high. "And I surely don't appreciate the way you're talking to me or about me right now, Clinton. I'm your mother."

At that, I bark out a loud, barrel-chested laugh. "Oh, are you? Because I thought mothers were supposed to take care of their children, not ask them for money time and time again, and then disappear and not talk to them for two years."

"Alright, Bear, I think that's—" Mr. Harrison starts, but he doesn't get to finish before I stand, towering over the fire and my mother on the other side of it.

"You're a liar, and an addict, and a piece of shit excuse for a mother, and I won't let you tear Clayton up the way you did me." I look at him then. "She won't be at your football games. She won't be here for your prom or senior night or graduation, either. Trust me when I tell you that she came back because she needs something." I turn on my mother again. "And as soon as she gets it, she'll be gone again."

Mom's bottom lip quivers, and I wish I felt a shred of remorse for what I said, but I feel nothing.

She stands, mumbling something about needing to get something out of her car before she excuses herself through the backyard gate. Mac's mom looks at her husband with worried eyes before chasing after her, and then I'm being shoved back by two surprisingly strong hands.

"What the fuck, Bear?!"

"Language, Clayton," Mr. Harrison warns, but he's already ushering Mac inside. "We'll leave you two alone, but just for the record, I don't appreciate any of that kind of disrespectful talk going down in my house. You understand me?" He looks briefly at my little brother, but his glare nearly burns a hole in my skull. "So, you two talk this out and cool down. Now."

I don't respond, but I do nod to let him know I've heard him, and a sliver of guilt seeps into my spoiled gut.

"Seriously, what the hell is wrong with you?" Clayton asks when we're alone. He's almost as tall as me now, with the lean and built body of a wide receiver, instead of the lanky one he'd had as a kid. I see the same shape of my eyes in his own, feel the same blood coursing through our veins, and though I know he's not a child anymore, I can't help but want to protect him like one. "We finally have her back in our lives, and you're doing everything you can to push her away."

"She left us," I remind him. "Our brother left *his* children, too. Now, they're back after two years of barely any word at all, and we're just supposed to listen to their stories, celebrate them, welcome them home with open arms?"

"People make mistakes, Bear," Clayton says. "Haven't you?"

I grit my teeth, looking away from him and at the half-open gate across the yard from us. Through the slit, I can see Mrs. Harrison holding my mother while she cries.

And it pisses me off even more.

"Yes, people *do* make mistakes. But unlike our mother, most people regret them. Most people do whatever they can to make amends and become a better person. But our mother, Clayton?" I point at the gate. "She is a fuck-ing train wreck. She cares about no one but herself, and I know you want to believe her when she says she'll stay, that she'll be a better mother, but believe me when *I* say that she's lying."

"You don't know that."

"But I *do*," I urge, stepping into him and grabbing both his shoulders in my hands. "Who has been there for you your entire life? Who used to feed you when that woman wouldn't, change your diapers, play with you, care for you when you were sick? Who made sure you got up in time for school and got on the bus? Who made sure you took show-ers and brushed your teeth? Who made sure you were okay when she bailed out of here?" I shake my head, begging him to see it. "I may not be perfect, Clayton, but *I'm* your family. I'm the one you should trust in — not her."

Clayton's eyes grow so tired in the span of my words, that I wonder if I've aged him, if it would be one of those moments like so many I had lived through myself that he'd look back on as a turning point.

"I do trust you," he finally whispers. "And I love you, bro. I do. And maybe you're right. Maybe she'll leave again or make promises she can't keep, but... I don't know. I think she's changed. I think something happened. She seems different, and I know she doesn't deserve it, but I want to give her a second chance. Okay? And that's my choice. Not yours. So if you want to write her off forever, if you want to be an asshole to her and never give her the opportunity to make things right, then that's your decision. I won't force you to do anything you don't want to do. But I'm asking the same courtesy from you."

His eyes are hard on mine, and he shrugs out of my grasp without letting me respond, jogging across the yard and through the gate to join our mother and Mrs. Harrison.

The next breath through my nose is icy cold, and I seethe with the overwhelming urge to run to him and hold him away from our mother and take him away from this place, even if he hates me for doing it.

But he's right.

I can't make choices for him, and he's grown enough now to know the possible consequences of the decisions he's making. And hadn't I done the same, given our mother chance after chance until she'd burned me enough times that I learned not to get close to the fire ever again?

I scrub my hands over my face, trying to soothe my uneven breathing enough to get through the rest of the night. My phone buzzes in my pocket, and I yank it out, expecting to see Becca's warm smile on my screen.

Instead, it's a black screen with the name ERIN XANDER in white letters at the top.

My stomach drops, and I stare at the vibrating device for what feels like an eternity with my heart in my throat. When I don't answer, she goes to voicemail, a *missed call* notification taking the place of her name on the screen.

But before I can put the phone back in my pocket, it rings again.

Erin.

I answer quickly this time, snapping back to reality like waking from a dream. "Erin? Are you okay? What's going on?"

"Hey," she answers softly, tentatively. "Oh gosh, yes, I'm fine, I'm sorry if I worried you. I just wasn't sure if my first call came through but... oh, you're probably busy. I'm sorry. I'll just—"

"Don't hang up."

A silent moment passes between us as my racing heart slows to its normal rate, and I run a hand through my short hair, turning away from where I can still see my mom and brother through the backyard gate.

"Did I catch you at a bad time?" Erin finally asks.

I want to laugh, because *every* time is a bad time for me — ever since the last night Erin and I talked.

"Why did you call me, Ex?"

I hear a shaky inhale on the other end, a shuffling of papers. "I'd like to talk to you."

"So, talk."

"Not on the phone," she explains. "I was wondering if we could have dinner."

My heart stops, skipping a few beats before it hammers back to life. "Dinner."

"If that would be okay."

I glance over my shoulder and see Mrs. Harrison and Clayton leading Mom back inside the house, and I nod to my little brother, signaling that I'll be right in.

"I'm out of town."

"Oh..." Erin pauses. "Okay. I'm sorry, I—"

"I'll be back next week."

I swallow, my stomach so fucked up from the emotions of the day, I'm not sure I'll be able to hold down the beer churning inside it.

"Okay," Erin whispers. "How about the Sunday after Halloween? Eros?"

Eros is a small Greek restaurant off campus, and one of my favorites.

"What time?"

"Seven okay?"

I nod, more to myself than to her, as if I need that assurance from myself that I can do this, that I can have dinner with Erin and somehow live through it. "See you then."

I don't wait for a response before I end the call, and I don't allow myself to simmer on the sound of her voice, or the fact that I'll be meeting up with her when I get back to Florida. Instead, I shove the phone in my pocket and put out the bonfire on my way back inside to suffer through whatever time I have left with my mother.

One monster at a time.

Skyler

"ALRIGHT, LET'S MAKE THIS happen," I say, blowing a whistle through my teeth when I flip over the bottom card in my dealer stack. The top one was a Jack of spades, and the bottom is a three of hearts.

"Come on, come on," Chelsea says from the edge of the table. I learned earlier tonight that she's in banking, and the hot stud next to her who can't be any older than me is James, her "friend" from out of town.

They've been making out all night between hands, and judging by the ring on her finger, I'd say Chelsea is up to no good.

But it's not for me to judge. My job tonight is to lose as many hands as the cards will let me.

Because the more the Blackjack dealer loses, the more she gets tipped.

Casino Boat 101.

I flip the next card, and it's a two of hearts, giving me a fifteen.

"Bust! Bust! Come on!" Roberto says. He's short and spunky and has been smoking like a chimney all night, but he's also been the only one tipping me between hands.

I like Roberto.

I cringe, eyeing the next card before I flip it with a satisfied grin.

King of clubs.

The table roars, everyone thrusting their hands up into the air and high-fiving each other as I pay out the winnings and clear the cards.

I've been working on the boat for a couple months now, and one thing I've figured out for sure — I love it. I love being on a boat with people letting loose for the night. I love the freedom we all feel in international waters, like nothing is off limits, like the night is forever young. I love the clouds of smoke and the dinging bells of the slot machines and the distant roars of each table when they beat the dealer or get a good roll in Craps.

I may be out of the professional poker scene, but this will always be a part of who I am.

It's my energy. It's my soul. It's the very blood in my veins.

And that's why I'm going to open my *own* casino company when I graduate.

It won't be a real casino, but rather one that can be hired out for parties and weddings and corporate events. I've already got the start of a business plan together, detailing how companies or hosts can purchase fake money that, in turn, the guests can use to gamble. The more money they have at the end of the night, the more entries they get into raffles, or the more they have to use to bid on auction items. It will all be legal, not gambling, per se, but gambling-ish.

And it will all be mine.

Until then, working on the casino cruise will give me more experience dealing different games, which I'll need when it's time to train my *own* dealers.

Plus, it's a good distraction from the fact that Kip is across the country.

He must know that I'm extra in my sad panda feels tonight, because as soon as I wrap up my shift on the boat, stepping back onto the dock and immediately unfastening the tie around my neck, my phone rings.

"Hello, handsome," I sing.

"Hiiiii."

At the long, drawn-out greeting, I grin. "Someone's been drinking."

"And someone *else* has not been sending nudes."

I bark out a laugh, pulling my keys from my purse as I cross the employee parking lot. "That's because someone else has been working."

"Boooooo. Ditch work. Come to California, instead."

"I will, baby. In less than a month now."

"That's so far away."

My heart squeezes. "I know. I miss you, too."

There's a long pause of silence, and then a hiccup that makes me smile again.

"Where are you?"

"At the A Sig house. We had a party tonight."

"Clearly."

"The whole week is a party around Halloween."

"Tell me about it. The A Sig Halloween bash is tomorrow on the sandbar. Everyone has been talking about it all week."

"What are you going to wear?"

"The girls and I are going as pin-up dolls."

There's a groan on the other end, and then what sounds like Kip slapping himself in the face and dragging his hand over it. "You're going to look so hot," he almost whines.

I chuckle. "I'll bring the outfit when I come next month."

"You better."

I sigh, and silence passes between us as I get in my car and fire it to life. There's a roar somewhere in the background where Kip is, and I smile, picturing the madness.

"You sound like you're having fun," I say. "I wish I was there with you."

"Soon," he promises.

"Soon," I echo.

I check the date on my watch, letting my head fall back against the head rest and closing my eyes.

Just twenty-four more days.

Cassie

"GOD, WHEN THEY SAID the Halloween party would be even bigger and better than last year, I doubted it," Skyler confesses, lowering her sunglasses down to the tip of her nose as she looks around the sandbar. "But *damn*, did Alpha Sig deliver."

I glance around with her, and while I can tell she's in awe, I feel mostly overwhelmed by the amount of students crammed onto one speck of sand off the east coast of Florida. The sandbar is usually vacant, save for the occasional boat that might stop there on the weekends, but today, it's crawling with people dressed in swimsuit Halloween costumes. Boats line every bit of the shore, anchored in place, with people standing or floating in the water between each one, and in the center of the sandbar is a DJ, hooked up to a generator and thumping music like a heartbeat out to every inch of the little island.

We couldn't have asked for a more perfect day. It's seventy-five and sunny, the breeze enough to cool us if we get too drunk and hot, but the water still warm enough for us to not freeze our asses off. Ashlei and Jess have already set up camp with their beach chairs and umbrellas and gone in search of booze, and Skyler and I set our stuff next to theirs, saving room for Erin, just in case she shows.

Fluffy white clouds pepper the bright blue sky, giving a slight reprieve from the sun as we splay out our beach towels, but I still pull out my sunscreen to protect my fair skin.

"Adam is really kicking ass as second-term president, isn't he?" Skyler asks, putting her hand out for the sunscreen once I have a dollop in my hand.

I pass it to her, still looking around and trying to ignore the pit in my stomach at the fact that I knew nothing about what to expect today since Adam and I have barely talked, let alone seen each other. "He is, indeed."

"I'm sure the pressure is insane," Skyler says, rubbing lotion on her chest. "No one has ever been president two years in a row."

My stomach twists again, but I force a smile. "Speaking of pressure, how is Kip doing in the film program at UCLA?"

"Oh, kicking ass and taking names, of course. He's working on a script for an online series right now that will go up in competition against the other students in his program. He seems pretty geeked up about it, but won't tell me much."

"When do you get to see him next?"

Skyler frowns a little at that, squeezing more lotion into her hands before passing the bottle to me. "Thanksgiving. I can't believe it's already been two months."

I reach over to squeeze her arm. "But hey, Thanksgiving is just a month away."

"Twenty-three days," Skyler corrects with a smile. "I hope he knows we're not leaving his dorm room."

I snicker. "And *I* hope his roommates have noise-cancelling headphones."

It's only a little past noon, and already the Halloween party is in full swing. Just looking around the island at the multitude of students doing beer bongs and keg stands and hammering back shots tells me most of them won't make it to sunset. Still, I love seeing how creative everyone got with their costumes, finding ways to dress up but in swimsuits. I spot an Indiana Jones, a group of Minions from the *Despicable Me* movie, animals of every kind, superheroes and Disney princesses, Barbies and musicians, even a few puns — like Bear's Little, Josh, who has a lampshade on his head and a box over his shoulders with a table cloth and some random items on top. The front of it says "*one night stand.*"

The girls and I decided to go for something sexy but classy, landing on pin-up dolls. For one, it was easy to transform that into a swimsuit costume, and for two, we could each dress in colors that complemented our different skin and hair colors.

I'm in an emerald two piece, the bottoms high waisted with a frilly trim, the top a shiny sweetheart cut with straps over my shoulders. I curled my short red hair and wrapped a matching green bandana around it to tie at my forehead, and painted my lips a cherry red.

Skyler, on the other hand, is sexy as hell in a yellow one piece that looks more like a man's shirt than a swimsuit. It's loose at the top, with a deep V that accentuates her tan cleavage and toned stomach, but it cinches at her waist and hugs her ass perfectly at the bottom. It looks like a cuffed sleeve where the straps hook around her neck, and the left breast has a pocket, like a work shirt. She's paired it with jean shorts that I'm sure will come off at some point, and her hair is braided into pigtails, each wrapped with yellow bows.

"Speak of the devil, if it isn't the big man on campus," Skyler says with a grin, skipping past me. I turn just in time to see her give Adam a big high-five before hanging her hands on her hips. "This is *bad ass*, my friend. Well done."

"Thank you, thank you," Adam replies, pretending to bow.

"How the hell did you get a DJ on a sandbar?"

"With a very expensive generator and a lot of possible disaster planning."

Skyler chuckles. "Well, it sets the tone, and the open bars, the kegs, the slip and slide..." She whistles her approval. "You've outdone yourself."

"Just wait until the fireworks show." Adam smiles, pride radiating off him. It turns me on to see him like this, exuding power and confidence, and I slide up to him, wrapping my arms around his bare torso.

"I agree," I say, kissing his warm neck. "You knocked it out of the park, babe."

He swallows, putting his arm around my shoulders, but I feel the hesitant way he does it, and it makes my stomach ache. "Thanks, Cass."

"I'm going to get a drink," Skyler says, pointing a thumb over her shoulder. "Want anything, Little?"

"Just a beer for me. And a shot of something fruity, if you're up for it?"

Skyler scoffs. "Like that's even a question. Be right back!"

She skips off, and then it's just me and Adam, and I turn to thread my hands behind his neck and press my lips to his. The kiss is a little too cold and short for my taste, but he keeps his arm around my waist when we break off.

"So... I thought you were going to wear green trunks to match me?" I tease, eyeing his red swim trunks. He has a whistle around his neck and a patch of white sunscreen on his nose, which tells me he went for a lifeguard. "We never do seem to get our Halloween costumes right, do we?"

It's a joke, referencing the fact that he dressed to match Skyler my freshman year, and then last year, dressed up like Prince Eric as if to make up for it, since I had been Ariel from *The Little Mermaid*. But of course, I hadn't worn the same thing twice, and was Cleopatra, with a matching Grayson as my Mark Anthony.

It seems we're always mixing signals, but here in his arms, I don't care. I'm just thankful we've finally gotten out of our own way to be together.

"Yeah, I didn't really have time to shop," he says coldly, shrugging out of my grasp. "I actually need to go check on something at the DJ booth, but I wanted to say hi. I hope you have fun today."

I swallow, shivering at the cool breeze once he's no longer holding me. "You say that like I won't be spending it with you."

Adam runs a hand through his hair, looking off toward the DJ booth before he looks at me again. Of course, I can't see his expression under his dark Ray-Bans, but I don't have to see his eyes to notice the avoidance in them.

"Of course, you will," he says unconvincingly. "But I'll be running around a lot, too. I have to make sure everything runs smoothly."

I nod. "Right."

Adam takes a step toward the DJ booth, but I reach out for his arm, spinning him in place.

"Adam, what's going on?"

He sighs, but before he can say anything, I hold up my hand.

"And don't tell me it's nothing. You've been a class-A prick to me since the night of your concert. I know you got ragged on for spending time with me, and that your fraternity brothers need you around as president. I get that, and I've been supporting it. But it's not fair to be a jerk to me, or to just ignore me completely. Just because you need to be more present at Alpha Sig doesn't mean I get placed on the back burner." I frown, stepping into him and wrapping my hands around his forearm. "I'm still your girlfriend."

Adam chuckles. "Oh, are you?"

"What the hell is that supposed to mean?"

"Oh, nothing — except I wasn't aware that girlfriends lied to their boyfriends about hanging out with their exes."

The blood drains from my face, but I still hold onto him. "I'm not trying to hide anything from you, Adam. I've been trying to talk to you for weeks about it."

"About what? The fact that you're hanging out with Grayson behind my back?"

I inhale a hot breath. "Not behind your back. Like I said, I've been trying to tell you."

Adam scoffs, ripping away from my grasp. "Do you hear yourself, Cassie? You're hanging out with your fuck-ing *ex-boyfriend* who cheated on you and oh, by the way, also came between us."

"I'm not *hanging out with him*, okay? We have a class together, and we've been assigned lab partners, and *yes*, he apologized to me about what happened and I listened, okay? He wants to try to be friends, and I've lost so many people in my life..." I swallow. "I just don't want to write someone off because of past transgressions."

"He's in your Genetics class?"

"Yes."

"And why didn't you tell me? I picked you up for lunch every fucking *day* after that class."

"I've been *trying* to tell you," I fume. "But you've been all caught up in Alpha Sigma stuff and hellbent on ignor-ing me."

"Oh, so now it's my fault."

"I don't even understand why this is a fight," I say, throwing my hands up.

"You do, Cassie, or you wouldn't have hidden it."

"I *didn't* hide it."

"Well, you certainly didn't tell me outright, did you?"

I know he has a right to be upset — I do, deep down in my gut. But for some reason, I'm defensive, and annoyed, and pissed off that he's accusing me, and that all this time that I thought he was focusing on his fraternity, he was really just ignoring me for sport. To make a point. To drive that point home.

That is *not* how a healthy relationship functions.

"Jesus, Adam," I say, holding my hands out, palms up. "You already won me. Okay? I'm yours. And that's not changing. But I don't want to have to hurt someone, either. I know it's hard to understand but... Grayson is my friend."

"No."

"Adam."

"No," he says again, shaking his head forcefully. "I'm not okay with that."

"He's not a bad guy, okay? I know he fucked up, he hurt me, he was an asshole to you, but he had a lot of shit going on that neither one of us knew about, okay? I mean, would you want someone to judge you in *your* darkest hour?"

Adam grinds his jaw but doesn't reply.

"He's changed," I continue, voice softer. "And he's not asking me on a date or hitting on me. He's asking to be my *friend*."

Adam laughs, crossing his arms as he tongues his cheek. "You actually believe the words you're saying to me right now, don't you?"

I frown. "You know he even asked about us? He asked how we were doing, Adam. He knows we're together, and he's happy for us."

"Bullshit," Adam says, his voice high-pitched and desperate as he thrusts his hands toward me. "It's all bullshit. Are you so blind, Cassie? Of course he asked how we were, because he's just *dying* for one little fuck up on my end so he can slip back into your heart, and then into your pants. He doesn't want to be *friends*. He wants you back."

"But I don't want *him*," I yell in return. "I love *you*, Adam. It's as simple as that. He is not a threat and you know it."

Adam's jaw clenches, and he looks away from me without a response.

My skin prickles with the memory of being in this position before, of having to choose between Adam and Grayson, and my stomach flips violently at the thought of it. I've already lost my best friend, and there was still a gaping hole I was convinced would never be filled again.

If I have the chance to fill the hole Grayson left in me, I want to take it — and I don't understand what I've ever done to make Adam second-guess that he can trust me, that I can be friends with another guy without it being a danger to us.

"There was a time he made me choose between you two," I whisper, crossing my arms over my chest. "Do you remember that?"

I don't miss the way Adam's jaw ticks. "How could I forget."

"Well, then you know why I'm so adamant about this. Making that choice... being in that position..." I swallow, thankful for the sunglasses hiding the tears glossing my eyes. "It *killed* me. It tore me in half. I swore to myself that I would never do that again. I *can't* do that again."

Adam nods, stepping into my space, and he removes his sunglasses for the first time, showing me the pain in his eyes as he stares down his nose at me. "So, you'll do it for him, but not for me?"

My next breath is shaky and burns me from the inside, stinging my nose and making my bottom lip quiver. How can he not understand? How can he not see that I can be friends with Grayson and still be in love with him, still be *his* — completely?

How could he ever ask me to choose, knowing the hell it put me through last time?

I'm not sure how long we stand there, nose to nose, chest to chest, each of us waiting for the other to break. But it doesn't matter, because neither of us does, and it's Adam who shakes his head and pulls back.

He slips his sunglasses back on, pausing when he's a few feet away like he wants to say something, but decides against it. Instead, he takes off toward the DJ booth, speaking into the walkie-talkie that was strapped to his hip, effectively dismissing me and slipping back into president mode.

And I just stand there, watching the muscles of his back as he goes, wondering how we always find ourselves back here, no matter what we do.

Jess

MY BEST FRIEND AND I are the most annoyed I've ever known us to be.

We are also at petty level one thousand.

But I don't care.

I don't care that we're both grumbling and being catty little bitches as we watch our respective targets from across the sandbar, each of us leaning back in our beach chairs and soaking up the sun as if it could do anything to warm our cold, black heartss in this moment. I don't care that we're shit talking about someone we don't know to make ourselves feel better. I don't care that we're making up stories in our head to fill in the blank spots for everything we're dying to know.

Sometimes you know you're being a little bitch, and you just can't stop yourself.

And that's where we're at today.

Ashlei's target? The new intern at *Okay, Cool*, who looks absolutely stunning in a flapper swimsuit costume, complete with pearls draped around her neck and a feather in her headband. She honestly looks so much like Lei that they could be doppelgängers, which is likely why my bestie wants to strangle her with the pearls around her neck. She looks like her, has her old gig at the agency, and seems to be making quite the impression on their boss — AKA, Ashlei's boyfriend.

And my target?

The *too-hot-to-be-in-college* Puerto Rican goddess currently hanging on Kade's arm.

I don't even know her name, and I don't need to. All I know is that Kade is making her laugh, and she's rubbing all over him, and he's holding her close, and I can hear his words reverberating like bells in an echo chamber in my mind.

"Might have to pull out all the tricks I've learned on some unsuspecting hottie at the Halloween party…"

I grind my teeth together, and then continue my petty party.

"I mean, honestly, who has tits that big in college? They're like a triple D, and she has a waist the size of a coffee cup."

"Did you know she has already been put on an event account?" Ashlei responds. "I mean, I had to *claw* my way to my own account."

"Sure, she's gorgeous," I continue. "But I bet she's vanilla in bed. He could do better."

"She's got this sweet little angel thing going for her at the office," Ashlei says, shaking her head before she sips on the bright pink straw sticking out of her tumbler. "But I know better. She's got an agenda, I just don't know what it is."

"And besides, *I* taught him everything he knows. So really, if she's falling for his lines, she's falling for me, *technically*."

"She's not even that good at her job." Another lie from Ashlei.

"Whatever, I don't care, he's just a fuck buddy and a free ride, anyway." Another lie from me.

We both fall silent, sipping our drinks angrily and swimming in our petty pool. After another stretch of me trying to ignore Kade and his "unsuspecting hottie" but always finding myself staring at them again, I stand, ditching my cover up on my chair.

"You know, maybe I'll go over there just to make him squirm a little."

"Good idea," Ashlei says, standing. "I think I'll go hang out with our perfect little intern, get better acquainted."

"Not that we care about either of them," I remind us both.

"No, of course not," Ashlei agrees, and then we storm off in the sand in opposite directions.

I don't realize it's a terrible idea, inserting myself into a situation that clearly makes me itchy, until I'm standing right in front of Kade with a fake smile on my lips. He doesn't even notice me at first, which pisses me off, but luckily, I'm patient, and I stand there next to one of his fraternity brothers, blending in until he sees me.

When he does, one eyebrow arches high up into his hairline, and a stupid smirk spreads on his dumb face. "Hey there, J-Love."

Hey there? I'm going to murder him.

"Hey, yourself," I say, still wearing the fake smile. "Nice costume."

Kade is dressed in bright red, flashy shorts that cut off down past his knees and hug him right under where that deep V cuts from his abdomen to the promise land. Around that waist, he's got a giant, heavyweight champion belt, and the way it pairs with the tattoos sprawled out over his entire body, he looks like a younger, hotter version of John Cena — if there even is such a thing.

"Thanks," he says, flexing his biceps, which makes me roll my eyes and wonder why I care that he's hanging all over someone else.

"I absolutely *love* yours," the unfortunately beautiful girl on his arm says, leaning forward to touch one of the curls in my hair without asking. "Pin-up, right? My dad *loves* pin-ups... he has calendars and posters and old tin containers and all kinds of stuff with pin-ups on them."

Ashlei, Skyler, Cassie, and I decided the pin-up idea together. My costume is a one-piece, black-and-white striped, with a cut out where my stomach and back are, the top and bottom connected only by scrappy fabric over my ribs and hips. The top has a zipper down the front of the cleavage, too, which is conveniently zipped low right now, boosting up my tits.

"Thanks, sweetie," I say, smiling at her even though it's killing me to watch her thread her arm through Kade's and draw a fingernail up and down his toned forearm. At first, I thought she was clueless, but the way she's holding onto him and smiling back at me with possession in her eyes tells me she sees me as a threat.

And she should.

I somehow manage to check myself before I can be a bitch, thanks to my feminist side reminding me that I should lift women up, not tear them down — even if I'm jealous of them. But I'm done playing games.

She has something I want, and I'm not leaving without it.

"Kade," I say, turning my attention back to him with my smile still in place. "Can I steal you for a second?"

He shrugs, oblivious, whispering something in his unsuspecting victim's ear before she giggles and runs her hand over his chest, slick with tanning oil. "Hurry back," she says, and then she grabs his junk over his shorts, right there in front of everyone, outlining the thick shaft that I had inside me just days ago.

I turn before rage can seethe through me, not checking to see if Kade is following, because I know he knows better than *not* to. I just stalk toward one of the tents set up for shade reprieve, and when I step inside it, I thank Adam and his fraternity brothers for being smart enough to put fans with water spritzers inside each one of them.

It feels like heaven.

I sigh, turning just as Kade joins me in the tent. It's a large one, with space for at least a couple dozen people, but most everyone is out in the sun or on a boat. There's a couple making out on one of the couches in the corner, but I snap at them and point to the tent flap, and without a word, they exit.

Then, it's just me and Kade.

I cross my arms, mouth twisting to the side as I wait for him to say something.

"Uh..." He looks around, cocking a confused brow. "Am I in trouble or something?"

"What are you doing?"

"Currently? Standing in a tent with you wondering why you look like you want to murder me right now."

"I mean, with Miss Tits for Brains out there." I cringe. "Sorry, I didn't mean that, I'm sure she's lovely and very intelligent and driven and resilient."

Kade chuckles. "I wouldn't know, I just met her."

"Well, you seem to be *very* acquainted, judging by how she just wrapped her hand around your cock in front of your brothers and me and God and everyone else."

A moment of silence passes, and Kade's smirk climbs higher as he crosses his arms over his chest, his stance even cockier with that damn belt hanging around his hips. "Jess... are you *jealous*?"

"No."

"No?" he asks, taking a step toward me. "Because it *kind of* seems like you might be jealous."

"I'm not."

"Then why'd you pull me in here?"

He's still walking toward me, and I take a few steps back, until I run into one of the several cocktail tables set up inside the tent. Just as I do, three Omega Chi brothers stumble into the tent. Kade turns around and points at the door they just came through, and they laugh, all drunk, throwing their hands up before exiting again.

"I haven't done anything wrong, have I?" Kade pushes again when we're alone. "We had a deal, did we not?"

"We did."

"You've been a great instructor; I was just testing out my skills."

I scoff.

His brow arches higher, and he moves into my space, trapping me between his hot, toned body and the table behind me. My hands press into his chest, and he places his palms flat on the table, staring down his nose at me.

"If you want to re-negotiate our terms," he husks. "I'm all ears."

I want to growl. I want to scream and slap him and shove him away and spit on him for good measure.

But I also want him to take those big bear hands of his and put them on every inch of me.

Jesus Christ, what is happening?

And it's then that I realize it.

I like him.

I fucking like him, and I *hate* myself for it, but it's true. Somewhere between all the teasing and fucking and fooling around, I started liking the time we spend together.

And he's right.

I am jealous.

Fuck.

"Fine. I still want to teach you," I say, dragging my nails slowly down his chest to his abdomen. Each inch lower makes his cock twitch, growing where it's pressed against me, and I instantly react to the power I feel from having that effect on him. "Because God knows, you still have a lot to learn."

"I'm sure I do," he says, his voice low and husky.

"But if I'm going to teach you, then I want to reap the benefits."

"And?"

"And…" I say, dragging my fingertips down lower. I slip them under the band of his shorts and revel in the stiff inhale it elicits from him. "I want to be the *only* one who gets to reap the benefits."

I try to shove my hand down his pants, but he stops me, wrapping his hand around my wrist with force. "Meaning?"

"Fuck you, Kade," I say, writhing in his grasp with my swimsuit so wet you would have thought I'd already been in the water. "Don't make me say it."

"If you want me inside you right now," he whispers, using his free hand to skate up the inside of my thighs. His thick knee presses between them, spreading me wider, my back aching where I'm pressed against the table. "You *have* to say it."

"Fuck," I moan, ripping my hands free of his grasp to hold onto his shoulder. His thigh rubs against my swimsuit, the friction heating my clit, and my eyelids flutter at the sensation.

"Come on, Jess," he teases, releasing the belt around his waist with one snap. In the next breath, he reaches into his shorts and pulls his cock out, holding it, throbbing and hard in his hand, right between my thighs. "What. Do. You. Want."

I'm practically salivating, and in that moment, I'd say anything to have his dick inside me.

I convince myself *that's* why I reach up on my tiptoes and bite his lower lip, sucking it between my teeth before

I whisper, "Be mine." My hand wraps around his cock, replacing his, and I grab his ass, making him thrust into my grip. "And make me yours, too."

Kade answers with a growl, whipping me around to face the table so fast I have no choice but to brace myself on it. My fingers have barely wrapped around the edges before one of his hands is crooking me at the hips, and the other is yanking my swimsuit to the side, and in the next inhale, I'm filled to the brim — all at once, brutally and punishing, a claiming thrust that kills me as much as it makes me feel alive.

"Oh *God,* you feel so fucking good," he groans, nipping at my ear as his hands find my hips and slam me onto him again. "All that talking made you wet, didn't it, babe?"

"Yes," I whimper, and I want to slap myself because I *don't* whimper for a man. But here I am, putty in his hand, legs shaking and orgasm already building from just a few thrusts.

I reach down and shove my swimsuit farther to the side, rubbing my clit as he pounds into me. It's fast and animalistic, and it takes everything in me to be fucking quiet so not everyone on the beach knows I'm getting railed inside this tent. Not that I particularly care, but I'm at least *trying* to be discreet.

Kade reaches down, hiking one of my legs up to where I'm balanced on just one foot, but he's holding all of my weight, allowing me to spread my legs open wider and rub my clit until I come in a burst of gasps and fire. I quiver and shake in his grasp, and his mouth claims mine, my neck bent so forcefully it hurts, but the kiss is too good to break. And Kade keeps going, pounding into me, forcing me to open wider and wider for him as I ride the waves.

When my climax recedes, I'm even more weak, and I know that if it wasn't for him holding me, I'd collapse to the ground. But we're still kissing, tongues and teeth clashing, biting and licking, until he grunts something that sounds like *coming* and rips himself out of me, whipping me around and forcing me into the sand on my knees.

I don't even think twice, just open my mouth and guide him into it just in time to catch his hot release down my throat. He shoves a little too far down and I gag, but he holds me there, and I squeeze my eyes shut in an attempt to focus and not gag again.

I'm so fucking turned on I want a round two already.

When he's spent, he pulls out of me slowly, trembling, and I swallow, looking up at him with a wicked smile and wiping the corners of my mouth.

"So, you're mine?" I ask, and he just laughs, a lazy smile on his face as he yanks up his shorts and collapses into the sand next to me.

Kade pulls me under his arm, kissing my temple, chest still heaving. "All yours, you devil woman," he says.

Then, he palms my tit with a grin.

"And *these* are all mine."

Bear

THE SUNDAY AFTER HALLOWEEN, an entire plate of hummus and tzatziki sits untouched between me and Erin, along with fresh, hot pita bread and a smorgasbord of vegetables. It's been there for at least five minutes now, but neither of us moves for it, and I've nearly drained my first beer as Erin has attempted small talk. The way her eyebrows are drawn together as she watches me from across the table, I have a feeling she's about done with that.

Thank God.

Now we can get this over with.

"Thank you for agreeing to meet me," she says, tentatively tucking a strand of hair behind one ear. Her hair is longer now than it was at the end of last semester, when her head was in the toilet and she told me unknowingly about our baby. She was an absolute wreck that night, but this evening, she looks... calm. At peace. She looks like she's getting sleep and eating.

Still, she watches me with worry etched in every feature, and I find that as fucked up as it is, I like that aspect the most.

Erin clears her throat when I don't answer, folding her hands in her lap with her eyes falling to the hummus plate. "I don't know how to start, so I'm just going to talk. And I know a lot of this might not make sense to you, but... I guess, I just wanted to talk to you. I wanted to explain what happened." She lifted her eyes to me then. "Why I made the choices I made."

I inhale a stiff breath, draining the last of my beer and signaling to the waitress for another. She delivers it promptly, seeing as how there are only a dozen tables inside the small restaurant.

Erin offers a gentle smile as I take my first sip, something like pity in her eyes now.

"When we slept together, neither of us really knew each other. I mean, I asked you to semi-formal on the heels of your fraternity being on probation, and then we accidentally got too drunk and..."

She pauses when I take three dramatically large gulps from my beer, belching before I set the glass back down on the table. Her eyes stick there for a moment before she swallows and continues.

"I mean, neither of us even really remembered it the next morning. Do you recall that? We laughed it off, promised not to tell anyone... it wasn't serious."

"Is there a point here?"

Erin blows out a slow breath. "Bear, we weren't in a relationship. We *still* aren't ready for a child, let alone back then. We're just kids ourselves. And when I found out I was pregnant... I did come to you."

"Bullshit."

"Let me finish," she says, holding up one hand. "I came to you, before I even took the test, actually. I wanted to do it together. I knew we could figure it out. But when I went to you... you were with Shawna."

I frown, tracing back through my memory for what she could possibly be talking about. "I don't understand."

Erin takes all her hair and wraps it over one shoulder, taking a deep breath. "I went back to your room, and I was knocking but you didn't answer, and when I walked in... I didn't know her at the time, but you and Shawna were..." She swallows. "Indisposed."

My gaze hardens.

"And, I don't know, Bear. I just, I felt so fucking silly. Like, we had a one-night stand, and I expected you to hold my hand while I peed on a stick? I mean, these were my *exact* thoughts." She shakes her head. "I felt like a fool. How could I expect that of you, of anyone in college?"

I take another pull of my beer in lieu of answering.

"Anyway, so I took the test alone, and... well... obviously, I was pregnant. But I lied to Jess, who was the only one who even knew I was suspicious about being pregnant. I told her it was a stomach flu. And then..."

She doesn't finish, and I squeeze the glass so hard in my hand, I wonder if I can break it like the Hulk.

Erin's expression softens, and she reaches forward, wrapping her hand around my wrist before I can flinch away. As soon as I feel her warmth, something inside me cracks, and emotion stings my nose, but I fight it back.

"I am so sorry, Bear," she says, her eyes glossing with tears. "I was a coward. I should have come to you. I know that now, but I also know it doesn't change what I did. At the time, I thought it was the right thing to do. And I'm sorry I didn't include you in the decision, but... it was my body. And ultimately, it was my choice."

I shake my head, tearing back from her grasp. "I know it was your choice. And I would have supported it, Ex — even more so if you would have just fucking told me."

She breaks at my words, swiping at the tears streaming down her cheeks furiously. "I know that now. I didn't know that then, but I do now. I know that you were the one who saw I wasn't okay before anyone else. I know that you were the one who saved me when Landon..." Her voice breaks, and another zip of pain splits my chest open. "When he raped me, when his brothers stole every ounce of innocence I had, you were there. You saved me. You kept my secret even when I knew it killed you." She rolls her lips together, more tears tumbling over her cheeks. "You are the most amazing man I know, and you are my best friend. And I am so sorry I hurt you."

Every muscle in my jaw is tight and burning as I fight off the emotion strangling my throat. I just shake my head, over and over, gaze lost in the distance before I finally pull my eyes back to hers.

"Listen. I know you're going to therapy, and I'm really fucking glad you are. Okay? I want you to be okay. I do," I say, and I mean it. "I also know that you're sorry," I continue, forcing a breath. "But that doesn't mean I have to forgive you. So, don't expect me to."

"Bear," her voice cracks, and she reaches for me again, but I'm already up out of my chair, abandoning my napkin on the table, as well as what's left of my beer.

"Excuse me," I murmur, and then I'm gone, out of the restaurant and in the first campus cab I see.

My heart is thundering in my chest as the car carries me to the other side of campus, and then I'm on Becca's doorstep, and as soon as she opens the door and sees me, she invites me in, wrapping me in a warm hug that I completely collapse into.

I'm not sure how long she holds me, how long I have to use every ounce of willpower I have to fight off the tears my body is desperate to let free, but eventually, she grabs me by the hand and pulls me back to her room. Her dorm mate doesn't seem to be around, which I'm thankful for as she closes the door behind us.

She sits us on her bed, wrapping her arms around me and leaning her head on my chest. For the longest time, we just hold each other, and she takes long, exaggerated breaths, cueing me to do the same.

After a while, she whispers, "Is this about the trip?"

I sigh, running my fingers over her hip where I hold her against me. Just feeling her warmth already makes me feel better. "Partly."

"How did it go?"

I swallow. "Well, Clayton is convinced I'm a monster because I don't believe our lying, sack-of-shit mother when she says she's back for good."

"Was she drugged out?"

"No," I admit. "She seems clean, actually. But I don't trust it."

"What's the other part?"

I sigh, debating how much I should tell her. "I just met up with Erin, and we... we had a fight."

Becca stiffens in my grasp, sitting up even when I try to hold her there in my arms. She shakes her head, looking out her window before her eyes land on me. "You saw Erin before you saw me?"

Shit.

I let out a long sigh. "She asked if I'd have dinner with her," I explain. "She wanted to apologize."

"For what?"

Fuck.

Another hot breath leaves my nose, and I roll my lips together, looking anywhere but back at Becca.

"I asked you last semester if there was anything between you and Erin, and you said there wasn't."

"There's not."

"Then why are you holding this..." She waves her hand in the air. "*Grudge* against her? You haven't talked to her or *about* her since the night of Skyler's poker tournament, and now you're meeting her for dinner for her to apologize for... what?"

I swallow.

"What *happened*, Bear?"

Still, I don't answer. And it kills me, because I know Becca is pissed, and hurt, and as much as *I* am angry with Erin, it's still not my place to tell anyone what happened.

Becca shakes her head, sliding off the bed before I can stop her. She stands, crossing her arms and watching me. "Maybe you should look at that."

I frown. "At what?"

"You told me about what happened with you and Shawna, how you never forgave her, even when she came to you *begging* for you to understand. And when you held a grudge against Skyler for half a semester. And how you wrote off your mom completely, and now that she's back and legitimately trying, you won't have any part of it."

Defensiveness prickles in my chest, and I stand up, too, ready to combat her. But she holds up a hand to silence me.

"And, on top of all that, whatever is happening with Erin that she needs to apologize, which — judging by the way you were acting when you first got here — I'm assuming you didn't accept either."

I clamp my mouth shut at that.

Becca shakes her head, her golden eyes thick with confusion and pity as she watches me. "You don't give second chances, even when someone maybe deserves one. Why is that, Bear?"

I blink at the accusation, skin hot and uncomfortable for the way it sinks into my gut like an anchor.

Becca holds her hands out toward me, palms up, desperation in her voice. "Have you never made a mistake? Have you never hurt someone?"

My little brother's words echoed on my girlfriend's lips.

She waits for me to answer and gives me plenty of time to do so. But when I don't, she just shakes her head, tears blurring her vision as she opens her door.

"I think you should go," she whispers, her eyes finding mine. "And maybe think about that. Because we're all human, Bear. We *all* fuck up. I know I have. And if I was never forgiven for my transgressions in the past, I don't know where I'd be today. Besides... holding onto all that anger, all the resentment?" She swallows. "It's tearing you up."

"I'm sorry," I say, moving toward her, but she flinches away, opening the door wider. "Please, don't make me go right now. I need you."

"No," she argues, looking at me pointedly. "What you need is time alone with yourself. You're just too scared to take it."

We stand there, watching each other for what feels like an eternity, and her words melt over me like lava, burning my skin, scarring my heart. Eventually, I nod, and as soon as I'm out her dorm door, she closes and locks it behind me.

For the first time since last semester, I don't feel numb.

For the first time, I feel all the pain, all the betrayal, all the resentment and anger I've been trying to work out of my system with weights and cardio and drinking.

Becca's right.

I do need to be alone.

But I'm fucking terrified of what will happen now that I am.

EPISODE 4

Ashlei

HERE'S WHAT I KNOW about our precious little shining star of an intern, Sophie Miller.

She's a junior at Palm South University, majoring in Public Relations with a particular interest in working as a publicist for high-profile executives. She's not in a sorority, but seems to be very *in* with the Greek crowd, thanks to dating the president of Zeta Rho Kappa her sophomore year and becoming affectionately known as "one of the guys" in that circle. She's a self-proclaimed country girl from Central Florida, and her favorite party trick is shotgunning a tall boy faster than any guy who tries to compete against her.

Of course, this was all learned at the Halloween party last weekend, when I casually found my way over to her group and infiltrated enemy territory. I shamelessly admit that I was looking for dirt, because Sophie Miller has been too damn perfect at work, and I wanted something to have even a small leg up on her.

Instead, I came to the conclusion that not only is she a stand-out intern, but she's also pretty fun to party with.

Currently, she's at the biggest *Okay, Cool* event of the year — our relatively small and intimate after-party for the Southeastern Advertising Conference held in Miami. It's invite only, costs a thousand dollars a head, with all proceeds benefitting a local charity, and it's reserved for the agencies my beloved boyfriend sees as leaders in the industry. Getting an invite as an agency is like finding Willy Wonka's golden ticket, and being asked to attend as an

Okay, Cool employee is arguably better than a ten-thousand-dollar bonus.

I know why I'm here.

I landed one of our biggest clients to this date while I was an intern. *I* completely dismantled and rebuilt our current project management team from the ground up, revamping old and outdated systems and ushering us back into our top spot in the industry. *I* am already building a reputation as one of the most competent and creative account managers and creative directors in Florida, and I haven't even graduated yet.

I've earned my spot in this bougie mansion, standing in my brand new, rose gold and crystal-covered Jimmy Choo heels next to a giant pool that no one at this party will enter.

What I can't figure out is why Sophie *Goddamn* Miller is here.

The party is in full swing, even though the conference just ended an hour ago. And though Florida may be immune to the rest of our country's quickly declining temperatures during the holiday season, we're still a victim to the days being shorter, so the sun has already set, and the party's up-lighting and pool-lighting and candles littering every table make for an elegant, sophisticated feel. A jazz trio plays music from the corner of the pool balcony, a pleasant background to the soft buzz of chatter and laughter coming from each little pod of people.

It's the networking event of the year, and that's what I should be doing — networking. I should be rubbing elbows with other creative directors, making proposals for how we could work together to bag large, out-of-our-league clients, or steal the most coveted ones from other agencies who are lacking what we have.

I should *not* be staring death lasers with my eyeballs into the intern, but it's all I can manage to do.

Presently, we're both in a small gathering of executives — including the CEO of Atlanta's hottest agency, *Ball & Pen,* the director of the conference, who also hands out the most sought-after agency awards each year, our CFO, and of course, Brandon.

He's who stands between me and Sophie, one hand tucked into his pocket, and the other wrapped confidently around a glass tumbler of scotch. He and the others are laughing at something, which I miss, because I'm too busy wondering how the hell Sophie weaseled her way into this event and, even more so, how she's standing here in this particular circle.

To make matters even more peachy, Brandon is bragging on her to the group. It's not over the top, just noting a few of her accolades as an intern, but it's enough to make me have to actively keep myself from tapping my heel in annoyance.

I'm debating ways I could make it look like an accident and shove her into the pool, when Brandon puts his hand at the small of my back and smiles down at me, flashing his dazzling smile that somehow looks even more charming in the low lighting and pulling me back to the moment.

"And this one," he says, shaking his head. "Not *only* did she secure the *Bare•ly* account as an intern, but she is also the lead on our top-performing campaign." He pauses, arching a brow at Mrs. Lambert, the CEO of the Atlanta agency. "And she hasn't even graduated yet."

Mrs. Lambert whistles through her teeth as the rest of the group smiles and nods their approval. "That's pretty impressive, Ms. Daniels. You ever get tired of working for this chump, you make sure you find me in Atlanta, okay?"

"Does Atlanta have a beach?"

The group chuckles at that, but Mrs. Lambert tips her glass toward me. "No beach, but if you ever thought about coming to work for me, I'd build one for you right in the middle of the city, if that's what you wanted."

"I'm flattered, Mrs. Lambert," I say, laying a palm over my chest. "But my home is *Okay, Cool.*" I look up at Brandon then. "As long as this one will keep me around, anyway."

Brandon pulls me into his side possessively. "Like I'd ever be stupid enough to let you slip out of my hands."

My heart blooms in my chest as he stares down at me, and then — in front of our little group and for everyone else to see, too — he plants a gentle, adoring kiss on my lips.

Fucking swoon.

He jumps right back into the conversation, steering them toward the conference and how they could improve upon it, but I'm still floating on a cloud with that kiss reverberating through my body. Ever since the end of last semester when the truth about us came out, we haven't had to hide our relationship — and being able to stand next to this man and proudly claim him, to have *him* claim me?

It's the most powerful drug in the world.

I'm still trying to contain the butterflies in my ribcage when my gaze shifts to Sophie, and I'm a little surprised to find her staring back at me, a small smile curved on her ballerina-pink lips. She tilts her glass toward me in a nod of acknowledgement, and I do my best not to frown, offering her my *this-isn't-a-fake-smile-I-swear* smile before I turn my attention to the current speaker in the group.

But Sophie keeps watching me, and when Brandon's assistant comes up to usher him away from our group and to another anxiously waiting to speak with him, the rest of the executives disband, and Sophie stands closer to me, sipping from her champagne glass as we both survey the crowd.

"This event is *wild*, isn't it?" she says after a moment, shaking her head as her bright eyes scan the crowd.

I hate those eyes, because they remind me so much of my own that I want to gouge them out of her head and claim copyright infringement. It pisses me off that her hair is the same platinum blonde as mine, that she has the same taste in high heels, and the same love for high fashion. Hell, we even look like we *planned* our similarities tonight, both of us dressed in sleek, form-fitting and short white dresses with heels that steal the show — mine being the dazzly Jimmy Choos, and hers the same Louboutins she was wearing the first day I saw her in Brandon's office.

She looks incredible, sexy but professional.

And I *loathe* her for it.

"I can't believe Brandon invited me to come," she continues, a longing sigh leaving her chest. "I feel like the luckiest girl in the world."

I growl low in my throat, though I'm praying it's not loud enough that Sophie heard me. "Yes. *Mr. Church* is lovely in that respect," I correct her subtly, reminding her that *no one* at work calls him Brandon — except for me. "He has *such* a big heart for charity."

It's a thinly veiled dig, but if Sophie notices it, she doesn't let me know it.

Instead, she leans in closer, lowering her voice. "I know I won't have much time alone with you tonight, since I'm sure you have so many people to see and talk to, but while I have you, I just have to say..."

And then, that conniving, sneaky little bitch wraps her silky palm around the inside of my elbow.

"The work you've done on the *Bare•ly* account?" She shakes her head in earnest, leveling her gaze with mine. "It is the most inspiring work I've seen done in any agency in the years I've been studying. I was wondering... I have this project I have to do for my cornerstone class on big moves in the industry, and I'd really love to spotlight you and that account in particular. It wouldn't require much, just an interview and maybe some behind-the-scenes brainstorm notes, if you'd be willing to give me access. Just enough for me to put together a ten-minute presentation."

Sophie pauses then, her hand slides down my arm, slowly, each fingernail making contact with my skin. Her eyes follow the gesture, her plump, smooth lips parted slightly, and when she glances back at me, there's something hidden in her lash-covered gaze.

Chills and confusion wash over me in equal measure, and I'm suddenly shocked still, throat tightening with how intimate the touch is. We're in a crowd full of people, but the way she's looking at me, it feels like we're miles and miles away.

"You're just such an inspiration to me," she explains, wrapping her hand around mine until our palms touch. She's not holding my hand, but rather sliding her skin over mine, and she holds my fingertips with her own for just the briefest moment before withdrawing entirely. "It'd truly be an honor to work under you, to get an inside look of what makes you tick."

If anyone were to ask me, I would never admit to my suspicion — but I *swear* her eyes flick to my lips, that there's heat in her gaze when it finds me again, that the curl of her lips is alluding to more than just her desire to use me for a school project.

I clear my throat, inhaling a breath that burns too much for my liking and taking a marginal step back from Sophie. Her grin intensifies, as if she's won some competition I hadn't realized we'd entered into, but I hold my chin high to let her know she hasn't won *shit* in my eyes.

"Thank you," I say first. "And I would be happy to help you with your project. Why don't you swing by my desk on Monday and we can discuss further?"

Sophie's manicured eyebrow inches up, that smile still cemented on her lips. "I'll do that." Her eyes wash over me suggestively, tongue sliding along the inside of her cheek as she does, and now I *know* I'm not imagining things.

This bitch is checking me out.

Is she... *is she hitting on me?*

"Have a good evening, Ms. Daniels," she says, tipping her almost-empty glass with a wink. Then, she plucks the toothpick with an olive at the end of it and pops it into her mouth, sucking on it in a way that makes her lips big and pouty before she turns and leaves me standing at the edge of the pool so shaken up that I'm in danger of falling into it.

And I *keep* standing there, completely alone, with a shocked face I can't even pretend to hide.

What in the ever loving fuck was that?

Erin

GAVIN LINDBERG HAS BEEN MIA from every session since the one when he so casually asked me to dinner.

Not that it matters, of course, because I've had my own priorities to focus on. I've spent the last month making amends, apologizing to everyone I've hurt and accepting that as much as I want them to, not everyone will forgive me.

Skyler was first, and she was the easiest — perhaps because she was the one in our group who always seemed to put her friends before herself. I don't think it's in her blood to hold a grudge, and I'm thankful for that, since we're now slowly working toward having a friendship again.

My mother was the next battle, and it was more like a war, because as much as I was apologizing to her for all the hell I'd put her through in the past year, I was also confessing to her that she was responsible for a lot of the deep-seated issues I'd been fighting all my life.

She did *not* like hearing that.

I'm thankful to my mom for how she helped me after Landon and his brothers gang-raped me. It's because of her that I clawed my way out of the deep, bottomless hole that night had put me in and took the reins of my life firmly in my hands once more.

But she also advocated ignoring what had happened and disguised that as strength. We never talked about it, and there was never any room for me to explore what that night did to me, how it permanently changed me, how I would never be the woman I was before. Hell, I wasn't even allowed to say the *word* rape — like I should have been ashamed of it.

To my mom, strength is standing tall and holding your chin high and never letting anyone see that you were a human being with feelings and flaws and hopes and dreams.

You must be steel — cold and hard and resilient.

So, opening up to her was not only difficult for me, but to her it was practically being forced to lie in a bed of needles. She wasn't just annoyed by my emotions, she was uncomfortable when they were aimed at her, which is why I wasn't surprised when she was less then receptive to them.

Still, she forgave me, and she seemed to at least somewhat listen to me, and I hope that, like Skyler, we'll move forward into a new, stronger relationship together.

I'd sat down and talked with everyone close to me — Lei, Jess, and Cassie included. I wasn't ready to tell them everything that had happened to me just yet, but I at least wanted them to know that I was trying.

And then, there was Bear.

I'm not surprised that he reacted the way he did when I asked him to dinner and tried, pathetically, to explain why I murdered our child.

I know it's not as callous as that, that I'm berating myself and not "being kind to myself," as my therapist would urge me to do.

But truthfully? In my heart? That's how I see it.

I took life from my own child, and I'll never forgive myself.

So why does it upset me so much that Bear won't forgive me, either?

He had every right to reject my apology that night we went to dinner, and still, I was shocked by it. Maybe it's because through all the shit I've faced in the past year, he has always been there for me. He's always been the one holding me and assuring me that it's okay, and that I'm not a terrible person, and that I will make it out of the hell I've been imprisoned in.

But he didn't hold me this time.

Hell, he could barely *look* at me.

And it killed me.

So, yeah, I've had plenty of my own shit to occupy my time and energy without worrying about going on a date with Gavin Lindberg.

But I'd be lying if I said I didn't notice he hadn't been around.

I'd be lying if I said I didn't take extra time getting ready for group the week we were supposed to go to dinner, curling my hair and putting on my makeup with precision and picking out one of my favorite fall outfits — dark, skinny jeans, a conservative silky blouse, and my favorite black high heels. And I'd be lying if I said my heart didn't deflate a little when he never showed that night, or the week after, or the week after that.

Maybe that's why I find myself slightly annoyed when he waltzes through the door two minutes before group therapy starts, casting me a smile and a wink as if we're buddies before taking a seat across the circle from me, outstretching his legs and shoving his hands in the pockets of his hoodie. His intense blue eyes watch me curiously, and I just glare back at him, letting my annoyance show until Jackie says we're getting started.

Then, I turn my attention to her, and I leave it there for the rest of the session.

I don't look at Gavin again, not even when he makes his sarcastic and ill-placed comments when someone else is speaking. Jackie warns him a couple times, and he finally shuts up — presumably because he's failing to get my attention like he so desperately seems to want to do.

When the session is over, I promptly grab my belongings and make my way toward the door, not bothering to stop by the table of coffee and donuts that I never touch, or stay back to talk to anyone else in the group.

I make it all the way to the parking lot before the distant sound of my name being called out stops me, and I take a deep breath, turning and finding Gavin slowing from his jog to a walk and eventually to stand just a few feet away from me.

It's dark in the parking lot, save for the streetlights casting warm circles over a few of the spots. Gavin is standing under one of them, and it leaves his face half-shadowed, but I can still see a tinge of remorse in his ocean eyes.

"Geez, you really bolted out of there tonight," he says. "Did I miss the fire?"

I cross my arms, shifting my weight to one hip.

Gavin sighs, grabbing the back of his neck and looking around at the otherwise-empty lot before his embarrassed gaze finds mine again. "Alright, I deserve the silent treatment. I'm sorry I bailed on our dinner. I have the tendency of being an asshole from time to time."

"How unfortunate," I deadpan, turning on my heel and making my way toward my car. I click the button to unlock it, sending a flash of taillights over the lot before Gavin jogs around to stand in front of me, holding his hands out, palms up.

"Erin, wait."

"Honestly, Gavin, I've been busy handling my own shit, okay? If you didn't want to go to dinner with me, you could have just said it. You didn't have to avoid group for almost a month."

"I *do* want to go to dinner with you."

"Clearly." I roll my eyes, pushing past him and opening my car door, but before I can slide inside, Gavin wraps his hand around the top of the window, serving as a barricade.

"I mean it," he says, brows furrowed together as his eyes search mine. "I'm sorry. Truly. I... I've had some personal things going on." He swallows, and I let my guard down marginally at the display of vulnerability. "And I *do* want to go to dinner with you."

I inhale, but otherwise don't respond, waiting.

"Let's go now."

At that, I laugh. "Now?"

"Right now," he says again. "If we go now, I can't bail out."

"Oh, how charming."

"I'm serious," he says when I try to push him out of the way to get in my car. His hand gently holds my forearm — not with enough force to stop me from brushing him off if I really want to, but with enough care to let me know he means what he says. "Let me take you to dinner. Right now. Anywhere you want."

The way he watches me is like he already knows who I am, and I hate that I love it so much. I hate that feeling like I'm being seen makes me want to say yes to any and everything this shadow of a man proposes.

"I don't really know of any good places to eat around here," I finally say. "I spend most of my time on the other side of town, near campus."

"What are you in the mood for?"

I shrug. "Sushi?"

Gavin grins, stepping out of the way and holding the car door open for me. "I know just the place."

"Why do I feel like I should be scared for my life or, at the very least, that I will be hugging my toilet later tonight?" I ask, eyeballing the dingy, roughed-up exterior of the brick building Gavin has guided us to. It's small and tucked between a bicycle shop and a barber shop in the part of downtown my parents specifically told me to stay away from when I first started school at PSU. The flickering neon sign above the blacked-out door says something in Japanese, and under it, a simple white banner reads SUSHI in black, all-caps English.

"Trust me, this will be the *best* sushi you'll ever have in your life," Gavin says, holding the door open for me. As soon as he opens it, we're hit with the thumping base of electronic music that would be better suited for a club than for any kind of restaurant, and a large group of people smushed inside, waiting to be seated. It's dim throughout the restaurant, with black lights and disco balls sending flares of light across the room.

I arch a brow, but don't move otherwise.

Gavin chuckles, reaching out for my hand. "Come on. Have a little faith."

Something about his smile makes my chest warm and fuzzy, and I smile in return, letting him take my hand in his and guide me inside. We mutter *excuse me* to several groups, squirming our way to the hostess stand.

Then, Gavin surprises me by speaking Japanese to the hostess, who smiles at him like she knows him — or like she wants to sleep with him, I can't be sure which — before leading us to a corner booth all the way in the back, where the music is a little softer and we have a view of the entire room.

Another surprise to me is that the place is *packed*. Every single table is taken, even though it's after eight now, and the table we're seated at was roped off like it was being held for a VIP. Judging by the long wait at the front, Gavin isn't the only one who's a fan of the sushi here.

I shrug off my jacket once we're seated, folding it once and laying it next to me in the booth. It's very rarely cold in South Florida, but we've been blessed with a cool front that leaves the evenings just chilly enough to wear the jackets and scarves we wear approximately three times a year and leave buried in our closet to stare at longingly for the rest of it.

A waiter swings by and asks what we'd like to drink, to which Gavin responds for me, ordering us both a water and a bottle of saki to share.

"So, you speak Japanese?" I ask when the waiter leaves.

"Surprised?"

"Very," I admit. "I take it you frequent this place a lot, judging by the fact that they gave us a roped-off booth."

"I roomed with the owner's son for a couple of months when I lived in Tokyo."

"You *lived* in Tokyo?"

"Briefly," Gavin says, shrugging as if it's no big deal. "I was thinking about teaching English there, so I stayed with a friend who was doing just that. Wasn't really my thing," he confessed. "But I loved the food, and the culture."

The way he said that, with a shit-eating grin and a wink, made me roll my eyes.

"Let me guess — culture is code for *girls*?"

"You said it, not me," Gavin deflects, holding up the menu with the writing facing me. It's just a simple, half-sheet of paper with a couple dozen items, and the menu is hand-written and photocopied. "Now, what you need to know about this place is that you can't go wrong with anything you order," he says. "But, if you really want to wet your panties, order the mackerel nigiri, the otoro sashimi, and the moon phase roll."

I laugh, folding my hands over my own menu rather than looking at it. "Okay. I trust you."

"Do you?" he challenges, and I love the way his eyes light up, the way his lazy smile spreads on his face.

"To order sushi for me, yes. To be respectful in group therapy or actually show up to take me on the date you asked me on?" I shrug. "Jury's still out."

"Hey, we're here, aren't we?" Gavin argues, gesturing to the restaurant around us.

"Just a few weeks late."

"That's fair," he says, and then the waiter drops off our water and saki, and Gavin pours two small ceramic cups with the hot liquid before passing one to me. "To overdue dates and the beautiful women who concede to them."

I roll my eyes, taking a sip before hugging the small cup between my hands. The smell and taste is delightful, and the warmth of the cup in my cool palms makes me feel oddly cozy inside this dim restaurant that could be a club.

"You were thinking about teaching English," I muse after the drink. "And you mentioned in therapy that you're a grad student. Is that what you're studying now?"

He shakes his head. "Psychology."

I chuckle.

"Fitting, isn't it?" he says with his own smile. Then, a shrug. "I want to be a different kind of grief counselor. I want to work with people who don't believe in the hippie ya-ya bullshit. People like me. People who need their therapy served a little hard up, like a shot of whiskey instead of a tall glass of sweet tea."

I tilt my head. "I like that analogy."

"We'll see how far it gets me."

The waiter stops by again, and Gavin places our order in Japanese before making small talk. By the time the waiter leaves, they seem like best buds.

"So, Erin Xander," he says once we're alone again. "Besides the fact that you're fucked up enough to need group *and* solo therapy, what else should I know about you?"

I nearly choke on my next sip of saki, but laugh despite it. "Wow, you really don't shy away from the dark, do you?"

"Why should I?" He shrugs. "We're all fucked up. It's the brave ones who actually admit it."

"And the ones like us who go to therapy for it, what do you call us?"

"Bored. Self-seeking." He pauses, his blue eyes locking on mine. "Lonely."

My eyes drop to the cup in my hand. "Well, if the fact that you know a little Japanese didn't make me think you were smart, that observation just did." I sigh, ignoring the pinch in my gut when I look at Gavin again. "As far as what you should know about me, I'm the president of Kappa Kappa Beta."

"I don't care."

The comment shocks me quiet, and I stare at smiling, confident Gavin for a moment before hesitantly continuing. "Um... I graduate at the end of this semester, and I'll be attending Grove Law School next summer."

"Don't care about that, either."

I frown. "I love country music, and going to the beach with my friends."

"Bor-ing," he sings, sitting back in his booth and sipping his saki.

"You are such an asshole," I spit, shaking my head. "Seriously, why ask me something and then react like that?"

"I asked what I should know about you."

"And I'm telling you."

He leans forward, elbows on the table and eyes boring into mine. "You're telling me things you think define you — positions you hold, schools you attend, your major, the music you like." Gavin's eyes search mine. "Tell me something real."

My chest is tight when I force my next breath. "I don't know what you want from me."

"Tell me. Something. Real."

Part of me wants to reach over and slap the stupid, knowing look off his face. The other part of me wants to shrink away from his gaze. And somewhere in the deepest, darkest hole of my heart, I see myself reflected in him.

It both terrifies and excites me.

I lean over the table, too — mirroring his stance and leveling my gaze with his. "I've been playing a part for so long, I don't know who I am past the labels I've been given and the credentials I can attach to the back of my name."

Those words linger between us for a moment, and Gavin's eyes soften, his next inhale long and deep.

"That real enough for you?"

Gavin swallows, and then he pushes out of his side of the booth enough to balance on his elbows and meet my lips in the middle of the table.

The kiss is so unexpected that I'm stiff at first, my eyes shooting open wide as he takes my face in his hands, holding me to his mouth, his lips soft and warm. In the next breath, before I can even catalog what I'm feeling or what we're doing, I'm melting into him, sighing into his mouth as I open mine and let his tongue sweep inside.

The lights dim somehow, and the music around us fades until it's no more than a thumping heartbeat pulsing through me. Gavin's hands are possessive and sure, holding me steady as his expert lips move in time with mine. It feels like the entire world has stopped spinning, like everyone in the restaurant has frozen in place in the name of this sacred moment.

When Gavin pulls back, he presses his forehead to mine, and we both exhale shaky breaths that meet between us.

Then, his hands gently release me, thumbs brushing my jaw softly before he sits back in his booth. I lean back in mine, too, and we watch each other for a beat before the world kicks into motion again, and the waiter delivers our order, and Gavin picks up his chopsticks like nothing even happened.

"Alright," he says, smirking with his eyes on me while I fight to catch my breath. He picks up the mackerel nigiri, dipping it ever so slightly in soy sauce before offering it to me. "Are you ready to have your mind blown?"

I think I already have, Gavin Lindberg.

I think I already have.

Jess

THE BEST PART ABOUT fall in South Florida is that while the rest of the country is already getting snow and temperatures well under fifty degrees, Florida is cooling down just enough to land us in that perfect beach weather zone. Almost every day is sunny, hovering between seventy-five and eight-five, with a cool breeze coming in off the coast.

I smile and soak it all in as the girls and I work on our tan in the back yard of the sorority house. We've all been so busy with classes and work and relationship shit that it's the first time the five of us have really been able to spend quality time together, and while the weather might be cooling down a smidge, it's apparent to me that the drama in our lives never will.

This crew couldn't escape trouble even if we tried.

So far, Cassie has filled us in on her and Adam's fight regarding Grayson, and to be fair, we've all told her that while we understood that she wanted to be friends with Grayson, we understood why Adam flew off the handle. Was he a little overdramatic? Maybe. But when I think back on how I reacted to Jarrett spending time with his female co-workers, I can't blame him.

Hell, Jarrett didn't even fuck those girls, and I was jealous and pissed off. I can't imagine how I would have reacted if I knew they had a past.

Still, Cassie is adamant that she's had to cut friends out of her life before and it's nearly killed her. She almost cried when she told us she couldn't do it again.

And I also understood that.

So, while we tried to help her through that whole ordeal, we also caught up with Ashlei and the weird intern drama going on at *Okay, Cool* and — though she's been mostly coy about it — Erin briefly told us about a new "friend" she's made at group therapy.

I have a feeling that *friend* is going to come with some benefits.

But we can all tell Erin's not ready to talk about it, because she brushes off the topic as soon as it's brought up and shifts the attention to Skyler.

"When do you see Kip next?" Erin asks, reaching for the sunscreen to reapply on her face. Erin has always been the one to take the best care of her skin — not just in the sun, but with her entire regimen that she's had since she was eighteen. If I had to make a bet on which one of us would age the most gracefully, all my money would be on her.

"I'm flying in to see him for Thanksgiving, actually," Skyler says on a longing sigh, fanning herself with her magazine. "And honestly, I'm a little nervous."

"Why?" Cassie asks.

Skyler shrugs. "It's hard to explain. I miss him so much, but I haven't seen him since he started school out there. I don't know... I guess I'm just worried that maybe I won't fit into this new part of his life."

Ashlei scoffs. "Are you kidding? I bet he can't *wait* for you to be there so he can show you around and show you *off* to all his film buddies."

"And *I'm* sure he can't wait to bang your brains out," I chime in. Then, I snap my fingers, leaning up in my chair so I can see her better. "Oh! Maybe you could make a movie of your own."

I waggle my brows, and Skyler rips out a page of her magazine, balls it up, and pegs me in the forehead with it. "Perv."

I stick my tongue out before reaching for my tumbler, which I told our sorority house mom had iced coffee in it but is actually filled with vodka and tonic and a splash of lime juice. "You love me."

"We all bear that curse," Erin agrees, and I reach over to smack her ass where she's tanning it to the tune of giggles.

"Speaking of the spell you've put on us," Cassie says. "Looks like Kade has fallen under the same one, huh?"

I try to bite back a smile, but fail miserably, and then *I blush* and I want to punch myself in the face.

"He's definitely hooked," I say, shaking off the butterflies in my stomach.

"And are you?" Skyler asks.

I sigh, flopping back in my chair dramatically. "God, I don't even know anymore." I shake my head, trying to find the right words. "He annoys the absolute *fuck* out of me. But... he also fascinates me, too. And *God*, the sex..." I pull down my sunglasses so the girls can see how serious I am. "The sex is out of this *world*."

"Better than with Jarrett?" Ashlei asks, and I know she means it as nothing more than a simple comparison, but my heart pounds once, twice, three times hard in my chest.

I swallow. "It was different with Jarrett."

"Different good or different bad?" Skyler asks.

"Just... different. We weren't just fucking. We had a relationship."

"Is that what you want with Kade?" Erin asks.

And the question hits me like a semi-truck.

I freeze, shock still, holding my drink in my hand with the sun warming my skin.

"Jess?" Erin asks.

But I can't respond. I'm too busy turning her question over and over in my head, like the winning numbers of the lottery just waiting to be plucked out.

Holy fucking shit.

Do I want a relationship with Kade?

I mean, obviously, I want more — that much was established when I dragged his ass into the tent during the Halloween party and told him I wanted to be his and for him to be mine. But, at the time, I'd been so focused on the fact that I didn't want him with any other girl, that I hadn't paused to ask myself what *exactly* I wanted from him — other than to fuck me exclusively.

And now that I'd asked myself the question, my reaction told me all I needed to know.

Skyler snaps her fingers in front of my face. "Earth to J-Love."

I groan, sinking back in my chair and abandoning my drink on the table so I can scrub my hands over my face. "Oh, God."

"What?" Cassie asks, worried.

I sigh. "I do."

The girls fall silent, exchanging glances.

"I *do* want a relationship."

At that, Ashlei laughs, reaching over to squeeze my forearm. "You say that like you just realized you're an alcoholic or something. Wanting a relationship isn't bad, babe."

My next swallow is impossible, like I've just eaten forty-five saltines without a glass of water to help out. "It is when I'm pretty fucking certain that is *not* what he wants," I argue. Then, I lock eyes with her. "And that the last time I was in a relationship, I had my heart shattered."

Again, the girls exchange glances, and then Skyler gets up from her chair and sits down at the foot of mine, leaning in to look me in the eyes. "Hey, love is fucking scary, okay? I think if anyone gets that, it's this group of girls."

Everyone nods, and my chest tightens with discomfort. I want to crawl inside a hole and hide forever.

"What if you just asked him?" Skyler suggests.

"Ask him what?"

"Ask him on a date," she says with a shrug. "Or, better yet, *tell him* you're going on a date. See what he says."

My instant reaction is to shake my head and scream out *absolutely not*, but her words slide over me like silk, and I lean into them, wrapping them around myself like a blanket.

Could it be that simple?

Could I just tell Kade what I want, and him reciprocate it?

Everything in my body screams a resounding *hell no*, but already, I'm up out of my chair, throwing on my cover up and sliding into my sandals.

"Where are you going?" Erin asks.

"To the Alpha Sigma house."

"To...?"

I look at all of them. "To tell that motherfucker that he's taking me on a date."

That earns me a burst of laughter, and they each smack my ass and holler out encouragements as I dash out of the backyard and down Greek Row.

I burst into the A Sig house just like I did that first time I came to tease Kade, only this time, the house is mostly empty — likely due to it being such a beautiful day outside. I head straight back to Kade's room, but find it empty, and I frown, hanging my hands on my hips.

Where are you? I text him.

The house. What's up?

Where at in the house?

Outside playing beer pong with the guys.

I weave my way through the house and outside, and there are at least a dozen brothers in their swim trunks, jamming to country music and playing beer pong and having an arm-wrestling competition at a nearby table.

At the sight of me, all the commotion stops.

Kade's right in the middle of a game, and before he can shoot the ping pong ball across the table and into his opponent's cup, I slide in front of him, taking it from his hand.

"What the—"

"I want more."

Kade's smile slips off his face at my words, and he shoves his sunglasses up onto the top of his head, cocking a brow at me. "Um... hi?"

"Hi," I say. "I want more."

"More what?"

"More than mind-blowing, toe-curling, name-screaming sex."

That earns a few whistles and *atta boys* from his brothers, and I flick them all off before crossing my arms over my chest and focusing back on Kade. The noise around us picks up again, as if everyone has gone back to their business while Kade smirks down at me.

"Okay, then," he says, leaning a hip against the table. "What do you want?"

"I want to go on a date."

Kade's eyes trail over me, locking on my cleavage still visible even in my cover up. When his eyes find mine again, his grin widens. "Friday?"

I clear my throat, aiming for nonchalance. "Fine."

With my mission accomplished, I turn, tossing the ping pong ball across the table. It bounces once and sinks into the right back cup, and the boys roar in approval.

I wink at Kade, who's laughing his ass off, and then I waltz *my* ass right on out of there with a victory smile on my face.

Adam

I AM THE MOST pathetic piece of shit.

I run another hand through my greasy hair, feeling that sentence sink into my veins like venom. I haven't slept more than a few hours since the Halloween party, when Cassie told me she wouldn't choose between me and Grayson, and to me, that meant she'd already made a choice.

And once again, it wasn't me.

Eating has been impossible. I've taken to drinking protein shakes with a shit ton of vegetables just to keep my nutrition up because solid food just isn't an option. And currently, though it's gorgeous outside, I'm in my dark bedroom all alone with Thirty Seconds to Mars blasting in my headphones.

I'm perfectly content to waste my day away. It's what I've been doing for the past week and a half, and every day I go without Cassie showing up at my door, I realize I'd be content to do this for the rest of my life. Who needs a presidency? Who needs a college degree? Who needs sunlight or friends or something to live for?

I've hit some lows in my life, but this might be the lowest.

Because for the first time, I've lost Cassie not because of something stupid, but because of something real that we couldn't see eye to eye on.

That we maybe never will.

And I have to decide if this is what will end it all.

I roll over to face my wall, but before I can curl into a fetal position, my headphones are ripped from my ears.

I don't even yell at the offender — especially when I see Jeremy's annoyed expression staring back at me in the dim light of my bedroom. I just sigh and face the wall again, resigned.

"You're wasting your time," I mutter.

"Yeah. And you're wasting your senior year." Jeremy reaches over me, ripping the navy-blue curtains on my window open before I can prepare for it. I shrink away from the sunlight, shielding my eyes and shoving him off my bed.

"Asshole."

"Get up."

He yanks the covers off me, and I try to rip them back, but he chucks them across the room before I can.

"Look. It's been almost two weeks. I'm tired of this shit, and so is everyone else. So, if you need to talk about what happened at the Halloween party, let's talk."

"I don't."

"You don't?" Jeremy deadpans.

When I say nothing, he shakes his head and pulls up my desk chair to sit in front of my bed. He straddles it backward, leaning his arms on the back of it with a heavy sigh.

"Fine. I'll talk." But before he says another word, he reaches over and thunks me on the forehead. "Why are you such a fucking idiot when it comes to Cassie McBee?"

I sit up, a bit stunned and a lot pissed, ready to slug him off his chair, but he easily dodges my fist and shoves me back onto the bed — hard.

"No, you had your chance to talk and didn't say shit. So you sit there and listen."

I'm panting, gritting my teeth, but I know Jeremy well enough to know he's not here out of disrespect.

If anything, he's here because he cares about me.

And that's a helluva lot more than I can say for anyone else.

"Look. I get it. If I had a girlfriend and she was hanging out with her ex-boyfriend, I'd be fucking livid, too. In fact, I probably would have run over to them the first time I saw them together and laid him out. But here's the thing — you sat on it *for weeks*, and grew all this resentment, so much so that by the time you two hashed it out, you were so heated and so far up your own ass that you couldn't even listen to her."

"What the fuck was I supposed to listen to?" I argued. "She told me that no matter what I said or did, she wasn't going to choose between us."

"Because she doesn't think she should have to! And honestly, Adam — do you?"

I blew out a breath like a dragon. "I don't think I even should have had to *ask* her."

Jeremy holds up his hands. "Just think about it for a second. Okay? Do you remember all that fucking shit that went down with her and our stupid asshat for a president?"

I swallow, because I'll never forget the night Cassie climbed into my window and into my bed and I held her against my chest while she cried. She told me I was right about Clay, who had been fucking around with her *and* her high school best friend at the same time. She found out in the crudest way possible at a party after her first semester at PSU, and I'd been there for her.

I'll never forget how crushed she was.

"I remember," I manage on a croak.

"Then you know that this is more than just a simple *him or you* scenario," Jeremy says. "This isn't about her wanting to fuck Grayson or ever be with him again. This is about the fact that she's lost people in her life and it *kills* her. I mean, you know better than anyone that Cassie is the sweetest fucking girl on the planet. She hates being hurt. She hates hurting others. So, when this guy she spent so much time with comes back around and apologizes and she has an opportunity to be friends with him? Of course, she wants to. And I hate to say it, brother," he says, shaking his head. "But it has nothing to do with you."

My chest tightens. "It does, though. It's not fair of her to expect me to be okay with that."

"Really? Just like it's not fair of you to expect her to be okay with you and Skyler still being friends?"

His words slam into me, hard and fast and unexpected, and I sit up slowly in my bed before leaning my back against my headboard. "Fuck."

"Yeah," Jeremy says. "Look, man. I know it's hard. You two have been through some shit, and you don't want to lose her. She doesn't want to lose *you*, either. And I know this is a big thing she's asking of you, to put aside your pride and your jealousy and trust her."

I bite my tongue against the urge to argue that I'm not jealous of that fucking prick, and Jeremy must notice, because he leans down until I look at him again.

"But whether you see it or not, she *already* chose you." He smiles, shaking his head. "Bro, you got her. You got the girl. She's all yours and has been since she came to this campus — regardless of the past."

A deflated breath leaves my chest.

"Do you trust her?" he asks.

"More than anyone."

"Then, what's the problem?"

I swallow, because as much as I want to argue that it's that fucking douchebag musician I don't trust, I know that negates what I just said. Because no matter what *he* tries, Cassie would never lean into it — into *him* — ever again.

Jeremy's right — that girl *is* mine.

And I can't fucking lose her again.

I scrub my hands over my face. "Goddamnit. How the fuck do I make this right?"

Jeremy claps his hand on my shoulder. "Step one, take a shower. You smell like shit, bro. And then, go *talk* to her. And listen this time, too."

I nod, looking at my best friend who should be so tired of my shit, he never speaks to me again, but instead, is always there for me. "I owe you a beer."

Jeremy scoffs, standing. "More like a keg."

"Thank you, bro. Seriously."

"I got you. Now, get your shit together and then come outside and hang with your brothers."

I nod, and when he's gone, I pull out my phone and immediately dial Cassie's number. My heart races in my chest as it rings, and after the seventh one, I'm sent to her voicemail.

"Cassie..." I say after the beep, but then I freeze.

I'm sorry?

I love you?

I take it all back?

Nothing seems right, and I sigh, leaning my forehead against the cool wall. After a few calming breaths, I decide if there's any way to make this right, it's not going to be with a simple phone call or text or trip down Greek Row.

I need to show her that I'm serious, that I'm sorry, and that I trust her.

"If you still love me," I say, my voice low and hoarse. "Then meet me at the marina this Saturday. One hour before sunset."

I stay on the line for a moment longer, as if somehow she'll feel me through the phone. When I finally hang up, I take a deep breath and drag myself into the shower.

And while I put together my plan, I pray that Cassie will give me the chance to make things right.

Ashlei

THE INSIDE OF MY thighs are tender and slightly bruised by the time I finish my pole session on Friday.

Getting back into dancing? Easy enough, just a little cardio training and getting my body to remember how it feels to move that way. Revisiting climbing the pole and head up tricks? Not too shabby, a little painful, but for the most part, I got this.

But once I got into training my leg hangs and thigh grips again, my body wanted to divorce me.

I've spent all afternoon upside down, working on my Extended Butterfly, my Scorpio, my leg switches and hip holds, and *God help me,* even my Superman. As much as it hurts to train like this, it also feels good, like I'm making progress and finding my passion again.

Besides, I need a break from my brain.

I haven't stopped turning over what happened between me and Sophie since the *Okay, Cool* after-party. It seems no matter how much I try to focus on work or school or sorority events or pole, that night keeps creeping up on me, and I find myself trying to dissect every word she said, every move she made, wondering if I made it up, or if she really was hitting on me.

And if she was... *what the hell?*

Was she bisexual? Was she just being a bitch, trying to fuck with my head since it's clear that I'm onto her and the way she looks at Brandon?

Did I make it all up, and it's *me* who's the psycho?

I sigh, peeling my high heels and knee pads off and shoving them into my gym bag with more force than necessary, like it's Sophie I'm shoving out of my life.

"Hey now," Karen says, arching an eyebrow as she lowers down to the floor next to me. "It wasn't *that* bad of a training session, was it?"

I offer her a smile. "I'm sorry. Just have a lot on my mind."

"That explains why you asked for two hours of torture instead of just one today." Karen pauses, watching me. "Ashlei, I know we talked about this a few months ago... but I really think you should consider competing again."

I swallow, trying to remain calm when I meet Karen's eyes. "I... I don't think..."

Karen folds her soft fingers over my arm, gentle and calm. "I know what happened with Kitty Heels."

I nearly pass out at the mention of the studio I left behind me, that I've tried to bury for years. In a flash, I see Leslie, Kya, Hayden, the drugs, the threats, the money, the club I tried to work at to save my ass, Jess coming to my rescue.

Another soft squeeze from Karen saves me from blacking out. "Leslie has made a name for herself in this industry — and it's not a good one. Everyone knows the sketchy shit she pulls, and trust me when I say you were the best thing to happen for her and that studio. I know she fucked you over... but don't let her steal this passion from you."

My eyes gloss, and I don't have a single word to say in response.

"You don't have to make a decision now, okay?" Karen says, standing and offering a hand down to help me up, too. "Just think about it. If not competing, maybe you could at least perform. Trust me — if you got on a pole stage?" She shakes her head once I'm standing with her. "You'd captivate the entire audience — me included."

I somehow manage a nod and a smile, and I thank her, grabbing my bag and leaving the studio with my mind whirling with even more thoughts than when I walked in. When I see Brandon's car on the curb, relief sinks into me like sweet honey, and I smile.

"I like this tradition of you picking me up after class," I say when I slide inside the passenger seat. I toss my bag in the back. "But I'm starting to think you might have a fetish for sweaty girls or something."

"I only have a fetish for *one* sweaty girl," he corrects, leaning over the console to give me a deep, passionate kiss. I'm breathless when he pulls back, and his golden eyes settle over me in appreciation. "I was thinking we could do dinner tonight."

"I like that idea."

"In Chicago."

I balk. "*Chicago?*"

He nods on a grin. "There was a last-minute cancellation at one of the most famous restaurants in town, and the owner called me and asked if I wanted the table. It's twenty-four courses of the finest cuisine you'll ever have." He shrugs. "And then, I was thinking I could fuck you on the balcony of my favorite suite in the city."

I lick my lips, crawling over the console enough to thread my fingers around the back of his neck and pull him into me for a kiss. "Are we flying commercial?"

"Come on now," he chastises, nipping my bottom lip. "You know me better than that, Miss Daniels."

I smirk. "Then *you* should know better than to think we'll wait until after dinner to fuck if you're taking me on your private jet again." I pause, letting my hand drop to his belt buckle and drawing a soft line over the seam of his dress pants before whispering. "Mr. Church."

A guttural groan rips from his throat, and then he breaks our kiss suddenly and swiftly, throwing the car in drive and speeding us across town to the airport.

I feel night and day better after an evening with Brandon.

Just like I suspected, we'd barely made it through takeoff before Brandon had me pinned against one of the leather couches on the private jet, and once we'd landed in Chicago, we'd spent all dinner staring at each other from across our intimately lit table, my heel tracing up and down his leg under the tablecloth, his eyes devouring me more than the meal.

By the time we get back to the suite downtown, I'm starving for his touch again. It seems I never can get enough.

I've never been to Chicago before, and I decide after just one day in the city that I love it. The architecture is unlike anything I've ever seen, buildings stretching up high into the sky and lining the river, the lake, filling the city with lights. But there are also dozens of parks and recreational areas, so while it's a city, it's somehow greener and fresher than Manhattan — at least, in my opinion.

I'm appreciating the view from our balcony and the crisp, cool air when Brandon joins me, wrapping his arms around me from behind. I rest my head back on his chest as he lets out a deep, content sigh.

"Beautiful, isn't it?" he whispers in my ear.

I nod, letting my eyes trace over the city lights glittering like stars, the river reflecting their glare and making for the most picturesque backdrop.

"You know, it's been almost a year since the first time you took me on that private jet," I remark.

Brandon chuckles, kissing my cheek. "It has, hasn't it? God, I wanted you so bad. I'm surprised I made it that long before touching you."

"You were trying to do the right, moral thing and not fuck your intern."

"Looks like I sold my soul to the devil, then."

I turn in his arms, threading mine around his neck. The way the lights reflect in his eyes warm my chest, and I trace his dark features, falling even more for him every second that we're together. "I'm so happy we found each other."

He nods, knuckles brushing my jaw. "Me, too. I can't believe you thought we weren't exclusive all that time, until you asked me in the spring after we told everyone at the agency about us."

"It's hard," I argue. "When you're my age, everyone plays games."

His eyes are darker when they meet mine again. "Do you know now that I don't?"

I swallow, nodding, leaning into where his hand frames my face.

"And do you know that I love you?"

I close my eyes, fighting back the tears those words drew from me the moment he said them. It's nearly impossible, though, for the joy that strangles me, the relief, the terror and otherworldly ecstasy that consume me at once.

"I do now," I say, opening my eyes and looking into his. "And I love you, too."

Brandon's lips are on mine as soon as I finish speaking, and I breathe in the kiss, the man holding me, the night around us, the moment I'll never forget. I'm so lost in the way his hands feel on my waist, and the way his lips move in time with mine, that I barely register him lifting me into his arms and carrying me inside.

The windows that surround the suite are floor to ceiling, still showcasing the breathtaking city view as Brandon deftly turns out every light and guides me to the California king bed. My knees hit the back of it once he sets me back down on the floor, and I press my hands into his chest, smiling against his kiss.

"I thought you said you wanted to fuck me on the balcony?"

I'm ready for him to give some smart ass comment in response, or to haul my ass back outside, but instead, he swallows, pressing his forehead to mine. "Not now," he husks. "Now, I'm going to make love to you in this bed."

My heart swells in my chest, my throat tight as I run my fingers back to hold his neck and draw him back to my lips. The kiss is gentle and sweet and unlike any other that I've had from this man, and I melt into it, resisting the urge to pinch myself to make sure this is all real.

He takes his time undressing me, peeling my little black dress over my head before reaching into my hair and slowly pulling out each bobby pin that holds it in place. Next, he unclasps my bra, and helps me step out of my heels before slipping my panties down over my ass, my thighs, my ankles, leaving them on the floor.

Between kisses and touches and sighs and licks, he undresses himself, too — and then his arms wrap around me, guiding me down on top of the plush comforter of the bed, the down pillows giving way to the weight of my head.

I don't realize I'm shaking until Brandon holds himself over me and my trembling fingers wrap around his thick, bulging biceps. I hold onto them as an unsteady breath slips through my lips, and Brandon kisses me gently, spreading my legs wider with his. Our bodies are hot where they touch — chest to chest, his arms surrounding me, and mine holding onto him, his thighs between mine, his shaft warm and hard where it slicks between my wet lips.

"Do you remember when I told you on my yacht that the only place I held any power over you was in the office?"

I nod, still holding onto him for dear life with my heart racing in my chest.

"Well, I've decided that's now a lie." He shakes his head, eyes flicking back and forth between mine. "In every possible way, in every place that exists, you are my everything. You hold the power, Ashlei, and I am yours — to bear or to break."

Tears flood my eyes, and this time I don't try to stop them. I have never felt anything in my life like I feel for this man, and I succumb to the feeling of him surrounding me — all of me — now and forever.

"I will never break you," I whisper, reaching up to press my lips to his. He answers me with a passionate kiss in return, and then with a flex of his hips, he's inside me.

I feel him all at once, all-encompassing, the bare length of him filling me up. I gasp into his mouth, and his hands wrap around my shoulders, giving him a better grip to thrust inside me again. Each time he withdraws and pummels in, his pelvis rubs my clit, and I spread my legs even wider, chasing the building fire ready to catch.

Brandon's mouth roams all over me — my neck, my jaw, my chin and lips and ears and breasts. I feel him everywhere, and I run my nails down his back, kiss his skin in return, praying that he feels me just as much.

How can it be that this strong, powerful, successful man wants anything to do with me? How can it be that out of all the women falling at his feet, he chose me to stand by his side, to be his queen, to say the three words every woman wants to hear?

This time last year, I was fighting every urge that begged me to give into my lust for him, and now, he's making love to me in a city halfway across the country, and everyone knows about us, and nobody dares to tell us we can't have each other.

I could never break him, I realize, because we're unbreakable.

As long as we're together, we can't be stopped.

Trembling and holding onto each other with slick, hot hands, Brandon makes love to me for hours in that bed.

And before we leave the next morning, he makes good on his promise to fuck me on the balcony, too.

Jess

THE LAST TIME I went on a date, it was with Jarrett.

I don't want to compare. Fuck, the whole *point* of dicking around with Kade was to distract myself from the fact that Jarrett had pulverized my heart. And the surprising fact is that it's been working... until now.

Because now, I'm staring in the mirror moments before Kade is picking me up for our first official date, and for some reason, it all feels wrong.

It feels wrong to be thinking about the way my stomach fluttered the first time Jarrett took me on a date, or how he made me come home with him when I was sick just so he could take care of me, or how he flew in from New York and hung out with me and my sorority sisters, which made them fall just as in love with him as I was.

It feels wrong because it's a past, not a future — and tonight, I start something new with *someone* new.

I sigh, rubbing the edge of my lip with my pinky to fix a bit of lipstick smudge. It's slightly cool tonight — for South Florida, at least — so I landed on my favorite pair of Spanx leggings, a burnt orange crop top, and my favorite black booty heels. I layered a cream, high-low cardigan over the top, and did my makeup mostly natural, except for the smoky eye. My blonde hair is down and curled, falling over my shoulders, and I stare back at the golden eyes in the mirror with a pit in my stomach.

Because as much as I'm thinking of Jarrett, perhaps what fucks me up most is that I don't think I miss him anymore.

I don't think my heart breaks as much when I think about him. I don't think I care what he's doing or who he's with anymore.

And more than anything, I don't think I'm sad that it's not him picking me up tonight.

The truth is, I'm *excited* for my date with Kade.

And for some reason, that fucks me up.

That's what feels wrong.

Skyler pops her head into the bathroom, dancing a little with her eyebrows waggling like a cartoon character. "He's here," she whispers. "And he's *smokin'!*"

"Are you hitting on my boyfriend, Sky?"

At that, her mouth pops open. "Oh, I didn't realize he was your *boyfriend.*"

My cheeks flame, and I grab the makeup remover wipe I'd used to correct my eyeliner and chuck it at her. She dodges it easy, laughing and teasing me all the way down the stairs. When I hit the bottom one, we both stop, Skyler watching me knowingly as I do everything in my power to keep my jaw from dropping.

Holy fucking shit.

The Kade I'm most familiar with is naked Kade. I'm used to seeing his tattoos sprawling out over every inch of his muscular body, his short hair messy and mussed, his grin goofy and playful. But tonight? Tonight, Kade is in dark, form-fitting jeans, an olive green polo that sets off the color of his hungry eyes, and a brown leather jacket, shoved up just below his elbows, showing off his toned and tattooed forearms. His hair is styled, and that grin that's usually so goofy and carefree is sultry and sexy as hell.

He looks like a *GQ* model, a celebrity, a rock star who could fuck me all the way up.

And I want *all* of him.

"Jess," he says, his eyes roaming over me appreciatively as he shakes his head. I shiver at my name on his tongue, and when his gaze finds mine, that tongue snakes out just enough to wet his bottom lip. "You look gorgeous." He pauses, lowering his voice to just above a whisper. "You always do."

I don't realize we're not alone until that exact moment, because a chorus of *awww's* and *oh my God's* ring out from the sorority sisters clamored in the living room.

That seems to knock me out of my daze, and I roll my eyes, taking the last step off the stairs and crossing my arms in front of him. "That's some line."

"Not a line," he assures me, that sexy smirk back in place. Then, he holds out his arm for me to thread mine through. "Ready?"

Oh, how I want to call him on his obvious show. But then again, I love the way he's holding out an arm for me, the way he came to the house to pick me up, the way he planned an entire night for us.

I meant it when I said I wanted a date.

And he's delivering.

I try to fight a smile, but fail miserably, weaving my hand through the hole in his arm and wrapping my fingers around his bicep. I glance back at Skyler and the other girls when we're at the door, and they're all holding up their thumbs and clapping quietly with glee.

"So, Mr. GQ," I say when I'm buckled into the passenger seat of his hot little Camaro — the one *I've* been driving all semester, thanks to our deal. "What's on the menu tonight?"

It's a purposeful line, one that sets him up to easily say *you* in return. But instead, Kade smiles, firing the engine to life. "I'm going to wine and dine you, beautiful. Just like you deserve."

His eyes find mine then, and then one hand reaches over to hold mine across the console, and he doesn't remove it the entire drive.

When Kade told me he was going to wine and dine me, I honestly thought he meant he was going to take me to the equivalent of a fancy Olive Garden downtown. I definitely *did not* expect him to take me to one of the most expensive restaurants on the water, one that sits at the top of a high rise and rotates.

No joke — the restaurant *spins*, giving you a three-sixty view of the city and the coastline as you eat.

On top of that, they're known for incredible tapas, of which Kade orders us a dozen, a rare collection of wine, of which Kade orders us not one, but *two* bottles, and a live jazz trio, to which Kade takes my hand after dinner and leads me out on the dance floor to enjoy.

It's the most magical night.

And it is absolutely not what I expected from him.

I can't help but stare at him when we're back at the table after a few songs, each of us sipping our wine and enjoying the music as we look over the dessert menu. Or rather, as *Kade* looks over the dessert menu and I study him, instead. He looks even more handsome in the candlelight, with the city glowing behind him, and I have to admit, watching him sip red wine turns me on *way* more than seeing him chug a beer at a frat party.

"I feel like I don't even know who you are."

The words blurt out before I can stop them, and Kade lifts a brow, casting me a glance before he's looking at the menu again. "What do you mean?"

"I mean, who the fuck are you?" I ask, gesturing to where he sits. "The Kade I know lives in basketball shorts and flat-bill hats. I didn't even know you had clothes like this in your wardrobe."

Kade chuckles, setting his menu down and lifting his glass to his lips for another sip. "Are you upset about it?"

"No," I answer quickly, shifting. "Just surprised, is all."

"I love surprising you."

"Seriously, Kade," I say on a sigh. "This is... a lot. I'm just... where is the kid who annoyed me at Spring Break last year? Where is the kid who thought telling me he wanted me to sit on his face was a good pick-up line?"

"I was a puppy then, remember?" he says, using the exact words I had. "I've been trained."

"I didn't train you to do all *this*," I argue, gesturing to the table.

Kade leans forward, resting his elbows on the table and folding his hands together. "You said you wanted to be taken on a date," he reminds me. "You also said you wanted to be mine, and wanted me to be yours. Am I missing anything yet?"

I shake my head.

"Well, for me, I don't take any of that lightly. If you're my girl, then I'm not just fucking you in my dorm room and eating burritos wrapped in foil — though that *is* a good time," he adds with a grin. Then, he shrugs. "If you're my girl, then I'm giving you the best that I can."

"Color me impressed."

"Oh, this is just the first date," he says with a grin. "The best is yet to come. And for the record, you may not have liked the proposal when I first gave it, but you *know* damn well that you love sitting on my face."

I roll my eyes, taking a sip of my wine just as the waiter asks us for our order. Kade takes over, ordering three different desserts for us to sample from, and once our menus have been taken and it's just us and our wine, his eyes land on me.

"So, you're graduating soon," he says. "What are you going to do next?"

I chuckle. "Why do you care?"

"Jess, if you want more, you've gotta give me more, too."

His eyes are sincere, and somehow that scares me more than anything.

I swallow another sip of wine, staring at the red liquid in my cup. "Hell if I know. I changed my major last year because one thing I figured out for sure, I do *not* want to go into politics."

Kade snorts. "I can't imagine that ever even being an option for you."

"I thought it was at one point," I admit. "I was a poli sci major, bright-eyed and bushy-tailed and thinking — like everyone else in that major — that I could someday change the world."

"What happened?"

"I'm not sure, honestly. I mean, the classes were hard," I admit, and a vision of Jarrett at the front of the class-room assaults me out of nowhere. I shake it off as soon as it hits. "But I think more than anything, I realized that — like Ashlei — I love to plan and organize events. I think I have more passion for that than anything else."

"So, do you want to go into corporate events and ad-vertising like Ashlei?"

I scoff. "Not a chance. I think... maybe... more like weddings."

Kade's wearing his shocked expression again.

"What?"

"Nothing," he says quickly. "I was just thinking how great you'd be at that."

"Really?"

"Are you kidding? Kappa Kappa Beta just had the best recruitment they've ever seen, thanks to you. And every time you host a KKB event, it's the best one. You have a great knack for attention to detail. Besides," he says, taking a sip of his wine. "If anyone can wrangle a Bridezilla, it's you."

"I'll take that as a compliment."

"You should."

I smile, still watching him with a mixture of confusion and appreciation. It's just so crazy to see this side of him when I'm so used to the other.

"When you blew me off this summer," I say. "You said there was some family stuff going on."

Kade's smile instantly falls, and his gaze drops to his hands. "Yeah."

"What was it?"

He lets out a long sigh, looking around the restaurant. "Remember how I told you last year that I was practically raised by two rowdy older brothers?"

"I do."

"Well... they're half-brothers. Technically. And their dad..." He pauses, jaw ticking.

"We don't have to talk about this if you don't want to."

"No, it's okay," he assures me, and his eyes meet mine. "I want to tell you. I want you to know more about me."

I smile at that, reaching across the table for his hand. And though I've touched every other part of him, this — holding hands across a candle-lit table in a room full of strangers — it somehow feels like the most intimate touch we've shared.

"Our mom got sick when I was really little," he says after a moment. "When she passed away, my brothers went to live with their dad, and I stayed with mine. And let's just say it put a rift in the family, because their dad was an addict and, frankly, a piece of shit. And my dad, while he took care of *me*, didn't really want to take care of my brothers — especially when he found out that my mom had been seeing their dad behind his back once she found out she was sick."

"Whoa."

Kade grimaces. "I know. Family drama is super fun, right?"

I squeeze his hand.

"Anyway, my brothers' dad just got into some trouble this summer, and they called me and asked me to help." He shakes his head, eyes lost somewhere in a memory. "It was the first time I'd seen them in years."

"That must have been hard."

He shrugs. "It was. But our mom was the glue that held us together. Once she passed... we all kind of fell apart."

The waiter brings our desserts then — a key lime pie, a cheesecake, and apple pie a la mode — but when I try to slip my hand out of Kade's to make room for the dishes, he holds fast to me, his eyes begging me not to let go.

So I don't.

We hold hands through dessert, turning the subject to lighter topics and feeding each other sweets and finishing off the last of our wine.

Kade is a little too buzzed to drive at the end of the night, so we take a cab, and when we make it back to the sorority house, he walks me to the door with his hands in his pockets.

"I had a great time tonight, Jess," he says softly when I slide my hands around his neck. His wrap around my waist in the next breath, and he lowers his lips slowly and carefully, the kiss sweet and a little too PG-13 for my liking.

"Well, the night's not over, is it?" I husk, running my hands down his chest and over his abdomen.

Before I can trace the outline of the thick cock I *know* his pants are hiding, he grabs my wrists, stopping me short.

I pout, which earns me a chuckle before Kade kisses me again, a little more passionately this time, which only fuels my desire to get him naked — and fast.

His lips move from my mouth to my jaw, to my neck, and I let my head fall back to allow him better access. When he kisses his way up to the shell of my ear, his breath eliciting chills over every inch of me, I practically pant in anticipation.

That is, until he whispers, "I don't fuck on the first date."

He pulls back with a sexy, knowing smirk, kissing my knuckles on each hand before releasing me.

"Gotta get to at least number three for that," he adds on a wink. "I'll call you tomorrow."

I'm still standing there in shock, mouth open, violet vulva throbbing in my pants. "You're fucking joking, right?"

Kade chuckles, rolling his lips together before he walks off the sorority front porch backward. "Goodnight, gorgeous."

I flick him off, which makes him laugh harder, and then he turns and leaves me there with a wine buzz and no orgasm.

That motherfucker.

But then, I smile.

I really have taught him well.

Adam

SHE CAME.

My heart that's been racing since I called Cassie earlier this week — with no reply — heaves a sigh of relief at the sight of her walking down the dock. Her short red hair is curled around her face, and she's bundled in a pair of leggings, an oversized KKB sweatshirt, and simple black boots. We rarely get weather cold enough to wear a sweater in South Florida, but tonight, the breeze is blowing in from the north, and we're on the water, which puts us perfectly in the sixty to sixty-five-degree range.

Perfect cuddle weather, I think.

If she'll let me get close to her, that is.

I jump off the boat and onto the dock, shoving my hands in my pockets as she walks the rest of the way. She stops a few feet in front of me, crossing her arms and looking over the boat before her green eyes find mine.

"Thank you for meeting me."

She nods, looking down at her shoes.

I want to pull her into me. I want to drop to my knees and beg for her forgiveness right here and now. But I rented the boat for a reason, and I've got way more in store for this girl than just a boy begging for forgiveness on a boat dock.

I reach out my hand for hers, and when she hesitantly takes it, I help her onto the boat before climbing on myself. It's nothing fancy, a little twenty-five-foot deck boat that would be perfect for a trip to the sandbar with a group of friends. But tonight, it'll take us to Boca Chita Key.

Cassie takes a seat at the back of the boat, and the fact that she's letting me take her off the mainland tells me more than any words do that I still have a fighting chance here. If I were past the point of no-return, she would have fought me on the shore — or not shown up at all.

So, I put on a little music, deciding on one of her favorite artists — Jack Johnson — and we cruise out into Biscayne Bay, quiet but for the boat, the water, and the melody of "Monsoon."

It only takes about forty-five minutes to get out to the key, and we're greeted first by the lighthouse — one that I hope to take Cassie up in tomorrow, if she doesn't demand I take her back to shore tonight. Chancing a glance back at her from where I'm driving, she's not giving anything away. There's no smile on her face, but she doesn't seem in a hurry to run away, either.

She's waiting for me to make my move.

I just hope it's enough.

After I dock the boat, I grab her hand and walk her quietly onto the tiny island.

"What is this place?" she asks, looking around in wonder at the mangroves, the small, sandy shore, the crystal blue water, made darker by the sun setting over the coast.

"Boca Chita Key."

"I've never heard of it."

I chuckle. "Well, we're in college. I think we focus a little more on classes and partying than on cool places to camp."

"Are we camping here?"

I swallow, pulling her to a stop along the shore. "I hope so." Then, I look behind her.

She follows my gaze, and when she does, a soft gasp slips from her lips. She covers her mouth, and I hold my breath, hoping that reaction means everything I've set up is paying off.

Camping on the island is first-come, first-serve — so I came here early this morning, setting up a tent and working throughout the day to make it the most amazing campsite anyone could ask for. It took a little planning and a *lot* of figuring out how to do everything I wanted with just the power on the generator I bought for the Halloween party, but I pulled it off.

The two-person tent is cast in an orange glow, both from the setting sun and from the white string lights I hung above it. Two chairs wait by the fire, along with everything we need to make hot dogs and s'mores in a cooler and a couple reusable bags. There's a bottle of wine in a bucket of ice that I set up just before going back to the mainland to pick her up, and two plastic wine glasses beside it.

Grabbing Cassie's hand, I guide her toward the site, refilling the ice in the bucket as she looks around more. One peek inside the tent, and I know she's seen that it's filled with blankets and pillows and rose petals for a romantic touch. She closes the flap once more, standing, eyes tracing each and every detail of the scene before she looks at me.

"You did all this?"

My hands find my pockets, and I nod.

Her mouth parts, and she looks around in wonder, shaking her head. "It's beautiful," she whispers. "Are we the only ones out here?"

I look around at the vacant campsites. "It's first-come, first-serve, and there are a few other spots to camp on the key. But it's not really camping season. We very well might be."

She nods, still taking it all in.

Everything about her is stunning in that moment — the glow of the sun on her fiery hair, the freckles dotting her cheeks, her wide, emerald eyes sweeping over the campsite. Everything inside me longs to hold her, and I decide I can't wait another minute.

I swallow, reaching for her and breathing another sigh of relief when she lets me take her hands in my own. "Cassie, I'm sorry. I am so fucking sorry for the way I treated you at the Halloween party — for the way I've treated you most of this semester. We're finally together, finally official, and I take the first opportunity to blow something out of proportion and fuck it all up."

Her eyes well with tears, and she looks between us, rolling her lips together. "No, you had a right to be upset. I should have come to you that first day that I realized Grayson was in my class. I should have just told you from the start, and then maybe we wouldn't be in this mess."

I tilt her chin with my knuckle. "Hey, it's okay. I mean, with the way I reacted... well, it's pretty clear why you were hesitant to tell me."

Cassie sniffs, nodding slightly. "I'm sorry I hurt you, Adam. But I promise — *nothing* is going on between me and Grayson. Nothing ever will again. I'm yours, and I know it doesn't make sense to you, but Grayson wanting to make amends and be friends... it's important to me. It gives me the chance to not lose yet another person in my life. And—"

"I get it."

Her green eyes widen. "You do?"

"I do," I say, smoothing my thumbs over her knuckles. "I didn't, not at first, but luckily I have some pretty great brothers who help me see clearer. I mean, I'm friends with Skyler, and you've *never* been opposed to that — other than when I put her before us, which was fair. But since we cleared that all out, it's been me and you, and Skyler being my friend has never been an issue."

"Of course not," Cassie says, like she's shocked I would think that at all.

God, I love this girl.

"Well, that's just one good example of why I shouldn't have blown up the way I did," I say on a sigh. "You trust me. And though my actions at the Halloween party say otherwise, I trust you, too, Cassie. I know you wouldn't do anything with Grayson, that your heart is mine. I guess I just... I was scared. I thought I was losing you again. And to be honest, I still don't trust that guy."

She chuckles at that. "That's fair."

"But again, I trust *you*," I say. "And that's what matters."

I pull her into me, and she lets me take her into my arms, burying her face in my chest as I breathe in the scent of her.

"So, we're okay? You're not mad at me?"

"We're okay," I tell her, kissing her hair. "I'm sorry."

"I'm sorry, too," she whispers, and then she hugs me tighter and I do the same, and we stay there for a long time, just holding each other while the waves lap at the shore and the mockingbirds sing us a song.

After a while, we peel apart enough for Cassie to ask more about the camping set-up, and I walk her through everything, pouring us each a glass of wine. We make hot dogs and eat s'mores by the fire, listen to music on the portable speaker I brought with me, and catch up on everything we've missed over the semester.

And finally, I feel whole again.

It's late when we climb into the tent, the moon high above us and casting its silvery glow over the water. We leave the flaps of the tent open so we can enjoy the view, taking advantage of the fact that we're alone, and Cassie lays her head on my chest where we lie in the fortress of pillows and blankets.

"I've been so miserable without you," she whispers.

I inhale deep, running my fingers through her hair. "You and me both."

"I hate how well I know that feeling," she says, leaning up on her elbow to look at me. "The feeling of losing you, of wondering if I've lost you forever."

"You could never lose me forever."

"Promise?"

I laugh, kissing her cheek. "I mean, as long as you can put up with my stubborn ass, I'll be around."

"Good," she says on a grin, but as soon as it comes, it falls, and her eyes search mine. She watches me for a long moment, and then in one motion, her hands grab my shoulders and she swings one leg over me until she's sitting in my lap.

Her mouth finds mine, passionate and sure, and as soon as we breathe into that kiss, all the blood rushes to where her center meets mine.

"*God*, I've missed you kissing me," she whispers, grinding her hips. "*Touching* me."

"I hate myself that I wasted all this time."

"Well," she says, rolling again. "You can make up for it now."

Leaning back, she pulls her sweatshirt over her head, leaving my face lined up with her perfect breasts barely covered in a lilac lace bra. I groan in appreciation, running my fingers along the edge of the fabric before I dip underneath and palm her completely.

Her head falls back, mouth open, and she grinds against my erection with just the right friction to have me ready to come in my pants.

Ever since the first time Cassie let me touch her, we've gone slow. We've gone easy. We've taken our time and explored each other, and I made sure — above all else — that she felt good and comfortable and safe.

But the way she's grinding against me, the way she's kissing me and biting my neck and running her nails down my back, I know she doesn't want easy tonight.

And I can deliver whatever she needs.

We're all arms and lips and heavy breathing as we take turns rolling on top of the other, stripping off articles of clothing and letting them get lost in the blankets. When we're bare, I back up into the pillows and pull Cassie onto my lap again, running my hand down between her legs and slipping my fingers between her wet lips.

She moans, arching her back and digging her nails into my shoulders as I press one finger inside without warning.

"Jesus Christ, Cassie," I curse, sucking her neck between my teeth. "You're so fucking wet."

"I want you inside me."

"I am inside you," I say, pressing another finger in to join the first.

I curl them to the tune of another moan, but then she presses her hands into my chest. "No, I want *you*," she says, running her hand down my abdomen until she's palming me in her grip. Just the feel of her sweet fucking hand around my shaft has me flexing into her grip, pre-cum letting her palm slide up and down me with ease.

"Fuck," I draw out, letting my head fall back. I revel in the feel of her for a split moment before I smack her ass and yank her off of me, rolling her down into the blankets and pressing a hard kiss to her lips. "Hold that thought."

It takes me seconds to find my pants and pull a condom from my wallet, and then the package is torn open and I roll it over my length, loving the way Cassie's eyes heat as she watches me. She licks her lips like she loves what she sees, so I stroke myself in the condom for her, until she's reaching for me.

"Adam…"

"Roll over," I command, and I see the surprise in her eyes before she does as I say. We've only ever fucked face to face, with me on top or her on top, lost in each other's gazes.

But tonight, I can feel her craving for more.

She wants something dirty and carnal. She wants me to claim her and remind her that she's mine.

When she's on her stomach, I straddle her calves and wrap my hands around her hips, yanking until her ass is up in the air. At the same time, I press one hand down on her upper back, keeping her chest and face pressed into the pile of pillows and blankets.

I run my hand over her spine, reveling in the chills that break in my wake, and then I lower to press my chest into her back, sucking on her earlobe as she rolls her ass against my hard-on.

"Are you ready to feel me deep, baby?"

"*Oh, God.*"

I smirk, that answer enough for me, and then I kiss the back of her neck and position myself at her entrance with just a breath of warning before I slam it home.

Cassie cries out, fisting the blankets and squeezing her eyes shut. "Yes," she breathes, and I withdraw, pummeling in again with just as much force.

Her cheeks are already flushed, and the sight of her bent over in the mess of blankets under the glow of the string lights is like something out of a painting. Every curve is outlined, and I run my hands along all of them as I position myself on my knees and take her hips in my hands, pulling her wet pussy over my cock again and again.

"Play with your clit, baby," I say, flexing my hips to fill her again. "Reach down there and play with your pussy while I fuck you."

I've never talked to her like this, and I'm rewarded with a moan and a whimper before one of her hands that was gripping the blankets disappears under her. She strokes that hand over where I'm entering her first, eliciting a sharp inhale from me before I feel her circling her clit.

"God*damn*, you're so hot," I husk, watching her squirm as I fill her.

Cassie's cries echo throughout the entire park as she rubs her clit and rolls her hips, meeting my thrust each time. I'm half-thankful we're alone, half-wishing there was someone else to witness the way my girl can be so sexy when she's completely uninhibited.

"Adam," she says, just above a whisper and just shy of a cry, and then her hips drop, thighs spreading wider as she chases her orgasm. I answer the call by falling onto my hands on either side of her and grinding in even deeper, sucking on her earlobe and kissing over her neck as she screams out.

Her pussy tightens around me, her hand moving fast and furious between her legs. And just the sound of her coming undone has me ready to do the same.

She falls limp when she's spent, her hand pinned under her as I slow just a little, kissing the back of her neck and her shoulders tenderly.

"You good, baby?"

Cassie chuckles. "I'm fucking *great*."

I smile against her skin, still pumping gently in and out of her tight, swollen, soaked pussy. "You ready for me?"

"Please," she cries.

"I don't want to come in this condom."

She stiffens at that, glancing at me over her shoulder as I still. "Where do you want to come?"

"Roll over," I say as I withdraw, peeling the condom off and tossing it to the side as she rolls onto her back. I bite my lip at the sight of the lights casting a glow over her breasts, her lean navel, her thighs, spread and waiting.

"Move down a little," I say, grabbing her hips and helping her slide down until her head is on the blankets instead of the pillows. Then, I crawl up her, straddling her breasts and feeling them against my balls as I grip my shaft tight.

Her eyes are wide, flicking back and forth between my cock and my face as she waits for my next move.

"If this is too much, tell me to stop, okay?"

She nods, and I run my hands through her hair, tugging until her neck is exposed.

"Open your mouth, baby."

When she does, I nearly come on the spot. It's so fucking hot looking down on her plump lips and wet tongue, her eyes watching me, waiting. I position my tip on her tongue first, sliding it around to get it nice and wet before I gently thrust inside.

I groan at the feel of her lips surrounding me, of her tongue sliding along my base, and my hands fall to the pillows above her head to keep me balanced. Slowly, carefully, I withdraw and press inside her again, fucking her mouth with as much restraint as I can manage.

She gags a few times, and I slow, making sure she knows she's in control. But she doesn't ask me to stop. Instead, she grabs my ass, her nails digging into the skin as she guides me inside her again.

"Oh, *fuck*," I groan, my breathing picking up, heart racing. "I need to go a little faster. It won't take long."

She answers by grabbing my ass and pulling me inside her throat deeper, and my eyes flutter shut at the all-encompassing feel of her letting me take her this way. It's so vulnerable and hot, and at the very base of it, it's her saying she trusts me.

Just like I trust her.

With my eyes still shut, I pick up the pace, careful not to go too deep but finding my release building with each wrap of her lips and slip of her tongue. "Oh, fuck," I grunt. "Coming."

And with one last thrust deep into her throat, I spill.

My body shakes, fire consuming me as I black out to everything that isn't Cassie's mouth around my cock. Faintly, I register her gagging, but she holds me inside her as I ride out every last pulse. I withdraw and push back in, again and again, until I'm empty and spent and trembling as I carefully roll off of her and onto my back next to where she lay.

I'm still seeing stars, panting and trying to catch my breath when I look over and see Cassie swallow, wiping the corners of her mouth and smiling at me shyly.

"Fuck *me*," I say, rolling over to pull her into me and kiss all over her. She giggles and wraps herself around me, too, until we're a tangle of slick arms and legs.

"Did you like that?"

"Do you really have to fucking ask?" I laugh.

"I liked it, too," she says, kissing my jaw. "And I liked you taking me from behind."

"That so?" I ask on a smirk. "My little innocent Cassie McBee, a fan of doggy-style."

Her nose wrinkles. "Don't call it that."

"I'll call it whatever you want, babe," I say, pulling her into my chest. "As long as we get to do it again."

She laughs in my arms, and as the world slowly comes back to us, our breaths evening out and the music and sounds of the night finding us inside the tent, I run my fingers through her hair and count my lucky stars that she came tonight, that she forgave me, that I didn't lose her for good.

"I love you," she whispers.

I inhale deep, holding her tighter and vowing to never fuck this up again. "I love you, too."

Erin

"ALRIGHT, LADIES," I SAY once the room is quiet, glancing over my notes for tonight's Chapter meeting. "I think that wraps up everything on the agenda. But we do have some visitors tonight. So, phones away, everyone give your full attention, okay? First up, the ladies of Zeta Pi Alpha."

My sisters sit and clap politely as Jess lets five girls from the sorority stand at the front of the room and tell us about their upcoming philanthropy event. I'm half-listening, half-watching my sisters with a proud smile. It's a bigger Chapter night with our visitors, so I booked us one of the large rooms in the Sciences Building. And now that our new members have been officially initiated, the room feels whole, and I love knowing that I'm a part of what made this organization what it is now.

After last semester, Kappa Kappa Beta was awarded the best GPA out of all the sororities on campus. With Jess taking over during recruitment, we had a brand new, all-star pledge class, and with each member of exec mentoring another sister, I have faith that when we hand off the torch at the end of the semester, it'll be with this sorority in the best shape it's ever been in.

I glance at Skyler, knowing that while things are still a bit rocky between us, she's leaning more and more into following in my footsteps — just like I followed in my Big's, and her in her Big's before that. Our family line had a long running as president, and I know it won't end with me.

But it just might end with Cassie.

She decided again not to take a Little this semester, and as much as that pissed me off when she didn't as a sophomore, I accept it now. So what if our line ends with her? If it did, I'd say we've had a pretty badass family line, and every single one of us has left a mark on this sorority.

Besides, I'm done trying to tell others what they should do or judge them based on their decisions.

God knows I wouldn't want anyone judging me based on mine.

After the Zetas leave, I announce that the brothers of Omega Chi are next, and I take a seat off to the right of the podium still in a slight daze.

Until Bear walks in first, leading a group of ten of his brothers to the front of the room.

I stiffen immediately at the sight of him, sitting up straighter in my chair. He winks at Skyler and smiles at various sisters around the room, but then his eyes find mine, and he keeps them on me until the moment he reaches the front of the room and turns to address the chapter.

"Ladies," he says, his booming voice commanding attention as always. "Thank you for having us."

And as he stands there, demanding that power, I can't help but appreciate the way he looks when he's cleaned up for Sunday Chapter. I love Bear in his basketball shorts and muscle tanks, but there's just something about seeing him in dress slacks and a button-up that makes it hard to swallow.

"We know you're busy, and that all of you probably want to get home to enjoy what's left of your Sunday before classes tomorrow, so we won't stay long. We just wanted to wish you good luck on mid-terms, and bring you a little something..."

At that, he looks to the back of the room where one of his brothers is still standing, and he nods, opening the doors. As soon as he does, more and more Omega Chi brothers pile in, each of them holding a dozen roses in one hand and a reusable bag in the other.

The girls all gasp and smile in delight as each Omega Chi brother finds a sister and gives her the roses and bag. A few of the guys are carrying two of each, and they bring the extras to the front of the room to the brothers who were already standing there. When Bear has his in hand, he turns to me, and the smile slips off my face.

The room is abuzz with girls laughing and squealing and kissing cheeks and pulling all the goodies out of their bags — chocolate, salty snacks, a couple of shot-sized alcohol bottles — but I'm so focused on Bear walking toward me that I barely register any of it.

I stand when he's a few feet away, and he pauses, extending the bundle of roses and goody bag. He doesn't say a word as I take them from his hands, but our fingers brush, and I inhale a deep breath at the contact.

"Thank you," I manage.

He nods, and there's something there in his eyes — something I can't quite put my finger on. He looks so sad, so tired, and... maybe a little sorry.

Our dinner flashes in my mind, and my cheeks heat as I tear my gaze from his.

It's all I can do to hold it together through the rest of Chapter once he and his brothers are gone, and as soon as I call it, I gather my belongings and force a smile through small talk with sisters until the room is clear.

I lock up behind me with one thought on my mind — *I need wine.* But when I turn and spot a familiar shadow leaning against the brick building, a completely different thought comes to mind.

"Gavin?" I ask, shaking my head. "What are you doing here?"

He kicks off the wall with a grin. "Picking you up."

"Picking me up?" I cross my arms and arch a brow. "It's a Sunday night. I've got class early in the morning."

"I won't keep you out too late." His eyes flick to the flowers in my hand, but he doesn't address them.

"I take it that means you're not taking no for an answer."

The crook of his lips is all I get as a response, and he holds out his arm, waiting for me to slip mine through it.

"I'm sorry," the girl on stage at The Black Lily says, looking around the dimly lit room at all of the patrons. Gavin and I are in the back corner, at a table for two, each of us sipping on warm Earl Grey tea.

I can't take my eyes off the poet on stage, and it seems Gavin can't take his eyes off *me*.

"I'm sorry for distracting you, my shoulders too bare, my thighs too exposed in these shorts. I'm sorry for speaking too loud, my words ugly with truth, your ears sensitive from ignorance."

Each word she says hits like a beat of a drum, the cadence powerful and seductive, and I lean into every line.

"I'm sorry for chasing my dream, how selfish of me, to not ask for permission first."

A few girls snap at that, firing up the energy in the room.

"I'm sorry for leaving you, how careless to stand on my own when you begged me to bend."

"Preach, girl!" someone calls out in the dark.

"I'm sorry for proving you wrong," the poet says, grabbing the mic and raising her voice as her haunting brown eyes sweep the room. "How embarrassing my smile is for you, I'm sure. I'm sorry the flower you tried so long to drown bloomed anyway — that stem, once so fragile and weak, now roots dug deep."

A few more snaps ring out, and I snap, too, completely lost in the moment.

"I'm sorry," she says, louder now, her eyes boring into the crowd. "That I was *never* sorry."

"Yes!"

"Go on, then!"

The poet pauses, lowering the mic back into the stand before she whispers, "And that I never will be."

Applause rings out as she takes a little bow and exits the stage, leaving the mic open once again for the next performer, and I shake my head in awe, leaning back in my chair with my muscles relaxing all at once like I was just holding onto a speeding train for my life rather than listening to spoken word.

"She's amazing," I whisper, glancing at Gavin. "All of these performers are."

"Open mic is pretty cool, huh?"

"Very," I say, reaching for my tea to take a sip. "You come here a lot?"

"Almost every Sunday. It's a cool place on a regular night, too, but... for me? Open mic is where you get the real. The raw. The brave." He nods toward the stage. "It takes a lot of guts to get up there."

"Do you ever?"

He shakes his head easily. "I'm more of the lurk in the corner kind of guy than the one who wants a mic in his hand."

"Fair," I say with a smile. "Thank you for bringing me here."

"Of course."

I study him for a moment while the next performer gets set up — a young man, no older than eighteen if I had to guess, with an acoustic guitar and a wide, unabashed grin.

"Have you thought about our little therapy assignment?"

Gavin frowns. "What assignment?"

I chuckle. "Don't you *ever* listen? Jackie asked us to think about what we miss about the old us."

"Oh," Gavin says with a frown. "Yeah, well, I instantly wrote that off as stupid and never considered it again."

"Why do you think it's stupid?"

"Why do you think it's *not*?"

A little laugh bubbles in my throat. "I don't know. I guess I'm open to any and everything therapy has to offer. I've tried handling this all on my own," I confess. "It didn't work out well."

Gavin watches me curiously. "Okay. Tell me yours. What do you miss about the *you before you were all fucked up*?"

He waves his hands in the air like a fortune teller with those words, making me giggle.

"I miss a lot of things, actually," I say, playing with the handle on my teacup. "I miss when my biggest worry was what to wear to a sorority event. I miss when all my friends trusted me and looked up to me." I swallow. "I miss wanting to have sex."

I can't look at Gavin when I say those words, and they hang between us for a long time before he responds.

"I just miss my sister."

My heart cracks in my chest, and I close my eyes, inhaling a breath before I open them to meet his gaze. For a long while, he watches me unashamed, but slowly, he lowers his eyes to the table, jaw ticking, nose flaring.

He looks so old and tired and broken in that moment that I can't help but reach over and shelter his hand with mine.

Gavin swallows at the contact, covering my knuckles with his thumb, smoothing skin over skin, his eyes flicking up to meet mine. I offer a small smile, squeezing his hand in return.

"Thank you for sharing."

I get a genuine smile for that, and Gavin shakes his head, bringing my knuckles to his lips briefly before he pulls his grasp from mine to reach into his back pocket.

"Alright," he says, slapping a twenty down to pay for our tea and leave a generous tip. He stands then, holding out his hand for mine again. "I promised to get you back early."

"I just need to use the restroom."

"Come on, I'll take you."

Gavin leads me through a dark hallway in the back of the venue, waiting outside the bathroom for me. Then, we slip out the back door, and it's just the two of us alone in the alley.

The breeze is crisp and cool, but my skin is so hot from the adrenaline and the tea that I revel in the feel of it, closing my eyes and inhaling deep.

Gavin slips his hand into mine, pulling me to a stop in the middle of the alley.

"What?" I ask, eyes fluttering open.

His eyes watch me carefully, flicking back and forth, a small crease just above them. He steps into me, slowly, backing me up until I hit the brick wall behind me.

My heart picks up speed with the way his demanding gaze devours me, and when my mouth parts, his fills the space, the kiss soft but sure.

Now my heart is thundering so loudly, it's all I can hear in my ears, and I grip Gavin's shoulders, so afraid I'll pass out at any moment that I can't do anything but hold on. His hands thread with mine, and he pulls them up to either side of my head, leaning into me and licking my bottom lip gently before his mouth captures mine again.

A spark of something hot and electric shoots down between my legs, and it surprises me so much that I stiffen and shy away from it, panic filling my chest.

Gavin seems to notice, and he slows his kiss, pressing his forehead to mine. "Is it okay that I'm kissing you?" he asks on a whisper, pausing with his lips over mine until I answer.

"Yes."

"You're shaking."

I swallow, nodding.

Gavin releases my hands, framing my face and searching my eyes with his. This close, everything about him surrounds me — his dark and soul-piercing eyes, the heat from his chest and his hands on my skin, his scent — vanilla and oak and tobacco, something like a leather shop and a bar.

"No one has touched you since that night."

He says the words softly, kind of like a question and kind of like something he just realized he should have known all along.

I swallow, not sure how to respond, but knowing that my silence is answer enough.

Gavin closes his eyes, blowing out a breath between us before his thumbs trace a line on my jaw. He holds me there for a long time, silent, our chests heaving, and bodies still pressed together in heat and want and — for me, a mix of fear, too.

"I may be a little fucked up, Erin," he says in the dark. "But I won't hurt you."

I close my eyes at his words, fighting back emotion, because against every ounce of logic I've managed to hold onto in my life, I want to believe him.

"Can I..." He swallows, waiting until I open my eyes to look at him again. "I want to touch you. I want to make you feel good." His hands slip down to circle my waist, and my next breath is shaky at the heat they funnel into me. "Can I try, if I promise to stop anytime you want me to?"

Panic zips through me, but it's overpowered by a want so fierce I can't believe I haven't felt it in almost a year now.

"I'll stop if you want me to," he promises again. "Just say the word."

Everything inside me wants to run and hide with as much urgency as I want to wrap myself up in him and lose myself in the way it feels to be wanted and touched and desired. I have no idea which one will win, which one holds the most power.

But there's only one way to find out.

Slowly, I nod, threading my hands back through his hair and pulling his mouth back to mine. He answers with a passionate, bruising kiss, and I surrender.

I'm still wearing my dress from Chapter, and as he slowly kisses me, Gavin slips one warm, rough hand underneath it. I grip his shoulders, holding on as he lifts one of my legs and balances it on his thigh.

His eyes connect with mine between kisses, and I know I'm breathing so loud they can probably hear me inside the club, but I can't control it. I can't do anything but hold on and try not to pass out as Gavin runs his hand up my inner thigh, cupping me over the lace of my panties.

The moment his warmth covers me, I gasp, eyes fluttering and head falling back.

"Are you okay?"

I nod, deftly, and Gavin kisses my neck softly and sweetly before moving the lace of my panties aside and running one finger between my folds.

I inhale stiffly at the feel of his skin on mine, of him touching me where I haven't been touched since the night four boys took what wasn't theirs. I've spent the last year trying to block out that night, to forget their touch, to un-hear their laughs and grunts and crude words as they took their turns on me. Most nights I failed. Most nights I laid awake with the nightmare burning in my mind so fiercely that it felt like it was happening all over again.

But tonight is different.

Tonight, as soon as the thought of them comes, it's whisked away by another kiss from Gavin. He holds all of my focus, so much that I can't think of anything else but the way he feels — his lips on mine, his finger pressing against the sensitive bundle of nerves between my legs, his other hand holding me steady, digging into my hip.

Gavin breaks our kiss, eyes on mine as he skates his finger up and down my slick lips, and then — carefully and slowly — he enters me.

I must have blacked out. I must have collapsed in his arms and lost myself in another universe with him. I must have found a piece of me I thought was gone forever. Something out of this world happened, because when I finally come to, Gavin is kissing me to keep me quiet as I ride out an orgasm on his fingers, bucking my hips and digging my nails into his shoulders and crying out against his lips.

The climax is so powerful and electric that I feel it in every muscle, in every bone, in every fiber of my being and corner of my soul. I forgot what it was to feel this way, to be touched and not be scared, to have a man inside me and not be crying and praying for it to end.

Instead, I prayed for it to *never* end.

But it does, and when the climax fades, and the cool breeze of the night sweeps across my hot, slick skin, I whimper, folding into Gavin's arms.

He catches me easily, his fingers withdrawing from inside me slowly and carefully. He puts my panties back in place, drops my leg back to the ground, and wraps me in his arms, surrounding me with his warmth and embrace.

And just when I thought I was okay, I fucking lose it.

Sobs rip through my chest, and I cling to him more, like if he even thinks of letting me go, I'll die. But he doesn't move away. He doesn't flinch or ask me what's wrong or demand that I stop crying. He just pulls me deeper into his chest, wrapping me in his arms as fully as he can and kissing my hair, repeating the same words over and over again until I can finally breathe.

"It's okay. I got you. You're beautiful. You're safe."

"It's okay. I got you. You're beautiful. You're safe."

It's okay.

I got you.

You're beautiful.

You're safe.

EPISODE 5

Bear

I AM THE EQUIVALENT to a dog with its tail tucked firmly between its legs when I knock on Becca's door a week before Thanksgiving.

My heart races in my chest as I wait for her to answer, knowing she's home since I asked permission before coming over. I haven't seen her since the night she booted me out and essentially told me to get my shit together.

And she was right — I did need time alone.

I was also right.

It sucked.

I spent most of the first week wallowing, turning to the classic things that always got me by: drinking, working out, and — since fucking was out of the question with Becca being so pissed off — masturbating.

I had zero shame, and I wasted away seven days without a single urge to do anything about my predicament.

But something happened on that seventh day, like God himself was yanking me up out of my bed and throwing me in the shower and telling me we had work to do. I drove out to the beach that morning and sat there for hours, watching the sun rise, listening to the waves, and — for the first time since last semester — not running from the thoughts inside my head.

I thought about Erin, about our unborn child, about how it hurt me that I hadn't been a part of the conversation and how I also understood how it wouldn't have been my decision anyway. I thought about how I'd been so focused on my own betrayal and hurt that I hadn't thought about the fact that Erin went through that just months before she was raped, and then she slipped into the darkest hole I'd ever seen her in.

She's been fighting her way out of that hole all summer and all fall semester long, going to therapy and trying to make amends with the people she hurt.

And I shut her out.

She's on my list of people to try to make things right with, and next on that list is my little brother.

My mother, too.

That long morning at the beach helped me see that a lot of my anger toward my mother rests in the fact that I'm jealous.

I'm jealous that she never got clean when I was a kid. I'm jealous that I can't be there to get to know her — sober — and have a relationship with her. I'm jealous that my little brother doesn't need me now, that he might very well move out of Mac's place soon and back in with Mom, and then where will that leave me?

And I'm scared.

God, I'm scared. I'm scared of her leaving unexpectedly again and fucking Clayton up. I'm scared of her starting to use again and him getting caught up in it, the way Carleton had. I'm scared of Clayton and Mom becoming close and leaving me somewhere on the outside looking in.

But something I decided that day on the beach was that I wouldn't let fear drive my life.

Over the past few weeks, I've been working on *me.* I've been studying, focusing on school, working out more but drinking less. I've been spending time with my fraternity brothers, video chatting with my family and trying to put my fear aside to form a bond with them in understanding rather than suspicion.

And I've been thinking about how to make things right with Becca.

A deep inhale is my only preparation, and then the door swings open, and I lay eyes on Becca for the first time in weeks.

Her hair is wrapped in an orange and blue bohemian turban, tied in a swirl knot at the front with just a few tendrils of curly hair peeking out around her ears. Her face is void of makeup and she's wearing leggings that I know have holes in the thighs from her wearing them so much, along with one of my hoodies, which nearly knocks the breath out of me because it tells me I have a chance before I've even spoken a single word.

She looks effortlessly beautiful, just like always.

And what makes her even better is that she's even more gorgeous where no one can see her.

Her heart.

Her mind.

Her soul.

"Hi," I whisper after a moment.

"Hey," she says, opening the door a little more for me to walk through.

I go straight back to her bedroom, and when she shuts the door behind us and crosses her arms, waiting, I take my shot.

"Becca, I am so sorry for the way I've been acting this semester. You were right to kick me out that weekend after Halloween. And you were right about me needing time alone."

"I didn't want to, you know," she whispers. "Kick you out. Not see you for weeks."

"I know," I say, and not overthinking it enough to talk myself out of it, I cross the room and pull her into my arms.

She's stiff at first, her arms still crossed between us, but slowly, she unwinds them and wraps them around my back, resting her head on my chest with a sigh.

"I've missed you," she whispers.

"Not as much as I've missed you. I promise you that."

Grabbing my hand, she leads me to the bed, sitting with her legs crossed by her pillows while I take a seat in front of her. "How have you been?"

I blow out a breath, looking around her room at the dream catchers, the moon phase tapestry, the old record player and an open dream journal on her desk. Incense burns on a small slate of wood in the corner, and I smile, loving that that scent will forever remind me of her.

"Shitty," I confess, capturing her golden eyes with mine. "But I've been taking a lot of time to work on myself, and to think about everything that's been fucking me up. I'm not one-hundred-percent better, but... I'm working on it. And that's a step."

"A big step," she agrees. A frown slips over her. "Anything you want to talk about?"

"Yes, but not tonight. If that's okay." I reach for her, pulling her into me as we lie down in her sheets. "Tonight, I just want to hold you, and kiss you, and touch you, and make you feel how important you are to me."

She smiles against my lips as I kiss her. "I like the sound of that."

"And I promise I'll talk to you about everything I've been working through. Oh, and I had an idea."

"Do tell."

"I did a lot of thinking about what you said." I swallow. "About Erin. And it made me realize that I don't know a lot about you and *your* friends, either. And I want to."

I don't miss the way Becca shifts in my arms at the mention of Erin, but I hold onto hope that this idea is a good one.

"What if we host a Friendsgiving?"

"A what?"

"Friendsgiving. It's Thanksgiving but with your friends instead of your family. Jess hosted one last year…" I frown. "Actually, it was kind of a disaster, *but* ours won't be. I was thinking I could invite Erin, and my Little, Josh. I would invite Skyler, but she'll be out of town. But you could bring your friends, too — your roommate, your best friend from high school. You said she'll be in town, right?"

Becca nods. "Yeah… she will be. Are you sure this is a good idea? Did you and Erin work through whatever weirdness is going on between you two?"

"Not yet," I admit. "But… I'm hoping this can kind of be the start of that. And I want you to be a part of it."

She peeks up at me from where I hold her then, a soft smile on her lips. "I think it sounds fun."

"Yeah?"

She nods. "Yeah. I'll let the girls know." Then, she presses her soft, warm lips to mine, leaving them there long enough to send blood rushing to my groin. "Now, you ready to make true on your promise to hold me and kiss me and touch me tonight?"

I groan, rolling her over until I'm pressed between her thighs, hiking one up high so I can nestle into her heat. "I've been ready since the second I walked through that door."

Becca answers me with her hands on my face, pulling me into her kiss, her heel digging into my ass and pulling me in closer. I roll my hips against her heat, and she shudders, gasping into my mouth which is enough to have my erection straining against my basketball shorts.

We took it slow for so long, that even a kiss has me hard and ready to go, and the memory of the first time I tasted her at the beginning of the semester makes me even harder. She was so slick and tight, and the thought of tasting her again is too much to resist.

I kiss my way down her jaw, her neck, helping her sit up enough for me to slide my hoodie over her head, and groaning in appreciation when I see she's not wearing anything under it. Immediately, I drop down on my hands on either side of her, bending to suck and kiss the soft skin of her swelled breasts. Her dark nipples pebble under the touch, and I gently bite each one, sucking the peaks between my teeth.

I'm on my way down her navel, ready to spend the rest of the night, and maybe the rest of my life, with my mouth between her legs when she grabs my shoulders to stop me.

"Bear..."

Her eyes hold mine, her mouth parted, chest heaving. And I know without her saying a word what she wants.

"Tonight?"

She nods, and I don't miss the hard swallow, the way her heart picks up its pace under my lips when I kiss her breast again.

Slowly, I peel her leggings off, dropping them on the floor and taking a moment to kiss up and down her thighs, her calves, even the bones of her ankles. She's completely naked and writhing under my touch, and I allow myself the pleasure of torturing her until she's shoving me to stand up and ripping my clothes off, too.

When we're both bare, she opens her bed table drawer and pulls out a golden foil package, ripping it open without haste and sliding the condom over my length.

It's the first time she's touched me, and her hand rolling that latex over me is nearly enough to make me come already.

I groan, holding her wrist to keep her there even once the condom is in place. Her eyes widen, and she looks up at me through heavy lashes, squeezing a little more, wrapping her small fist around my shaft as best she can.

"Does that feel good?" she whispers, and *that* from her mouth has me groaning and flexing into her hand, my climax building before I've even pressed my tip inside her.

"Yes, baby. Grip it tighter."

She answers my demand, and her lips find my neck on the next thrust into her hand, leaving me biting my lip and imagining how good it's going to feel to finally fuck her after months of taking it slow.

"Do you want me to suck it?" Becca asks in my ear, and I swear to God I have to yank back and throw her on the bed because I feel my orgasm edging for release. She smiles wickedly at me, balanced on her elbows, her legs falling open, perfect brown pussy waiting.

"I don't fuck the way I eat," I say, grabbing her by the hips and yanking her down until her ass is hanging off the bed. I grab my cock in my hand, stroking it once before I line it up at her entrance, both of us moaning at the feel of her slick heat covering the tip. "This won't be gentle."

"Shut up and fuck me already."

I answer with a slam of my hips, filling her to the brim, and she cries out in what I know is both a mixture of ecstasy and pain. And it's not that I want to hurt her. It's just that I don't know how else to take her but hard, fast, and rough — my favorite fucking way.

I groan at the feel of her tight pussy wrapping around me, withdrawing and sinking back into her even deeper. Becca's back arches off the bed, fingers wrapping in the sheets and twisting, neck exposed.

I wrap my hands around that beautiful neck, gripping just enough to hold onto her as I pound without cutting off her air supply. Her fingers wrap around my wrist where I hold her, but the way her eyes heat when they look at me, I know she doesn't want me to take my hand away.

She loves it.

She wants more.

I squeeze just a little tighter, capturing her lips in a bruising kiss and reveling in the way the breath coming from her mouth into mine is strained.

"You like when I choke you, don't you, baby?" I hiss, slowing my pace just a little, just enough to feel every inch of her as I pepper kisses on her jaw. "I know you can't answer me, but the way your pussy is tightening is all I need to know."

Something of a whimper escapes her lips, and her eyelids flutter shut, her thighs somehow opening even more. That tells me she's chasing her orgasm, and I answer that plea by sliding my free hand down between us.

I skate my hand over my cock when I pull out of her, slicking it in her wetness, and then I cup her, rubbing my fingers up and down her clit in time with my thrusts.

"Oh, God," she manages, her voice still strained where I hold her neck. I grin, fucking her harder and rubbing her clit mercilessly the same way I sucked it the night I went down on her.

I don't need verbal affirmation that she's coming. I feel it in the pulses of her walls around my shaft, in the way her nails dig into where she holds my wrist, in the way her eyes roll up, like a spirit is taking over her body.

And if I had any doubt, it's erased when she squirts all over me.

Her eyes fly open at the sensation, and I know without her saying anything that she's never done it before. That makes it even fucking better, and I keep my pace on her clit, loving the way she covers me and the bed and the floor with her desire.

When she's sated and shaking and tapping on my wrist to release, I let her go gently, slowing my pace a little and bending to kiss her neck where I'd held her. I was careful enough to know I wouldn't leave any marks, but I still know it was rough, and I want my tender kisses to assure her she's safe.

"Oh my *God*," she finally breathes. "I fucking squirted."

"Hell yeah, you did," I growl, biting her earlobe before I stand again. Then, I wrap my hands around her thighs and pull her down the bed again, picking up my pace. "It was the hottest fucking thing I've ever seen."

"I've never done that before. I've never... *oooh, shiiiitttt.*"

Whatever she was going to say is stolen when I start pounding into her deeper and harder, ready for my own release. Her tits bounce wildly, her hands gripping the sheets, and the sight of her writhing and moaning does the trick.

"*Fuuuuck.*"

I burst into the condom so hard I worry I'll break it, the release I've been holding for weeks finding itself inside Becca. It's all I can do to stay standing as I empty, stilling and letting my climax pulse out inside her as I hold onto her thighs for dear life. Stars and numbness take me over, take me under, and by the time I'm finished, there's nothing I can do but collapse on top of her, and she wraps her arms around me, holding me, taking me, kissing my slick skin over and over and over.

I'm not sure how long we lie there, half on the bed, half off, both of us panting and sweating and sated. It's not until she giggles that I manage to pick my head up enough to look at her.

"Well, seems all that waiting had a pretty explosive outcome."

I smirk, using all the effort I have to discard of the condom before rolling us into the bed and wrapping myself full around her. I kiss her forehead, a deep and content sigh leaving both our chests at the same time.

"You're my favorite," I whisper.

Becca nods, holding me tighter, and I know she feels the same.

Cassie

EVERYTHING IS PERFECT.

It's a bright contrast against the dark place I was in just a few weeks ago, when Adam and I weren't speaking and I was convinced it was over for us. Completely and utterly over. It seemed we were at an impasse, with him firm in his righteousness and me firm in mine.

But then, just like he always does, Adam surprised me.

His apology and camping night on Boca Chita Key was everything I've come to expect from him, and yet somehow, it still takes my breath away. Because even when I don't deserve his love, he gives it to me — as if he has no other choice.

I knew what I was asking of him was hard when I asked it. Accepting that I wanted to be friends with my ex-boyfriend? That's a sticky demand for *anyone* to make, let alone with the history the three of us had.

But whether it was talking to Jeremy or realizing that he was still friends with Skyler without me having an issue with it, he came around. And more than anything, he showed me that he trusts me, that even if he doesn't love the idea of me being friends with Grayson, he understands why I want to be, and why it's important to me, and most importantly, that he can trust me to keep that friend zone firm.

It means more to me than anything else in our relationship, that earnest trust and support.

And it's a giant step for us as a couple.

My heart has been afloat on the wings of butterflies ever since that night in the tent on the key, and a permanent smile is my favorite accessory. I'm wearing said smile the Sunday before Thanksgiving as the girls and I shop for semi-formal dresses, each of us filtering through the racks at our favorite dress boutique and piling hangers on our arms.

"Well, I'm glad you two worked it out," Skyler says, eyeballing a red, glittery dress before putting it back on the rack. "I was worried there for a second."

"Me, too," Erin confesses. "But then again, I don't think Adam could ever let you go — not now that he finally got you."

I blush, passing up an emerald floor-length dress that caught my eye and running my fingers over a white one, instead. "Well, I want to hold onto him, too. So I guess that's a good thing."

"Indeed, it is," Erin says, squeezing my arm as she passes.

"Gah, why does every dress make my ass look so large?" Jess huffs, dramatically exiting the little dressing room with the curtains flying up behind her. She hangs her hands on her hips, turning around to show us said ass in a tight-fitting and rouched gold dress. "I mean, *look* at this."

She grabs both her cheeks and jiggles them to the tune of our laughter, and Ashlei smacks her ass for good measure. "I'd hit that."

"I'm sure Kade won't mind your ass being highlighted," Skyler remarks, arching a brow before making her way into the dressing room next to Jess.

"He might if it busts through the fabric and everyone else gets to see it, too." Jess mumbles to herself, shaking her head and flinging the curtains back on the dressing room, slipping inside it again.

"How's that going, anyway?" I ask, taking a seat on the bench outside the row of dressing rooms once I have an arm full of dresses. "How was your first real date?"

Jess pokes her head out, giving me a thoughtful look. "Honestly? It was... surprising."

"How so?" Ashlei asks, joining us from where she'd been picking out a couple of short numbers from the return rack.

"He was such a gentleman... all dressed up and fancy. Took me to this super nice restaurant. We talked, laughed, shared feelings and things." She wrinkles her nose. "And, he wouldn't fuck me at the end of the night."

Ashlei balks. "What? Why?"

"He said he won't until the third date."

Erin barks out a laugh from the dressing room. "I like him."

"Anyway," Jess says, disappearing behind the curtain again. "I had a great time. I just also am ready to get these next two dates over with so we can bang again."

I snort a laugh just as Skyler walks out in a rose gold baby doll dress. Ashlei and I both shake our heads in unison.

"Too innocent," Ashlei says. "You look like you're twelve."

"Aw, I thought the color was pretty," Skyler says on a pout, twirling and watching herself in the mirror. When she stops, she nods. "But, you're right. Next!"

"Are you excited for your trip to California on Tuesday, Little?" Erin asks beside her.

"Ugh. I'm *dying*. I feel like I've been staring at the clock since I booked my flight last month." She sighs. "I just can't wait to be in Kip's arms."

"I bet *he* can't wait to be in your pants," Jess murmurs.

I chuckle. "Honestly, I don't know how y'all do it. Just being apart from Adam for a couple weeks drove me insane. And we were still on the same campus. Like, if I *wanted* to see him, I could." I shake my head. "It's got to be maddening to have so much distance between you guys."

"It sucks. A lot," Sky confesses, emerging again at the same time Erin does. They look at each other and burst out into laughter when they see they're in the same dress, and then they're gone again, a wave of curtains floating behind them. "But," she adds. "This is the way it needs to be for now. I've got another year here, and he's just getting started at his dream school. We can make it work."

"Do you think you'll move out to California with him once you graduate?" Lei asks.

Skyler pops her head out of the curtains, frowning. "I hadn't thought of it... but honestly? Maybe. I could get down with the other coast."

"Maybe you could go from paddle boarding to surfing," I suggest.

"What's going on with that intern, Lei?" Jess asks, coming out in a breathtaking high-low sunshine yellow dress. It highlights her bronze skin and showcases her cleavage with the sweetheart, shell bust, and the flowy layers of the skirt seem to swish and sway with every tiny move she makes.

"Oh, Jess," I whisper, still gawking. "*That* is the one."

"Agreed," Ashlei says. "You might as well stop looking now. You won't find better than that. *God*, you look stunning!"

"Is that a *blush* I see?" Skyler teases, poking her head out to see what all the fuss is about.

"Shut up." Jess waves her off, but she can't hide her glow as she looks herself over in the three-split mirror. "It really is pretty."

"You're getting it," Erin says definitively, and then she steps out in a poofy purple dress that we all go silent at before bursting out into a chorus of laughter.

"Yeah. That *ain't* it, sis," Jess says.

Erin's shoulders deflate. "I look like a bridesmaid from 1982."

That earns her another roar of laughter, and when she's in the dressing room again, Jess and I turn to Lei.

She sighs. "The intern is... fine. I guess. She was great at the *Okay, Cool* party, and she said she wants to interview me for some project. She really is good at her job, but... there's something off about her. She's like a fox. I don't trust her." She pauses. "And... I think she might be into me."

"What do you mean *into you*?" Jess probes.

"I mean, I think she might have hit on me at the party."

We all widen our eyes at that.

"I know, I know, it sounds crazy, and maybe it is," she confesses with her hands up. "I don't know. I'll keep y'all posted when I know more, because right now, I'm just confused and jealous."

"Nothing to be jealous of," I assure her. "Especially since Brandon told you he *loves you*."

I sing the last words, and all the girls chime in with *ooh's* and *aww's* that have Ashlei flicking us all off.

"I think I'm seeing someone, too."

We all turn in unison to look at Erin, who's looking back at us in the mirror as she assesses the long violet dress she's wearing. She does a little turn, stopping when she's facing us.

I don't think a single one of us blinks.

"His name is Gavin. He's in my therapy group."

She adds that last part with a little clearing of her throat at the end, and we're all completely silent for a moment longer before Jess squeals and wraps her in a hug.

"Ex! You sly dog, you. Why haven't you told us?"

Erin blushes. "I don't know. I *kind* of told you when we were sunbathing behind the house."

"Ah, the *friend*," Jess teases.

Erin shoots her a glare. "Well, I wasn't sure what it was at first but... we've gone on a few dates and... I don't know. I think I like him."

"You haven't dated anyone seriously since Landon," Skyler observes. "Well, other than my boyfriend, but that was a hot mess."

We all shift a little uncomfortably at that.

"Too soon?" Skyler asks with her arms out.

Erin chuckles. "Yeah, I know... it's been..." She goes silent for a long time, a shadow passing over her eyes, and the girls and I exchange worried glances.

"You know you can talk to us," I whisper, standing to touch my Grand Big's arm. "Whatever it is you've been through, we'd understand."

"I know," she whispers, tears flooding her eyes. "And I will. Someday. Soon."

We all nod, and then Lei wraps her in a hug. "Well, I for one am glad this Gavin guy has caught your attention. I can't wait to meet him."

"And I can't wait for him to fuck your brains out so you'll loosen up a bit in Chapter," Jess adds.

Erin launches at her, tickling her sides before Jess breaks free and takes off. Erin chases her around the dress shop while we all watch and laugh.

Skyler and I exchange a beaming look, and I know we're thinking the same thing.

Our sisters are fucking crazy.

But *damn,* do we love them.

Later that night, after Sunday Chapter, Adam and I walk the beach licking on our respective ice cream cones. Mine is mint chocolate chip, his is moose tracks. Our hands that aren't holding our dessert are clasped between us, swinging lightly as we walk.

The stars are non-existent, the clouds wispy, glowing from the moon behind them and adding a moody tone to the beach. It's quiet but for the waves, and our occasional laughter.

When we finish our cones, Adam pulls me into his arms and kisses me breathless, his warm lips a contrast between the cool sand under my bare feet.

And when we sneak away under the pier to make love, that same fluttering of wings sets my chest afloat.

Everything is perfect.

Ashlei

"SO, YOU TOOK THE lead, pitched the launch event to Mrs. Delure from *Bare•ly*, and then *she* asked for you to be the lead event planner on the account?" Sophie asks, leaning on one elbow with stars in her eyes.

We're in one of the smaller conference rooms at *Okay, Cool*, finishing up what has been almost an hour of her asking me questions. We've covered everything from how I first became interested in event planning to my studies at Palm South University, from my first day of the internship to my duties today. I've never been watched with such reverence before, never been asked so much about myself as if I had something to offer that wasn't just a pretty face and an occasional creative event idea.

Sophie is making me feel special, like my role here actually matters.

And as the hour ticks by, I wonder if I've made a mistake about her.

I chuckle. "Yeah, that's pretty much exactly how it went."

"Wow," Sophie remarks, sitting back in her chair with a shake of her head. She clicks the top of her pen back and forth, jotting down something in her notebook. "That's pretty impressive. I mean, I feel like I've made strides as an intern, but I can't *imagine* being offered the event planner position on an account. I mean, there's a lot that goes into that."

"Oh, more than you can even think of or try to list out. I had more than a few times where I was sure I was going to land flat on my ass, but somehow managed to pull the event off by the hair of my teeth." I smile. "That was the first time I realized that working in event planning is a lot like trying to put out a house fire with nothing but a bucket of water and a handful of prayers."

"I'm sure you're selling yourself short," Sophie says, tapping her pen on my knee. "From what I hear, you've been rocking that account since the day they placed the first binder of information in your hands."

Appreciation settles in her fierce eyes, and those eyes trail the length of me, her tongue wetting her lips a little as they flow over my legs. I'm dressed in a rose gold, silky blouse and my favorite white pencil skirt, complete with hose underneath, and nude stilettos. Sophie nearly matches me in a skirt and blouse of her own, except her skirt is short, her blouse revealing, and where I'm all light and airy this afternoon, she's all mauve and black, dark and severe, all the way from her black heels to the dark blood shade of her lips.

And the way she just licked them, it looks like she wants to have me for lunch.

The trust she's built over the last hour fizzles out of me like the bubbles of a champagne bottle, and suspicion cools its place, making my skin prickle.

I clear my throat, gathering up the notes and files I'd brought for her to browse through for the interview. "Alright, does that about do it, then?"

"I think so," she says, but I don't miss the disappointment in her voice. "Thank you for taking time out of your day to speak with me. Truly. I appreciate it."

"No problem. You'll have to let me see the final product."

"Absolutely." She clicks her pen, still watching me as I pack up. "Can I ask you one more question? Off the record."

"Sure."

"Are you bisexual?"

I drop the files I'd been about to shove into my bag, sending papers flying around our heels on the floor as I watch her wide-eyed.

"Excuse me?"

"I'm sorry, I know that's forward," she says hurriedly with a blush. "I just... Well, you see, *I'm* bisexual. And I guess I just thought I had a knack for sniffing out another bi. My friends and I always joke that I have a radar of sorts."

She chuckles, and on the surface, she looks pleasant and friendly and like she genuinely is just curious.

But my insides shrivel up in warning.

I swallow, standing and holding my skirt tucked against the back of my thighs as I slowly lower down onto my knees and begin picking up the papers that fell from the file.

Sophie doesn't move an inch to help me.

She just sits in her chair above me, her crossed knees level with my face.

"I don't know that that's work-appropriate conversation," I murmur, focusing on getting the pages back in place.

"I didn't mean any offense. Honestly, I don't think being bisexual is offensive. Do you?"

"No, of course not," I answer quickly.

"Then, what's the big deal?"

What is *the big deal?*

I try to find the answer to that myself but come up empty. What is it about her that sets me off? What is it about her that makes me want to strangle her and be best friends with her all at the same time?

I grind my teeth. "I am."

"You are what?"

I huff, sitting back on my heels and looking up at her with half of the spilled papers in my hands. "Bi."

Her lips curl up slowly. "I knew it."

"But, I'm with Brandon now," I quickly add.

Sophie chuckles. "And I don't blame you for shouting it from the rooftops any time you get a chance. Mr. Church is..." She shakes her head, whistling. "Let's just say I'd let him put it where no man has put it before."

"Watch it," I warn, jaw tight.

"Oh, don't get me wrong," Sophie quickly adds, and then right in front of my face, she uncrosses her legs, spreading them just wide enough to show me a flash of her black panties before she leans forward and balances her elbows on her knees. Her eyes skate over the features of my face before they meet my gaze. "I'd let you fuck my ass, too. If you wanted."

A zip of something hot and electric shoots straight down between my legs.

Sophie's lips part, just barely, enough for her tongue to dart out and wet her lips again as she watches me. From this angle, I can see the mountains of her breasts, the black lace of her bra from where her silk blouse gapes at her neck.

And I'm rendered completely speechless.

Get up.

Get the fuck up and get the fuck out of this room.

But I'm under her spell.

Sophie spreads her legs again, this time lowering one knee to the ground, and then the other, placing one knee between mine. Her leg is warm and smooth as she presses my knees apart, just a little, and she picks up a few stranded sheets of paper as if that's why she was on the floor.

But her eyes don't leave mine.

And when she hands them to me, I hold onto them without moving an inch to put them in the folder, and her eyes flick to my lips.

She leans in.

I lean back.

At least, I want to. I *should*. But maybe I don't at all. Maybe I sit there completely still, shocked, knowing I should move but not knowing how.

Maybe... I lean in, too.

And in what feels like a stolen breath of time, Sophie kisses me.

I know I feel the kiss.

I know I feel her lips on mine, slightly dry from her lipstick but warm and soft all the same. I know I feel her hands shakily resting on my thighs for balance, and her hot breath on mine, and the silk of her blouse as I hold onto her, too. I know I hear her whimper of a moan, and taste that moan on my tongue.

I know I'm present for every searing moment of it.

But I awake on the other side as if I'd blacked out, as if someone had drugged me, as if I'd been betrayed and violated in the worst possible way.

"No!"

I shove her backward, sending her flying to her elbows with a shocked curse. I stand as soon as she's off me, swiping what's left of the papers off the floor and hastily shoving them into the folders before I shove them into my bag.

"Fuck, Sophie. *Fuck*. What the hell was that?"

I'm still packing up my shit, and I wait for her to say something. To apologize. To leap up and beg me not to overreact, not to tell, not to freak out or hold it against her.

I expect her to blame it on a moment of passion, or a late night, or a connection she felt through the interview.

But when I finally tug my bag onto my shoulder and look down at her, she's not making any excuse at all.

She's just lying there on her elbows staring up at me.

With the most wicked smile I've ever seen.

I shake my head, frowning at her with a mixture of horror and astonishment whirling inside me. It's like she's the devil or a witch or both wrapped into one, and I can't reconcile the fact that I just fell victim to her spell.

"Stay away from me," I warn.

And then I run out of the conference room to wash her lipstick off my mouth.

Skyler

I WAS AN ANXIOUS bundle of nerves the entire flight from Miami to LA.

It had been all I could do just to sit still, to drink the mimosas I'd ordered to help me cope with the fact that I was more nervous than I'd been in recent memory. And now that I'm on the ground in California, tugging my little carry-on luggage behind me in the airport and looking for Kip, I feel equal parts sick and elated.

I haven't seen Kip since we parted ways after the summer, him coming here to UCLA while I went back to Palm South, and as silly as it seems, I'm nervous.

What if he's changed?

What if he's forgotten about me since he's been here?

What if I'm a burden, if he doesn't want me here, if he wishes I would have just stayed in Florida?

What if it's weird between us?

What if we're not meant to be?

I don't know when I became this person, the kind who cares and loves someone so much that these are the kind of thoughts that plague me. Gone is the girl I used to be who could bang a stranger on Spring Break and not think twice about them. Gone is the Skyler Thorne who couldn't be tied down, no matter who tried. And absolutely gone is the version of me who couldn't be hurt by a breakup.

If I lost Kip, I'd lose my mind.

And my heart.

And my soul.

And my grip on life.

That much I know for sure.

I try to school my breathing as I roll through the airport, following the signs for passenger pickup. My stomach is still in a fierce tangle of knots, though.

Until the very moment I see him.

My blond hair, blue-eyed boy is leaning up against his shiny new BMW Z4 — the one he'd bought for himself after winning it all in Vegas — with his hands in his pockets and a sexy smirk on his face. Dark Ray-Bans cover his eyes, and when he sees me, he kicks off from where he's been leaning against the car, strutting toward me confidently in his dark blue jeans and casual, pistachio green long-sleeve, relaxed fit tee.

To anyone else in this airport, he's just another guy. He's just muscles and tan skin and a smile that might make them look twice.

But to me?

He's everything.

I walk slowly at first, returning his smile until the butterflies in my stomach are too loud to ignore any longer. With a laugh, I take off in a jog, abandoning my bag behind me when I'm just a few feet away from him and launching myself into his arms.

He catches me with an easy spin and an easy smile, our lips connecting like magnets, my arms threading around his neck while his hold fast to my waist.

And the moment we touch, the moment I'm in his arms, every nerve and anxiety settles into absolute peace.

In his arms, I'm home.

"Hey there, Ella Mae," he whispers against my lips before capturing them again. A deep and longing sigh leaves his chest when he finally puts me back on the ground, but he doesn't let me go. "Was it just me, or did that flight seem to last years?"

I scoff. "*You* weren't the one who had to sit through the torture of being on it."

"Trust me, it was just as sucky here on the ground waiting for you to land." He kisses my lips too briefly for my taste, squeezing my hand before grabbing the handle of my suitcase and wheeling it to his car. "You ready to see California?"

"I'm ready to see your bedroom," I murmur.

Kip chuckles, opening the passenger side door for me and stealing one last kiss from me as I slide inside. Then, he joins me in the driver seat, laying one hand on the inside of my thigh and the other on the steering wheel and driving us across town to UCLA.

Kip's room in the small house he shares with nine of his brothers is almost exactly like his apartment he had when he was at PSU, except it's much smaller, much darker, and has the faint scent of an old library.

The area they refer to as A Sig Quad is a little collection of five houses and a cottage on the same block, each one housing Alpha Sigma brothers close enough to campus to be convenient and yet far enough away to host parties that don't have to follow campus rules. Kip gave me a little tour of the courtyard and common living areas on our way upstairs, and now it's just me and him in the room he shares with Rick.

I smile, fingers gliding over the old wood paneling of the built-in shelves as I look around. "You know, as a millionaire, I'm a little surprised you didn't want to live in some fancy condo on the bay."

"And miss out on this glory?" he asks, propping my suitcase in the corner before waving his hands over the room. "It wouldn't be the same experience to live that far from campus. I mean, look at you. You could easily get your own place on the beach, but you stay at the sorority house."

"Fair. I guess we're both weirdos."

"At least we can be weird together." Kip points a thumb over his shoulder at the door. "You hungry? Want me to make us a couple sandwiches?"

"Oh, I'm hungry, alright," I say with a devious grin, stepping into him and winding my fingers into his hair. I kiss him deeply, inhaling his scent and reveling in the familiar feel of his lips against mine.

He grins. "That's not exactly what I meant."

"When does Rick get home?"

I'm already unfastening his belt, my fingers curling under the hem of his sweater so I can peel it up over his head.

"He's staying with his girlfriend tonight," Kip answers, letting me tug his sweater off before his lips find mine again.

"So it's just us?"

"In this room, yes," Kip says, slowly unwrapping the scarf around my neck. He pauses when it's unwrapped but still over my shoulders, tugging on it until my neck bends and my lips tip up toward his. "But as you saw, there are brothers all over this house."

"I'll be quiet," I promise.

But Kip smirks, shaking his head before he whispers in my ear, "Liar."

I just grin, done talking and joking now that I've got my nails raking down the ridges and valleys of his insane abdomen. I remember watching Kip workout when he was at PSU, and he's somehow bulked up even more here in

California, which makes me jealous of all the girls who have been in the gym with him.

That jealousy stings in my chest, fueling me to kiss him harder, drag my nails deeper as they trail over his shoulders and down his back. He hisses in through his teeth, grabbing me by the waist and backing me into the corner of his desk.

A grunt leaves my chest when we hit it, but the next breath is stolen by Kip's lips, and we're a flurry of hands and mouths, undressing and kissing and sucking and biting. Any time I moan or whimper, Kip's hand covers my mouth, and he clamps that hand hard over my panting.

Even still, nothing could muzzle the pleasure coursing through me at feeling him touch me for the first time in months.

When all that's left is his boxer briefs and my panties, Kip flips me around, walking me over to his full-length mirror on the back of the bedroom door. I brace my hands on either side of it just in time to stop my face from hitting it, and Kip grins from behind me, our eyes connected in the mirror.

It's a sight that sends waves of chills over every inch of me, seeing Kip towering behind me, his bare, bulging muscles encompassing me. One arm wraps around my waist and up to palm my breast, and he groans in approval with the full weight of it in his grasp, squeezing and kneading as his lips find my neck and suck hard. His other hand is behind me, and I feel it slowly trail down and over my ass, his fingers slipping between my legs and roughly sliding my lace panties aside.

"God*damn*, you're wet, Sky," he pants, his fingers easily sliding between my lips. He skates them deeper, centimeters at a time, but never enters me — not even a fingertip.

I writhe against the touch, pushing my ass back and up so I can get those fingers inside me. But every time I try, Kip pulls them back just enough to keep me empty and begging.

His hand retracts altogether on a shudder and a sigh from me, but before I can beg for more, I feel Kip shed his briefs and press his length against my ass. His long, thick, pulsing cock lines up in my crease, spreading me open as the hand that was on my breast slides up to grab my neck.

"Open your eyes," he commands, and when I do, the smile on his face is wicked and sexy as hell. "I want to see you when I fill you for the first time in months."

And that's all the warning I get before he slides in, hard and punishing and all at once, filling me to the brim as I shake in his grasp.

The moan that escapes me is impossible to quiet, and Kip squeezes my throat a little tighter in warning, withdrawing his hips just to slam back into me again.

"Shhh, baby," he says in my ear, sucking the lobe between his teeth.

I bite my lip to keep from crying out again, focusing on keeping myself braced over the mirror, my eyes fluttering open and closed again and again, little glimpses of Kip's hand around my throat, his other hand holding my hips as he plows into me from behind.

The way his cock curves, the way he squats just enough to fill me up completely on each thrust, has me seeing stars within seconds. Every new thrust hits that magical spot deep inside me, and the slight pressure of his hand around my neck sends all the blood rushing between my legs.

Fuck, I've missed this.

But I want more before I come.

Peeling his fingers from around my neck, I twist away from him and press my hands into his chest, shoving him backward.

He's panting, chest heaving, cock hard and erect and glistening with my pleasure as I guide him back to the bed. I shove him again until he's on his back, and then I climb up, taking time to slide my pussy over his cock before I continue my trek up, up.

And then, I sit on my boyfriend's god-like, too-handsome-for-his-own-good face.

"Make me come, baby," I whisper, and Kip answers with his hands gripping my ass and pulling my clit to his mouth.

His tongue lashes me like a whip, making me shudder with the way it flicks over that sensitive bundle of nerves. I grab his headboard and hold on for dear life, and when he sucks me, gently, over and over between his teeth, I rock my hips against the pressure, needing more.

"Fuck, I'm close," I groan.

Kip slips his finger inside me long enough to wet it, and then with his mouth still punishing my clit, he slips that same finger right into my ass.

I barely have time to gasp, to let my mouth fall open and my eyes shoot wide and my fingers curl into the headboard before I'm flying off into an orgasm like none I've ever had before. It's not the same as just having my clit rubbed or my g-spot hit. It's shocking and forbidden and a little painful as it rocks through me.

But I fucking love it.

I sit back a little, taking his finger deeper in my ass as I ride out my climax. And I don't give two flying fucks about the other brothers in the house. My screams are loud and wild and desperate, and I give in to every single one.

I've been living on masturbation alone since August.

I'm not being quiet during my first male-generated orgasm in months.

I'm still seeing stars, shaking and pulsing around Kip's finger when he gently removes it, kissing the inside of my thighs.

But I don't have time to rest.

He flips me over, kissing me with lips and a tongue that taste like my pussy before he hikes both of my legs up. My ankles on his shoulders, he slides back inside me, both of us growling at the sensation of him filling me again.

"Oh *fuck*, Sky," he says, pulling out and pressing in all the way. I twist my fists in the sheets and arch into him, begging for more.

He delivers with a harder thrust, a faster rhythm, and his hands reach out to palm both of my bouncing breasts as he fucks me like a man who's been in prison for years.

I see it the moment he crests, the moment that spark catches fire and his orgasm releases. His face screws up, a grunt escaping his lips, and he drops his grip on my tits, pulling his cock out just in time to spill hot cum all over my stomach, my chest, some even shooting up and hitting my chin.

My lips curl into a smile as I watch him come undone, and when he shudders his last breath, holding his wet, still pulsing cock in his hands, his eyes flutter open to find mine.

And I hold his gaze as I swipe a finger through the cum on my chin, sucking that finger into my mouth to taste him.

"*Fuck*," he groans, shaking his head, and then he's on top of me — sated and limp — while I giggle and kiss all over his shoulders.

We lie there for a long while, both of us coming down from our highs, our muscles already sore and aching for more.

Then Kip leans up on one elbow, his eternal blue eyes searching mine, and he sweeps my hair out of my face, gaze full of adoration.

"I love you," he whispers.

"I love you, too."

It's the sweetest, most tender moment, sealed with a perfect, gentle kiss.

And then a roar of applause breaks out downstairs, hoots and hollers and *atta boys!* so loud it sounds like we're at a football game.

Kip and I lock wide eyes, and then I blush furiously, burying my face in his chest as he laughs and kisses my hair.

"I told you to be quiet."

Indeed, he did.

Whoops.

Bear

"AW, LOOK AT US," Becca teases, kissing my cheek while I carve the turkey. "We're so domesticated."

"Totally. Cooking a half-ass Thanksgiving meal in a frat house kitchen. *So* adult."

She pats my ass, then gets back to whipping the mashed potatoes.

"Yeah, as much as this is awesome for a college Thanksgiving dinner, I have to admit — it ain't my mama's cooking," Amber says, eyeing the green bean casserole suspiciously.

Amber is Becca's best friend, a short little thing with curves for days, wild and beautiful curly black hair, warm brown skin, and a birth mark above her lip that makes her look like a glamorous Hollywood star from the twenties. She and Becca have been friends since they were toddlers, and the way they act together, the way they even mirror each other's gestures makes them seem more like sisters than friends.

Amber goes to school in Boston, but is visiting for the holiday, and watching her with Becca makes my chest warm and fuzzy in a new and unfamiliar way. It's one thing to see her undressed, or to have her all to myself in bed, both of us in sweatpants and lazy smiles. But it's another thing completely to see her with the ones she cares about, the ones she loves, joking and laughing and reminiscing on old stories.

"My mom always makes this *amazing* sweet potato pie," Becca says, still working on the mashed potatoes. "She's given me the recipe, but I swear it never turns out the way hers does."

"That's how my grandma is with her recipes," Amber chimes in. "I think they leave out important ingredients or steps so that we keep coming home for holidays. My grandma's homemade stuffing?" She clicks her tongue, shaking her head. "That shit is *magical*. But she'll never give away her secret."

Becca smiles, giving me a wink when she catches me staring at her. But I just can't help it. Seeing her in the kitchen like that — apron around her waist, natural curls bouncing with every laugh and turn of her head, smile wide and bright and full of love... it hits me hard in the chest, like a fist more than a feeling.

Because I can see it.

I can imagine us together, not just now but in the future, too. I can see her in our house, in our kitchen, with our family and friends gathered around us.

"What?" Becca asks, hanging a hand on her hip the longer I stare.

"You're beautiful."

I steal a kiss from her just as Amber makes a gagging noise. "Alright, that's enough mush for me. I'm going to go watch Josh try to hit on Pamela."

Becca and I chuckle at that. Pamela is Becca's roommate, a sweet, shy, petite little white girl with dark freckles and long, brunette hair she always lets hang a little in front of her face, like she's trying to hide from any and everyone.

Josh has been shooting his shot since the moment she showed up, and it's been the entertainment of the day.

I told everyone that we'd have dinner around four, but that they were welcome to come to the house ahead of time to watch football and hang out. Most of our brothers clear off campus for the break, visiting their families, so we have the entire place to ourselves today.

Becca, Pamela, and Amber got here early, helping prep the food and cook and bake and set up the table. Josh stumbled out of bed around noon and plopped his ass down on the couch to watch football — and try his best to make Pamela uncomfortable, which was undoubtedly working.

But Erin hasn't showed yet, and I can't help but wonder if she will at all.

She'd been surprised to say the least when I called and invited her to Friendsgiving. But after asking if I was sure and if she could bring a friend, she'd agreed, and I'd be lying if I said my stomach hasn't been in knots all day thinking about being around her tonight.

When Becca finishes mashing the potatoes, she washes her hands and dries them on a towel, looking around at the feast we've prepared. "I'd say we make a pretty good team, Chef Pennington."

"You're the chef," I correct her, taking her in my arms and planting a kiss on her nose. "I'm just the big-fisted dummy you boss around to help you."

She chuckles, threading her hands together behind my neck. "This was a good idea, Bear. The girls are having fun — even Pam, despite Josh being up her ass."

I laugh. "Are *you* having fun?"

"I am." She pauses, swallowing. "Is Erin still coming?"

I take a deep breath. "Your guess is as good as mine."

As if on cue, there's commotion from the living room, and Becca and I round the corner to find Erin giving Josh a hug before immediately introducing herself to Pam and Amber.

Herself, and then the tall, brooding guy she brought with her.

"This is Gavin," she explains, and he shakes everyone's hands with an easy grin before tucking his hands back in his pockets. He listens as Josh and Erin chat, his eyes wandering the room.

Until they land on me.

Then, they don't budge.

He and Erin couldn't be more opposite. Where Erin is sunshine embodied, from her shining blonde hair to the mustard yellow dress slimming her waist and cutting off below her knees, he's like the dark side of the moon, dressed in black distressed jeans and a black long-sleeve shirt with the name of some metal band I don't recognize sprawled across his chest.

He nods his chin at me after a moment, and it's as if that notion knocks me out of my spell.

"You must be Bear," he says, stepping around the couch to where Becca and I are. He extends his hand on a comfortable smile. "I'm Gavin, Erin's boyfriend."

I hope I'm hiding it. I hope my jaw isn't as tight as it feels, that my eyes didn't just shoot open as wide as I think they did when I snapped my gaze to Erin's.

She's still standing by the girls and Josh, holding a casserole dish in her hands, her wide brown eyes watching me.

I hope an uncomfortable amount of time hasn't passed as I force a smile and reach out for Gavin's hand, both of us engaging in a crushing grip that tells me he's threatened by me and whispers that I might feel the same about him, too.

"I didn't realize Erin *had* a boyfriend," I comment, and I want to kick myself for how petty it sounds.

"Yeah. From what she tells me, you two don't talk much anymore," Gavin comments. Before I can reply, he pulls his hand from mine and extends it for Becca. "Thanks for having us over."

"It's our pleasure," she says, shaking his hand. "I'm Becca." Then, her eyes land hard on me. "*Bear's* girlfriend."

I know that look. It's the one that says *why the hell didn't you say this before I had to?*

I clear my throat, rounding the couch to where Erin is standing with the casserole dish. I reach out for it. "I told you you didn't have to bring anything."

It comes out harsher than I mean for it to, and I internally curse myself. *Snap out of it, big guy.*

"It's just a sweet corn casserole," she says softly, tucking her hair behind her ear when her hands are free. "It's my mom's specialty."

My stomach tightens.

It seems like everyone has a memory of their mother on this holiday, fond thoughts of cooking in the kitchen and famous recipes.

The only things my mom ever brought around on Thanksgiving were drugs and strangers.

At least, that was always the case when I was younger. But earlier this afternoon when Becca and I were cooking, I got a video call from my little brother, showing me that they were all gathered at Mac's house — including our mother and my older brother and *his* family — laughing and playing games and getting ready to eat their own feast.

Without me.

"Well, thank you," I say after a long pause, shaking off my own shit to focus on the whole reason I had this get-together in the first place. I owe Erin an apology, but not now. Not in front of everyone.

Erin and I watch each other, her shifting her weight before the gaze becomes too much for her, and she looks behind me.

At Gavin.

Who promptly returns to where she's standing, putting his arm around her waist. What pisses me off most is it's not possessive or territorial or aimed toward me at all.

It's comforting and calming, meant for Erin only, and she leans into that touch with a sigh of relief that makes my chest tighten for a completely new reason.

"Alright, let's get this into the kitchen and I think we should be ready to eat," Becca says, taking the casserole from my hands with a warning glare. "Everyone grab your plates."

It's all laughter and catching up and getting to know each other as we fill our plates and gather at the table — a folding table usually used for flip cup and beer pong that has been disguised with a tablecloth, some flowers, and a few candles. The frat house always smells faintly of beer, but the candles help cover it a bit, and though it's far from something Martha Stewart would approve, it's not bad for a college Thanksgiving set-up.

I'm mostly a quiet bystander as everyone talks while we eat — Josh bragging about his IM football stats, Amber and Becca telling us stories from their raucous high school days, Erin and Pamela bonding over their shared love of well-organized planners.

And then there's Gavin.

He's almost as quiet as I am, chiming in time to time only to lay out a well-placed joke or to ask a question about something someone's talking about. Like he cares.

And maybe he does.

Maybe he's a perfectly cool dude with perfectly good intentions with Erin.

But after what she's been through, I can't help but watch him like the big brother she never asked me to be — arms crossed, gaze hard, jaw ticking as I fight back the questions I really want to ask.

Like:

Do you have a criminal record?

How many girls have you cheated on or broken up with?

When was your last serious relationship?

What plans do you have for your life?

What makes you think you deserve the most amazing girl in the world?

I shift uncomfortably as that last thought flitters through me, chugging half my beer in one swallow with Becca's eyes watching.

"So," I say when I set my glass back down, staring at Gavin. "Gavin. How did you and Erin meet?"

Erin smiles at him when he turns to her, and even without being able to see it, I know he grabs her hand under the table and gives it a squeeze.

"She was walking on the beach at sunrise, her hair and skirt blowing back behind her in the breeze as she watched the horizon. And I watched her. I mean, how could I not, with the morning glow on her face like that? I was just out surfing, but I didn't care about the waves once I saw her. I had to know her name. So, I paddled in and hopped off my board and walked straight up to her and said..." He pauses, looking at Erin with a bent brow and making his voice deeper. "*Hello, my queen. It is I, your King, and I have searched this world high and low for you.*"

Erin shoves his chest with a roll of her eyes, still smiling when she looks at me. "We met at therapy."

The girls all laugh, and Amber holds up her glass to Gavin. "You had me going. I was leaning in like *oh my God, what did she say to that?!*"

"I was just about to start taking notes, see if I could pull the same stunt on Perfect Pam here," Josh added, which made the group chuckle again. Well, except for Pam, who blushed and hid behind her hair.

And except for me, too, because I couldn't find it in me to so much as smile.

"What are you in therapy for?"

The room goes silent at my question, and Becca pinches me under the table. "*Bear*," she warns.

"Do you have to be in therapy for one specific reason?" Gavin asks, taking a sip of his wine, completely calm and cool and collected.

"Isn't that kind of the point?"

"The goals of therapy differ greatly, depending on the person. It can be focused on healing, growing, resolving issues, surviving trauma."

"So what's yours?"

"*Bear*," Erin says this time, her eyes wide.

"A little of everything, I suppose. Do you go to therapy, Bear?" Gavin asks.

"Of course not."

"Oh, so you're perfect? Nothing wrong with you at all, huh? No shit to work through, nothing holding you back from being your best self?"

I don't have an answer to that, which makes me grip my glass harder as I lift it to my lips and drain the last of my beer.

"I think it's great," Becca says, somehow managing a smile when she finally peels her murderous glare away from me.

"Me, too," Amber agrees. "And I think it's awesome that you two met at your most vulnerable. Not a lot of people can say that, you know? We all play games when we first start dating. We hide who we really are in the name of being who we *think* the other person wants us to be."

Becca sips her champagne silently, glancing at me with a sullen look in her eyes as Erin and Gavin smile at each other.

"It is pretty awesome," Gavin agrees. "There's a side of this girl that she doesn't show to anyone but me. And I'll admit, I'm a greedy bastard when it comes to that pile of gold."

The girls visibly swoon, but I just grind my teeth, not able to hold back my sarcastic grunt.

Gavin turns to look at me, arching one brow. "Something else to say, Bear?"

"Not to you."

"Whoa, bro," Josh says, smiling at everyone to try to make the moment lighter. "What's with the hostility? Gavin, did you steal the last of the cranberry sauce or something?"

"Actually, I think I stole the girl he never thought to make his. And now he's regretting his inaction and thinks he can piss on her to scare me off."

My chair grinds against the wooden floor when I stand, towering over Gavin as everyone jumps. I point my finger straight into his chest. "Listen here, you disrespectful little fuck."

"Oh, I'm listening. Go on. Tell me I'm wrong," Gavin challenges with a smirk, not even so much as puffing his chest back at me. He's not threatened, and that somehow pisses me off more.

"I think we should go," Erin says, standing and folding her napkin primly before laying it carefully next to her plate. "Becca, I hope you don't mind if we don't help with clean up."

"Not at all," Becca says, standing too. Only she doesn't fold her napkin — she bunches it in her fist and throws it down on the table with her eyes on me. "In fact, I think Bear can clean up this mess on his own."

She storms out of the room without another look at me, her friends on her tail, Pam looking at me with pity, while Amber's glare matches the one Becca had been giving me all night.

Gavin stands slowly, helping Erin put her camisole sweater on before grabbing her hand and leading her toward the door. "Thanks for dinner," he says to me, winking. "It's been a real treat."

My muscles work before my brain does, and the only thing that stops me from launching at that motherfucker and beating his face in is Josh's hands wrapping around my arms and quickly holding them behind my back in a stiff lock. I shrug against it to no avail, which makes Gavin shake his head with a look like he pities me.

Then they're gone, and it's just me and Josh.

"Damn, bro," he says when they're gone, releasing me. "What the hell was all that?"

And I just breathe like a bull, chest heaving, wishing I knew the goddamn answer myself.

Cassie

I HAVEN'T BEEN TO Cup O' Joes since Grayson and I broke up, and sitting here for the first time in almost a year, I remember why.

Everything about this place reminds me of when we dated.

I remember the first time I met him, when he bought my coffee and asked for my number and made me blush with his unapologetic gaze.

I remember watching him play a set, looking around the room at the way the girls visibly swooned with every note he played and every word he sang.

I remember sitting in this very seat, at this very table in the back corner of the room, so I could watch but not *be* watched.

Of course, Grayson never let me slide under the radar for long. He loved to call attention to me when he was on stage, or as soon as he got *off* stage, striding back to me and wrapping me in a hug or planting a big kiss on my lips to let everyone in that room know he was taken.

At least, that's what I'd thought.

My stomach sours when I remember something else — that the entire time I'd trusted him, he'd been lying to me.

Shaking that thought off, I take a sip of my coffee, reveling in the sweet taste of their famous caramel mocha that I haven't had since Grayson and I broke up. I've missed it, and the atmosphere of the shop, with students studying and chatting and listening to Grayson play.

He's on stage, crooning out a Maroon 5 song and winking at every girl who casts her wide-eyed gaze up at him.

I can't help but chuckle, noting that while he's changed, some things never will.

It's Monday evening, the first day back on campus for most students who went away for the Thanksgiving holiday. With the sun setting earlier now, it's completely dark in the shop, save for the dim industrial lighting and the candles at each table. With Grayson singing and strumming his guitar and the Christmas lights already being hung across campus, there's a feel of the holiday season in the air, and I breathe into it with a smile.

Grayson asked me to come watch him play while we were walking out of lab earlier. He wanted me to be there when he played his newest song, the one he'd been writing and giving me previews of for the past few weeks. I agreed, of course, and invited Adam to join me — which I knew he appreciated as much as he hated.

He doesn't love Grayson and me being friends, but he understands it. He respects it. And that means more to me than he could ever know.

I'm excited for him to see that Grayson and I really *are* just friends, that anything there was between us is firmly in the past. I hope it will set his mind at ease.

And hey, he can kiss me right here in front of Grayson and everyone else.

I don't mind him claiming his territory.

Heat flushes my cheeks at the thought of his kiss, the kind that always burns me and leaves a mark, and I check my watch anxiously. He should have been here by now.

Grayson announces he's going to take a little break, and when he comes back, he'll play a brand-new song. That earns applause and hoots and hollers from just about every girl in the place, and when I look around, I wonder how many of them are here for Grayson, alone.

His hair is tied at the back of his neck, and he's dressed in a leather jacket, forest green relaxed-fit t-shirt and dark jeans. His combat boots set off the rock-star look, and he strides toward me with an easy smile, like he doesn't realize every girl's neck is breaking to watch him as he passes.

"Great set," I say when he sits at the table. "Want me to get you a coffee?"

He opens his mouth to answer, but before he can, the barista drops off a hot Earl Grey tea and a tall glass of ice water. "The usual, Grayson," she says, casting me a cautious glance before she smiles at him again. "You were great up there. Can't wait to hear the new song."

"I'll play it just for you, Wendy."

She bites her lip on a flush, excusing herself without another word.

When Grayson looks at me, he shrugs. "What?"

"Just watching Casanova in action," I say, chuckling.

"Hey, I'm just being nice."

"Mm-hmm." I sip my coffee. "So, your parents know you still play here?"

His eyes darken with the question, and he dunks the bag of tea a few times, watching it steep. "Yeah. Dad says he doesn't care, as long as I've let go of my *fantasy* and am getting good grades."

"I'm sorry, Grayson."

He shrugs. "It's whatever. As long as I keep working on the plan *they* think is best for me, I can play my music. And that's all that matters to me."

"Do you think you'll go back to music once you graduate?"

Another shrug. "I don't know. I want to, of course, but... I mean, maybe it really is a fantasy. Look how many musicians never make a name for themself."

"Do you have to make a name for yourself?" I ask, sitting up straighter when he looks at me confused. "I mean, what if it was always just like this. You and your guitar, small coffee shops, playing music and making people feel good."

Grayson nods. "That'd be alright, I think."

"Then maybe you can have both — the life they want for you, and the life you want, too."

"I guess I never considered that the two could marry."

I shrug. "Just a thought."

"You always were smarter than me."

I scoff at that, biting my tongue to resist the urge to point out that I wasn't smart enough to know he was cheating on me all along.

My next sip of coffee is bitter. *Why the hell do I still care? Why does that thought still bubble to the surface every time I'm with Grayson, making me feel prickly as a cactus?*

I frown.

Will my new friendship with Grayson always be shadowed by that cloud of betrayal?

"What's on your mind?"

I blink, clearing my throat when I realize Grayson has been watching me. "Nothing."

"You've also always been a terrible liar."

"I guess I was just thinking. This place brings back a lot of memories."

Grayson's face slacks. "Yeah. It does for me, too."

The way he watches me now is with a longing so fierce, I feel it like a vibration in the air. I swallow, looking away from him and out at the quad where students are dressing the giant Christmas tree they put up there every year.

"I can't believe it's almost Christmas. This semester has flown by."

"Cassie, don't change the subject."

I frown, looking back at him. "I didn't realize we were on a subject."

"The shop. The memories." He pauses. "You and me."

"Uh…"

Grayson scoots his chair closer to mine, his eyes earnest as they watch me intently, and warning bells ring loud and shrill in my ears.

Oh no…

"I invited you tonight because I wanted to see if you felt it, too — the rush of what we used to be. Because every time I walk through those doors, every time I play here… it takes me under like a tidal wave."

"Grayson," I whisper, shaking my head. "I just came here to support you. As a *friend*."

"You and I have never been friends," he says, covering my knee with his hand. "And you know it."

I swat his hand away quickly, scooting back. "Grayson. Stop. Now. I mean it."

"Don't pretend like you don't miss me," he hisses, frowning and shaking his head like I'm in denial. "I see it. I feel it. And whatever is going on between you and Adam, it's not what we had."

"You're right," I say. "It's so much more than what you and I could ever have even *hoped* to have." I scoff, my chest on fire. "God, I can't believe I fell for this. I can't believe I thought you actually, *genuinely* wanted to be my friend."

"I do want to be your friend," he argues, scooting his chair closer again. Mine is pinned now, and I curse myself for picking that same back corner table I'd always sat at before. "But I want to be more, too. I want you back. I want to prove to you that *I'm* the one you should be with — not that asshat."

"I love him," I whisper-yell. "How *dare* you say these things to me. I stood up for you, you know that? When you didn't deserve it. When Adam questioned me. When he told me I was an idiot for thinking you could ever be just my friend." My mouth falls open, and I shake my head in disbelief at my own stupidity. "He was right. How did I not see it?"

"He sees what I see. What I know you see, too." Grayson puts his hand on my knee again, and this time when I try to swat it away, it doesn't budge. "We're meant for each other, Cassie. And I'm not letting up until you realize you never stopped loving me, and I never stopped loving you, and this — you and me — we're real. We're inevitable."

He takes his hand off my knee, but then it moves for my face, sliding back into my hair with his lips on track for mine.

I rip away, panic searing my chest. "Grayson, no!"

Crack.

I don't register what's happened, not until I blink several times, taking in the people gasping and screaming around us.

And then I see Grayson on the floor.

And Adam on top of him, fist in the air, ready to plow it back into Grayson's already bleeding nose.

"Adam, don't!" I scream, flying out of my chair and down to him. I wrap my arms around his waist and pull, knowing I wouldn't be able to budge him unless he actually wanted to be budged.

Luckily, he lets me pull him up to stand, but his chest is heaving, glare murderous, his eyes nearly popping out of his head as he stares down at Grayson. "YOU MOTHER-FUCKER," he screams, grabbing him by the shirt. "HOW DARE YOU TOUCH MY GIRL."

Grayson spits a mouthful of blood to the side before grinning up at Adam. "My girl, first."

A growl rips through Adam, and he lays another crack to Grayson's jaw before I can stop him. I'm screaming and crying and tearing at him to let Grayson go. When he finally does, it's to the tune of the manager yelling for us to take it outside or she'd call campus police. And so, Adam drops his grip, letting Grayson fall back onto the floor.

Then, he storms out without even looking back at me.

I scramble to get my purse where it's hanging off the back of my chair, plucking a twenty out and leaving it on the table before I fly out after Adam. He's already halfway across the quad, and I scream his name over and over, jogging to catch up.

It's not until we're by the reflection pond that Adam stops and turns, and when the weight of his gaze hits me, I stumble back, eyes blurring as I cover my mouth.

"Adam, it's not what you think."

"Oh, it's not?" he challenges, stepping into my chest as I shrink away. He points a finger back at the shop. "So that *wasn't* your so-called *friend* hitting on you, touching you, trying to kiss you?"

I cringe. "I swear, I didn't do anything."

"No, *you* didn't. But that motherfucker sure as hell did."

"I told him not to touch me. I told him to stop."

Adam roars out a growl that makes the students walking by us glance our direction with wide eyes before they scurry off. He throws his hands up in the air, lacing them over his head as he paces.

"What did I tell you? Huh?" Adam throws his arms out toward me, and I wince at his already swollen and bruised knuckles from where he hit Grayson. "I *told* you he didn't want to just be your friend. I *told* you he wanted more, that he had something up his sleeve. But you didn't believe me. You picked him over me."

"That's not fair," I defend. "I didn't *pick* anyone."

"Yes," he argues, stepping into my space again. "Yes, you fucking did. You may not have said the words *I choose Grayson over you*, but that's exactly what you made clear when you told me you *wouldn't* choose me. When you dug your heels in and proved that being friends with that asshole *who cheated on you* was more important than making me feel safe and comfortable."

"You're friends with Skyler!" I scream out, desperation flowing through me. I know the argument is weak before I even finish making it. "How is this not the same?"

"SKYLER DOESN'T TRY TO MAKE OUT WITH ME!"

My nose flares, and I look around at the attention we're calling, reaching out for Adam to calm him.

But he backs away before I can connect.

His chest heaves with the next breath, and he beats on it like an ape. "*I* don't hang out with Skyler after every single fucking class. Hell, I don't even hang out with her *period* — not anymore, not unless we're in a group setting in the same place. And if you asked me right now, right here, to not be friends with her because it made you uncomfortable?" He shakes his head, as if it's obvious. "I would never see her again. No questions asked."

"Adam," I beg, eyes blurring. "I'm sorry. Okay? I was wrong. I thought..." My voice is strangled, and I shake my head. "I... I really thought..."

"That he wanted to be your fucking *friend*? That you two would braid each other's hair and drink coffee and study together and he wouldn't be using every minute to plan how to get your panties on his bedroom floor?"

My chin quivers. "Okay. You've made your point."

"Have I?" He steps into me, staring down his nose. "What's my point, Cassie?"

"I didn't kiss him!" I say loudly, pressing my hands into his chest. "Okay? I didn't come onto him or ask for any of that back there. I didn't do anything wrong. I can't control what *he* did, but why are you so fucking mad at *me*?"

Adam watches me for a long time, breathing slowly, eyes dancing between mine. After a while, he shakes his head, looking at me like I disgust him, like I'm an idiot he feels sorry for, like he can't believe he ever trusted me.

"I'm not mad, Cassie," he says, his voice soft, resigned. "I'm tired."

"Of what?" I ask, throwing my hands out, exasperated.

"Of choosing you when you refuse to choose me back."

I frown, my next breath stuttering out of my chest like the exhaust of a busted old car. His words slice me into ribbons, each piece of me cut so thin and weak that I'm afraid I might blow away in the next breeze.

I hurt him.

I hurt the boy I love.

And all for what?

"Adam, I'm so—" I try, reaching for him, but he just shakes his head, giving me one last hurt look before he turns and walks away.

I cover my mouth, squeezing my eyes shut and freeing the tears before I open them again and watch him walk away from me, his hands in his pockets, head hanging between his shoulders.

And I just let him go.

Because I know in that moment that I don't deserve to ask him to stay.

Skyler

"I'VE MISSED THIS," I say on a wistful sigh, drawing circles on Kip's chest while he plays with my hair. I'm balanced on one elbow, looking down at the masterpiece that is his body. It's early in the morning, and the sun is casting the hills and valleys of his abdomen in shadows and bursts of light.

Perfect.

"What, staying up all night having sex?"

"Well, yes, that," I admit. "But I mean *this* — lying next to you, cuddling, talking." I tap his nose. "Getting to see you in these specs."

Kip smirks, adjusting his black-framed glasses higher on his nose. "I can't see your beautiful face without them."

"You wore contacts a lot this weekend."

I pout with the realization, and Kip laughs, leaning up to kiss my lips briefly. "I didn't realize you loved my glasses so much."

"My four-eyed blond thief."

"Thief?"

"Yeah. You stole my heart."

Kip smiles, shaking his head before he pins me in the sheets and slides between my legs, kissing all over my neck. "That was so fucking cheesy."

"But you loved it."

"I did," he agrees. And then he props himself up on his elbows, his sea blue eyes watching mine. "And I love you."

I answer with another long, telling kiss, inhaling him in and wishing we could stay just like that forever. But my plane leaves in four hours, and by the end of the day, I'll be across the country again.

My chest splits with the anxiety of being away from Kip, especially after having the most perfect week together. He showed me around the UCLA campus, let me get a sneak peek of his current film project, introduced me to all his brothers — who he complained liked me more than they did him. We played beer pong and flip cup and had a very college Thanksgiving, complete with pizzas and whiskey instead of turkey and wine. We spent time at the beach, taking a surf lesson that made me realize I much prefer the warm water of the Atlantic to the freezing water of the Pacific. Not that we don't get glimpses of cool water during the winter months, but for the most part? It's perfect.

Here, you need a wet suit. And that's not nearly as much fun as a bikini.

As much as we saw over the past week and as much as we did, my favorite moments were the ones just like this — me and Kip in his bed, holding each other close, saying more with silence than we ever could with words.

I met Rick the second day I was here, and once we became quick friends, I told him I'd book him a room downtown *and* give him five-hundred dollars if he'd get lost for the week and not tell Kip what I did.

Let's just say I'm a little selfish when it comes to this boy, and I wanted all the alone time we could get.

Kip groans when we break our kiss, holding me tighter. "I don't want you to go."

Another zing of my heart.

"I don't want to go, either."

We both sigh, then fall silent, knowing there's no other choice.

"What if you came to semi-formal in a couple weeks?"

Kip brushes my hair from my face, frowning. "I wish I could, babe. It's finals time, and I've got to submit this project. It's going to take up every hour of my day once you leave."

"Did I distract you this week?"

"Yes," he says quickly, kissing my nose. "But it was worth it."

I sigh, tracing the muscles of his shoulders and traps with my finger. "I'll ask Bear. He's always down for a good time. Although, he's been sort of distant this semester."

"Family stuff?"

"I think that's part of it. But I also think there's more." I pause. "I know it sounds crazy, but... I think something might have happened between him and Erin."

"Erin?" Kip asks, arching a brow. "As in Ex?"

"The very one."

"Why do you think that?"

"I don't know. They just... *look* at each other weird. I know that sounds stupid, but they formed this random friendship, which was odd enough, and now they barely talk and when they're in the same room, it's awkward. I can't explain it."

"Well, let me know what you find out on that."

I sigh. "I will. Erin and I have been talking more, hanging out more... we have a lot of stuff still to work through, but it's getting better."

"Have you made up your mind about the presidency?"

I smile then, my stomach flipping for a completely different reason. "Yeah. I'm going for it."

"Yeah?"

I nod. "I really want to be president, to continue our family tradition. Not even for that reason, honestly. But because I think I could make a difference. And I love KKB. I want to leave a mark before I go."

Kip kisses my neck, tickling my ribs as I giggle and kick him away. "You'll leave one hell of a mark."

From all my writhing, my legs are tangled around his waist, and even though we've been insatiable all week long, I feel him growing hard between my thighs.

I hum my approval, sucking the skin of his neck as I climb my way up to his mouth. But just as we lock into a needy kiss, my phone rings.

"It can wait," I murmur against his lips.

But before we can even get some heavy petting going, my phone rings again.

"Okay, maybe it can't," I groan, rolling over until I can swipe my phone off the nightstand. I frown. "It's Ashlei."

"Answer it."

I nod, hitting the green phone button and putting Ashlei on speaker. "Hey, babe. Kind of indisposed at the moment. Everything okay?"

"No."

As soon as I hear her choked voice, her sobs, I shoot upright. "What happened?"

She cries for so long that I debate texting Jess and telling her to get her ass to wherever Ashlei is — and fast. I'm texting it out when she finally speaks.

"I fucked up. *Bad*, Sky. I don't know what to do."

"Whatever it is, we can figure it out. Take a deep breath."

She does, but then she's crying again. "Sophie... the intern..."

I freeze, Kip and I exchanging glances. I'd filled him in on that whole situation when I first got here. "What did she do?"

"She... she kissed me."

"She *what*?"

"I shoved her off me as soon as I realized what was happening, but I can't even believe it happened *at all*. And when I pushed her back, she had this shit-eating grin, like she'd won something. I have been trying to make sense of it all week, trying to figure out how to tell Brandon. And this morning…" She pauses, a sob breaking through. "This morning, I realized…"

"What, Lei?"

She sniffs. "She was interviewing me for her project. And I just forgot…"

"Forgot *what*?"

Another pause. "She was recording it. She had her phone set up on a tripod to record so she could pay attention to what I was saying."

My heart tripled its pace in my chest, Kip and I sharing another look. I know what she's going to say before she can even get the words out, and the way Kip is looking at me, he knows as well as I do that this is bad fucking news.

"She has our kiss on video, Sky."

Ashlei lets out a long, painful sigh as I scrub a hand back through my hair, trying to think.

"What do I do?"

"It'll be okay. I have a plan," I lie, kicking the covers off and hopping out of Kip's bed. "Just… call Jess. You don't need to be alone right now. And don't talk to Brandon yet. I'll be home by seven tonight, and we'll figure this out."

"I can't lose him," she whispers, her voice breaking again. And I look at Kip, knowing that if I were in her shoes, I'd be ripping at the seams, too.

"You won't."

And I pray that that's not a lie, too.

EPISODE 6

season finale

Cassie

"ALRIGHT, MY FAVORITE LITTLE redhead," Skyler says, grabbing my toes from where they stick out from under my comforter. "What do you say we go for a walk?"

"That sounds awful."

She chuckles. "Yeah, well, I'm sure showering does, too, but that's next. Come on."

Skyler rips my comforter off of me before I have the chance to grab it, and I groan, thrashing in my sheets and making a big show of my unhappiness at being forced out of bed.

"Please, just let me sulk in peace. I don't do this often."

"It's been long enough, babe. I let you do nothing but go to class and then come back here and mope for over a week now. But it's time to face the music."

I roll over, face half buried in my pillow. "What if the music really sucks? Like a third-grade orchestra concert kind of suck?"

Skyler smiles, sitting on the edge of my bed and sweeping my messy hair off my cheek. "You just need to talk to him, Little."

"I've tried."

"Tried what, exactly?"

"I texted him after he left that night. I tried calling."

"And then?"

I frown. "I mean, he made it pretty clear he didn't want to talk."

"*Didn't*," she echoes. "Past tense. It's been over a week now. He's had time to cool off and think. And so have you. What's stopping you from going down Greek Row and staying in his room until y'all work this out?"

I sigh, forcing myself into an upright position with more effort than should be necessary. Once I'm leaned back against the headboard, I meet Skyler's gaze. "Honestly?"

She nods.

"I feel like maybe this is a sign from the universe."

"What do you mean?"

"I mean that Adam and I have been a train wreck since forever. When we weren't together, when we were with other people and trying to be friends, when we finally became more than friends... we just keep hurting each other, over and over. We always have some kind of drama, some kind of misunderstanding, some kind of fight." I swallow, eyes flooding with tears when I remember how he turned his back on me by the pond. "That can't be healthy, can it? I mean... are we ever just going to be *okay*?"

Skyler offers a soft smile, scooting over until she's right next to me before pulling me into her arms. I lie there limp for a long while, quivering lip and blurry eyes, and then I finally wrap my arms around her, too.

"You're too smart to think love will ever be easy, Little."

I sigh, resting my head on her shoulder. "But should it always be this hard?"

Skyler frames my arms, pulling back so she can look at me. "You and Adam spent *years* denying what you had between you. Okay? And you were both so damn good at it that I didn't even see it — and I dated the guy." She chuckles. "To go from that, to being together... it's not an easy transition. You have years of history, of hurt, and now you're in this fragile time of building trust."

"And I blew that trust to hell..."

Skyler frowns. "Well, not the words I was going to use, but... kind of."

I sigh, scrubbing my hands over my face. "I don't deserve him."

"Yes, you do," she argues. "And he deserves you. If any two people in the world were meant for each other, it's you guys. But, here's the thing... he's right. You have to choose him over everyone, and he has to do the same. That's the only way you're going to shake your feet free of this muck that's got you guys stuck in the past."

"I didn't choose Grayson over him."

Skyler crosses her arms, releasing mine. "Don't get defensive with me. I'm calling you on your shit, so accept it."

I huff. "I hate you sometimes."

"Why was it so important for you to keep a friendship with Grayson, anyway? The guy cheated on you, Cassie. He was a pretentious asshole, too."

I lean my head back against the headboard. "Do you remember when Clay fucked me over my freshman year, and I lost Paris because of that whole ordeal?"

She nods.

"I never got over that. And it wasn't even Clay I was upset about. Not really. I mean, did he deserve my virginity? No. But what girl loses her innocence in some perfect, magical way? That's not what I was hurt over. What hurt me the most was losing my best friend." My eyes fill with tears again. "I don't like losing people. I just want everyone to love me and stay forever."

Skyler smiles, reaching out to rub my elbow. "That's understandable. We all want to be loved for who we are. But the truth is... you're going to lose people as you grow. A lot of them. Friends, family, people who you thought would be a part of your story forever. The older we get, the less we give a shit about what other people think, and the more we start coming to terms with who we are, what we want, what we stand for." Skyler shrugs. "It's natural to lose people in that process."

I nod, sniffing. "I guess I just believed Grayson. When he said he was sorry, that he wanted to be friends... it felt like getting a second chance. Like I could have Adam and Grayson both."

"Sounds like a lot of work to me," Skyler says. "To be devoted to your boyfriend and also friends with your ex."

I blink. "God, it sounds so stupid when you say it like that."

"It's not stupid," Skyler says gently. "But it was maybe a lapse in judgment. It was acting on the desire to hold onto something in the past, rather than to embrace a new and brighter future."

"A future I blew to smithereens," I say on a sigh.

"Talk to him." Skyler stands, squeezing my shoulder. "Go for a walk, take a shower, and make a plan. Figure out a way to reach him even when he doesn't want to be reached. Because I promise you, he's just as miserable as you are right now. If there's anything I know about Adam, it's that he loves you more than he loves himself. More than he loves Alpha Sigma. More than he loves anything in this world." She smiles. "He doesn't want to lose you, either, Cassie. You guys just have to get out of your own way and stop the bullshit."

"Such wise and kind words of advice," I remark with a grin.

"Feel free to leave a tip in the jar." Skyler winks, patting my arm once more before she leaves me alone with my thoughts — the very ones that have plagued me since the night Adam walked away from me.

God, I'm so thankful for Skyler.

The universe knew what it was doing when it placed us together as Big and Little. I smile, thinking back to the first night we met, that night by the reflection pond when I was torn between which sorority to choose as my home. And now, we were about to be the only two left out of our little group of five. Erin, Lei, and Jess would all be graduating in just a few short weeks.

Everything is about to change.

And it only makes me want to hold onto her and Adam even tighter.

My chest squeezes, because I know Skyler is right — about everything. I know this is a mess that I made. And I know it's on me to figure out how to clean it up.

When it comes to Adam, there's only one way I can think of that I might be able to reach him.

I just hope he'll let me in.

Bear

BECCA SOUNDS A LITTLE like the teacher in the Charlie Brown cartoons I used to watch with Carleton as a kid.

I know she's saying shit I need to hear. I know I should be latching on to every word, nodding, letting her know I hear her and I understand what she's saying.

But I can't.

Everything feels distant, foggy, like I'm on a cloud of having an out-of-body experience as I sit next to her on the bench by the reflection pond. It's hot and muggy and so far from what December was as a kid growing up in Pennsylvania. It doesn't feel like Christmas is around the corner. It doesn't feel like winter.

And it definitely doesn't feel like Becca is breaking up with me.

But she is.

And I can't even find the words to try to convince her not to.

"Are you even listening to me at *all* right now?" she asks, waving her hand in front of my face before she lets it fall to her thigh with a slap. She sighs, sitting back on the bench, shaking her head with her eyes on the pond. "I don't know why I'm surprised."

"I'm listening."

"Mm-hmm."

I turn to her then, pinning her with my gaze. "What more do I really need to hear past the part of this conversation where you said you don't want to be with me anymore?"

Becca swallows, eyes softening, her eyebrows tugging together to meet in the middle of her forehead. "You do realize I don't *want* to break up with you, right?"

"Not what it seems like right now."

"What choice have you given me?" She throws up her hands, exhausted. "Bear, that Friendsgiving shit... that was the most embarrassing moment of my life. My roommate and my best fucking friend hang out with you for the first time — this guy I've been telling them I'm so head over heels for — and you show your ass being possessive over *some other girl*." She holds her hand out like she's serving me my own ass on a silver platter. "Do you see how this is a problem?"

"I wasn't being possessive."

To that, she only scoffs and crosses her arms, tonguing her cheek when she tears her eyes from me and focuses on the pond again. "Unbelievable."

Shame and guilt sizzle in my chest, like I've just thrown my heart on a grill. I know it's a lie just as much as she does. But I refuse to admit it, because if I admit it to her, I'd have to admit it to myself.

That I care about Erin.

That I care about her as more than just a friend.

That I can't stand to see her with someone else, even if *I'm* with someone else.

That until I work through my feelings with her, I can't be with anyone.

I keep my mouth shut, zipping my lips tight in an effort to keep all those thoughts hidden forever. I'd rather die with them buried inside me than live with them out in the open.

"Look... maybe you should go home for the holidays. Work things out with your family. With *yourself*," she adds, turning and waiting for me to look at her before she continues. "And then, *maybe*, we can talk about being together when you get back. But I don't want to be with you if your heart belongs to someone else, Bear. That's not fair to me *or* to her. So... if you want her, maybe you should tell her that."

My stomach sinks so violently that I nearly retch, because I care for Becca so much that it makes me physically ill to think she can see right through me, that I can hurt her so badly without even meaning to.

"I want *you*, Becca," I say, voice cracking.

"I know. But you *love* her," she says matter of factly, with a shrug in her shoulder. "And as long as that is true, you can't have me."

I suck in a stiff breath, shaking my head as emotion strangles me from the inside. My chest is tight, my jaw thick with tension, my knee bouncing uncontrollably.

I have to stop her.

But I can't.

She's right.

But I can't admit it.

Slowly, Becca leans over, wrapping her arms around my neck. She presses her lips to my cheek, and I close my eyes at the contact, savoring what I know will be our last touch.

"You're a good man, Bear," she whispers. "But you can't keep running and hiding from your truths."

When she pulls back, it's with a sniff and a swipe of her hand over her cheek to wipe away her tears. I wish it was *my* hand wiping them away, but it's not me who gets to comfort her anymore.

I'm not sure I ever really did.

She doesn't say another word. The *goodbye* doesn't ever come. She just stands and bolts, her feet carrying her quickly away from me as I watch her go.

I let out a gasp, one that I can't replace with my next inhale. I'm trying to get oxygen into my lungs and failing every time. Scrubbing my hands back through my hair, I let out a loud, lung-collapsing scream that echoes across campus.

And once again, I am alone.

I somehow make it back to my room at the Omega Chi house.

I somehow manage to peel my damp clothes off, the ones I sweated through, and drag myself into the shower.

And when I finally collapse into my bed, I somehow pull out my phone.

And I call Erin.

My heart is in my throat as the line rings, over and over, again and again, with no answer. I hang up when her voicemail clicks on, immediately redialing her number.

"Please," I beg, rolling my lips between my teeth. "Please pick up, Erin."

When her voicemail clicks on again, I sigh, sitting up and moving to the edge of my bed. My legs dangle over, and I stare at my bare feet, waiting for the tone.

"Erin," I say when it clicks, and just saying her fucking name has that same tight emotion gripping my throat. I let out a shaky breath, and with it, anything else I could have said.

Please, I need you.

Come over.

Help.

Instead, I hang up, and dial Skyler.

It takes less than five minutes for her to show up at my door, and she doesn't knock. She just pushes through it, kicks off her sandals and climbs into bed with me.

Usually, it's me curling around her, or holding her to my chest, but this time when she climbs over me, she drags my back to her chest and wraps her tiny arms around me as best she can.

Never in my life have I ever been the little spoon, and I almost laugh out loud at the stupidity of it.

But that laugh comes out as a sob.

And with it, I break.

Skyler doesn't try to shush me as I fall apart. She doesn't try to control my shaking body in her arms or my piercing wails as they rip through the quiet night around us. And if any of my brothers hear me — which I'm almost certain they do — they're wise enough to stay away, to not ask, to pretend like they didn't hear a thing.

For the first time since I was a kid, I cry myself to sleep.

Skyler is still there holding me in the morning.

Ashlei

"YOU CAN DO THIS," Skyler assures me on the phone as I press the button that will take me up to Brandon's penthouse.

"You sure about that?"

"He loves you, Lei. Remember? He's not going to walk away from you."

I sigh, leaning my head back against the elevator wall and praying the call doesn't drop on the way up. I need Skyler's voice to keep me calm. "I'm such a fucking handful. Why would he stay? After what happened in the spring… and now this…"

"*This* was not your fault. And dating your boss is not a crime, however taboo it may be."

I shake my head. "I'm trying to put myself in his shoes, if he came to me with this. And I gotta say… I wouldn't be happy."

"Look, he might be mad, okay? He might be hurt. *But*, again, *he loves you*. He's not going anywhere. You two are a team, and you'll figure this out together. Right?"

Silence.

"Lei, I need you to say it."

I sigh. "Right."

The elevator dings, and I force a slow exhale. "I'll call you after."

"You've got this," she says again, and then I end the call just as the elevator doors open.

Brandon's penthouse is unlike any place I've ever been in my life. The first time he brought me here, I had stood in this very elevator and gaped at the expansive space for what felt like an hour while he watched me and chuckled to himself.

The skyrise is right on the bay, with floor-to-ceiling windows that overlook Miami's beaches and beautiful teal water. His floors are a polished white marble, and the exposed air ducts and concrete give it an industrial feel like a New York apartment, but with the elegance and heat of Florida. He'd hired an interior designer to bring his vision to life, which was to make the entire place feel like an art museum. And it's not just the breathtaking art that decorates the walls. Each piece of furniture, each vase, each light fixture — every single aspect of the apartment is art.

And as soon as you walk in, you're part of the show, too.

Tonight, with the soft glow of candles and the fireplace in the center wall where the sitting room is, you can't even see the beaches or the water at all. Instead, it's dark outside the windows, save for the few boats in the distance.

And Brandon is sitting on the couch in front of the fire, scotch in hand, his eyes watching the flames and one ankle crossed over his knee.

It's Friday evening, so it doesn't surprise me that he's still in the same chocolate dress slacks and ice-blue button up that he wore at the office today. Even on casual Friday, the man always dressed to impress.

He was the boss, after all.

"Hey," I say tentatively, setting my purse on the kitchen counter before I make my way over to him.

I seem to shake him out of a spell, and he looks up at me with glazed eyes, accepting the kiss I bend to press on his lips.

"Thanks for letting me come over," I say, folding my hands in my lap once I'm seated next to him.

He nods, but otherwise doesn't say a word, his eyes back on the flames of the fire. I can't blame him for drinking and avoiding eye contact. After all, who responds well to the dreaded words...

We need to talk.

I sigh. "Brandon, something happened that I need you to know about. And it's going to sound crazy, but you have to believe—"

"I already know."

My mouth is still open, ready to recite the speech I'd practiced with Skyler all week — the one where I explain how Sophie had been quietly hitting on me, how she'd plotted out a way to get me alone, how she'd kissed me and made sure to get it on film. I was fully ready to get him prepared and on my side, ready to fight her attempt to take me down.

But those words are all stuck in my throat now, and confusion sweeps over me instead.

"What?"

"You and Sophie made out," he said, taking a sip of his scotch and hissing through his teeth.

"Um..." I think I'm in shock. I think my heart might actually give out. "Well, that's not *exactly* what happened, but—"

"It's not?" Brandon challenges, his eyes finding mine. "Because I saw the video, and I'm *pretty sure* that's exactly what happened."

Confusion turns to defensiveness in my chest as his scowl deepens, and I frown right back. "Why do I feel under attack right now?"

"Oh, I don't know. Maybe because you kissed our intern? Maybe because you cheated on me? Maybe because you waited over a week and *until I already knew* to tell me about it?"

My jaw drops. "Okay, first of all, *she* kissed me. I did not kiss her. And I certainly didn't *cheat* on you."

"No? What is it called when you kiss someone who isn't your boyfriend?"

I grind my teeth together, heart racing in my chest. "I didn't kiss—"

"Goddamnit, Ashlei," he yells, standing and slamming his glass onto the coffee table. What's left of the amber liquid inside sloshes out onto the wood, and Brandon threads his hands over his head, pacing until he's staring out the massive windows over the dark beach.

I just watch him, breath shallow, mind racing trying to catch up.

"I saw the video," he says quietly, turning to face me as his hands slowly come down. "She might have made the move. She might have been the one to lean in. But let me tell you, I've been in that position — when a woman makes a move on me that's unwanted. And what I do in those situations and what *you* did are vastly different. *I* pull away. *I* quickly tell them they are out of line. *I* remind them I'm happily taken, and that they need to respect my boundaries."

"I did the same thing. I told her to stay away from me, I asked her what the hell she was doing."

"*After* you kissed her and grabbed her blouse and moaned like your panties were fucking soaked."

I blink, over and over, my mouth hanging open.

Brandon just shakes his head, turning back toward the window. "We don't have anything to discuss. I took care of it."

"Took... took *care* of it?"

"Sophie came into my office earlier this week and showed me the video," he says, turning to look me in the eyes when he nails me with those words. "She knew what she was doing. She wanted to blackmail you, to blackmail *me*. She said it was sexual harassment and that I had until the end of the week to fire you and hire her, or she'd blast it to every news station in the city."

I stand, picking up the nearest pillow and chucking it across the room. "That little *bitch!*"

Brandon just holds up his hands, closing his eyes and forcing a breath like I'm a petulant little child he's highly annoyed with. "Like I said, it's handled."

"How?"

"Well, lucky for *you*, we record every call our interns make. I had MyKayla scrub all her calls to see if she could find something, and though Sophie might be cunning, she's also conceited. And she told her entire plan to one of her friends on her work cell."

I smirk. "Stupid cunt."

Brandon watches me for a long moment, like he can't believe me, like he doesn't know who it is standing in his living room at all.

"So, she has nothing," I say.

"She has nothing," he echoes. "I played the call for her and told her if she left quietly, I'd write her a letter of recommendation."

"What?" I shake my head, crossing the room to where he is. "Why would you do that?"

"To save your ass!"

My head snaps back at his words, but he's already turned away from me, scrubbing his hand over his face with his eyes focused somewhere on the water.

I sigh, closing my eyes. I knew this was going to suck, and I was right. Still, relief washes through me that Brandon handled it.

I don't know why I'm surprised, why I ever thought he wouldn't.

We're a team, just like Skyler said.

Wrapping my arms around his waist, I rest my cheek on his back, holding him to me. "I'm so sorry this happened. Thank you for handling it."

It's quiet after that but for the crackling of the fire, and I take what feels like my first breath in ages.

"Well, now that that's over with," I say, rounding until I'm standing between him and the window. I thread my arms around his neck, kissing his chin. "Are you ready for your first sorority event tomorrow?" I chuckle. "The girls are going to lose their shit when you show up to semi-formal."

Brandon's jaw ticks, but otherwise there's no response, and my stomach drops with the silence.

"What's wrong?"

"I think we should take a break."

My heart stops. "A... a *break*?"

Brandon closes his eyes, grabbing my hands where they rest behind his neck and peeling them off of him. "Ashlei," he says when his eyes open again. "Consider this your two-week notice to *Okay, Cool*."

Again, I find myself blinking repeatedly, as if I can erase what he just said with my lashes. "You're *firing* me?"

"No. You're resigning. Because you have opportunities elsewhere," he says, looking away from me. He crosses back to the coffee table and picks up what's left of his scotch. "That's the story we're telling. And if you go with it, I'll give you a letter of recommendation to take with you, too."

"A letter of rec—" I nearly vomit, my desperation propelling me forward until I'm in front of Brandon again, my hands around his bicep, urging him to look at me. "Brandon. I don't want a fucking letter of recommendation. I want *you*." Panic sears through me. "I want *us*."

He closes his eyes, and I see the emotion strangling him just as it is me.

"I love you," I whisper.

Brandon grits his teeth at my words, looking up at the ceiling, but I grab his chin and force him to look me in the eyes.

"She kissed *me*."

"Yes. She did," he agrees. "But you're lying to both of us if you say you didn't kiss her back."

I shake my head, tears flooding my eyes in an instant and spilling out over my cheeks before I can even think to stop them. The panic I felt before is a full-on storm now, swirling in my chest, crackling like lightning in my heart, the thunder so loud in my ears I can't hear his words through it.

"It was a mistake," I cry, holding onto him tighter. "I *love you*."

Tears gloss his eyes, but he rips away from me before they fall, leaving me standing in the middle of his living room as he storms across the marble back to his bedroom. "You should leave."

"*Brandon*," I plead.

And then, in one swift moment, he launches his glass across the room.

It hits the corner of the kitchen island and shatters, making me scream and jump back, covering my mouth with eyes as big as saucers.

"GET. OUT." His chest is heaving when his gaze finds me. "NOW!"

I press my other hand over my mouth, crying so hard my chest burns.

"You said you'd never break me," he chokes out, turning away from me before his emotion can show. "And you fucking lied."

"I didn't mean to—"

"Get out," he says, and then he starts beating his fist on the window. "Get out, get out, get out, GET OUT!"

I bite my lip as more tears trickle over my cheeks, but there's no use in trying to make him understand now. All I can do is leave him alone, like he's asking me to.

I rush to the kitchen counter and grab my purse, not even trying to be careful to avoid the glass. At this point, if I get cut, I deserve it.

I deserve every ounce of pain I'm feeling right now.

It doesn't take long for the elevator to ascend, and then I'm in it, and my back is to the wall, eyes on where Brandon stands across the penthouse. He has one hand on the giant window and the other scrubbing back over his head, his shoulders tense and rigid.

He turns just as the elevator doors begin to shut, and he forces a breath, covering his mouth with his hand as the first tear falls down his perfect face.

My eyes close before the doors do.

I can't bear to see the pain I've caused.

I can't bear to watch the only man I've ever loved cry because of me.

And on the way down, I realize it doesn't matter if I watch or not. It's still real. It's still happening. It's still true.

I've lost him.

And I know before the doors open again that I'll never get him back.

Adam

THEY DON'T MAKE NOISE-CANCELING headphones strong enough to drown out how loud the Alpha Sigma house can get on a Saturday night.

It's especially difficult on this particular Saturday night, when half the sororities on campus are having their semi-formals, and half our brothers are pre-gaming, trying to get drunk enough to not care that they have to wear a tie all night.

Another roar of laughter, followed by the chanting of *Chug! Chug! Chug!* makes me grit my teeth and rip my headphones off, tossing them on my desk as I kick away from it. I don't know who I'm trying to kid. Like I could sit here and study knowing that Cassie is down Greek Row getting ready to go to the Kappa Kappa Beta semi-formal.

Without me.

My chest squeezes hard, but I don't lose my breath this time. In fact, I've become used to it, that aching hollowness inside me that likes to remind me from time to time that I'm alive and suffering.

Cassie and I haven't spoken since the night I walked in on Grayson trying to kiss her at the campus coffee shop.

It's not that she didn't try — at least, at first. She texted me when I left her there at the reflection pond. She tried calling. Once.

But then?

Nothing.

And I know I have no right to be pissed off. If I wanted to talk to her, I should have answered.

I guess I just expected more effort.

I expected her to try harder.

And more than anything, I expected her to choose me the same way I'd chosen her.

Another sickening wave rolls through me, the same one that's made it damn near impossible to eat or sleep since that night. I'm fighting down the urge to dry heave when there's a soft knock at my door.

"Hey, Prez," Kade says, leaning against the door frame. He tucks his hands into the pockets of his slacks, watching me with a sympathetic smile. "You doing okay?"

No one knows the specifics of what happened between me and Cassie, but with Grayson having a broken nose, and Cassie staying away from the house, they could do some simple math and figure it out.

"I'm good," I lie. Then, I whistle, waggling my brows. "Look at you, all cleaned up."

Kade stands tall and adjusts his tie. "I look dapper as fuck, don't I?"

"I'm surprised you can fit those massive biceps of yours into a suit jacket, to be honest."

He shakes his head, staring at said muscles. "I'm going to split a seam by the end of the night."

I chuckle.

Kade relaxes again, leaning against the door frame and nodding to me with his chin. "What about you? Where's your suit?"

I swallow, pretending to go back to the very important papers on my desk. "In my closet."

"You're not going tonight?"

"You already know the answer to that."

Kade sighs, walking in to sit on the edge of my bed. "I know you and I aren't exactly best buddies, Adam. Fuck, if I'm being honest? I hated your ass as a pledge last year."

"Gee, thanks."

"But," he continues. "You've earned my respect since then. And one thing I like most about you is how openly and honestly you love Cassie."

His words surprise me, and I turn in my chair to face him.

"I mean it," he says, smirking as he runs his hand back through his hair. "It's not easy to do that. I am much more of a play games, crack corny pick-up lines, and hide all emotions kind of guy. Or, at least, I *was*."

"Until Jess."

Kade sighs, shaking his head. "That woman will be the death of me."

I smile. "Something about those KKB girls."

"Right? Anyway, I don't know exactly what happened between you and Cassie. But I hope you guys work it out. You make a good pair. And from what I hear, you two went through a lot to get here. I mean, hell, she used me as a pawn last year to cover up the fact that it was actually *you* she was falling for."

I held up my hands. "Don't get me started on what a train wreck last semester was."

Kade laughs, standing. "I won't. Just wanted to let you know I'm here if you need to talk or anything. And, for what it's worth, I think you should crash semi-formal. Show up in a suit and sweep that girl off her feet. She can't say no to you in a tie."

I smile. "Thanks, man. I appreciate it. Have fun with Jess tonight." I tilt my head, assessing him. "You're really into her, aren't you?"

Kade grabs the back of his neck, nodding sheepishly. "On a scale of one to fucking idiot, where do I land if I say I'm already head over heels for the girl?"

"I don't think you're stupid at all."

"Something tells me it won't last," he says, but he shrugs before the moment can get too serious. "But I guess that means I should just make the most of now."

I stand, clapping him on the shoulder. "I think that's the best way to look at it. Besides," I add. "For whatever it's worth, I've never seen her show another fraternity guy the kind of attention she shows you. I think she's just as into you as you are into her."

He smiles, squeezing my shoulder, too, and then he's out the door and I'm alone again.

I sigh, collapsing back into my chair and sinking down until my ass is hanging off it. I stare up at my ceiling as the house grows quiet, all the brothers leaving to hop into their various limos that will take them out tonight.

I debate Kade's suggestion the entire time.

I *could* crash the semi-formal, show up and demand that Cassie talk to me. But... what would I say that I haven't already?

Nothing has changed.

I still want her to choose me.

And the fact that her friendship with Grayson was more important than her relationship with me isn't something I can just forget about — especially if she doesn't even see it the way I do.

You're being stubborn, my brain sings to me for the fiftieth time this week. I don't have time to tell it to shut up before there's a soft rap of knuckles on my window.

My head snaps toward the noise, and I frown, wondering if I imagined it.

When it comes again, I rush out of my chair and leap onto my bed, yanking the cord on my blinds.

And when they open, I'm face to face with Cassie McBee.

She's an absolute vision in the last glow of the setting sun, casting her red hair aflame and igniting the flecks of gold in her emerald eyes. I blink away my shock at the sight of her, opening my window and holding out a hand to help her inside.

She's not wearing a dress, or makeup, or a head of curls like I imagined she would be tonight. Instead, she's in worn-out navy-blue sweatpants and one of my long sleeve Alpha Sigma shirts that she stole from me over the summer when she was cold one night.

And on her feet are the same Keds she wore the first night she crawled into my window two years ago.

That was when she was a freshman, and I was a sophomore, and my room was down the hall and on the other side of the house. That was when my bed was against the wall opposite my window. That was when I was with Skyler, and she'd just had her heart broken by my asshole president.

That was before we were us.

And yet, we'd *always* been us — no matter how we tried to fight it.

Her hand is cold in mine as I help her inside the window, which is a little tougher since my bed is right up against it. But she shimmies in, and once she's inside, she kicks out of her shoes just like she did that first time. I leave the window open, the breeze blowing through the strands coming loose from her messy top knot, and for the longest time, I just watch her and wait.

"Hi," she whispers after a while, pulling her legs to sit criss-cross on my bed.

"Hi."

I want so badly to reach for her, to pull her into me, to kiss her and tell her she doesn't have to say a word. And I decide after approximately two seconds that that's exactly what I'm going to do.

I reach for her at the same time her little bottom lip quivers, and she launches into my arms, letting me wrap her up and cradle her. I inhale her scent, breathe in her heat and her love, and the first relieved sigh leaves my chest since the night we parted.

"I'm so fucking sorry, Cassie."

"*You're* sorry?" She shakes her head, which is still buried in my chest. "It's *me* who was the idiot."

I chuckle. "You're not an idiot."

She pulls back, her eyes meeting mine. "You were right. You were right about Grayson just like you were right about Clay my first semester here. How is it that your asshole radar is so strong and mine is completely broken?"

"Hey, I'm kind of glad it's broken," I tease. "If it wasn't, you might never have started dating me."

She smiles, burying her head in my chest again. "God, I've been so miserable without you."

"Why didn't you come talk to me?"

"I wanted to, but…" She huffs, looking up at me again. "Honestly? I don't like being wrong. And when it comes to me and you, I'm not used to being in this position."

I scoff, tickling her sides as she writhes in my grip. "Wow. You saying you're always right and I'm always wrong?"

She's still laughing, shoving my hands away from her ribs, but then she curls up in my arms even more. "See? I even suck at apologizing."

I kiss her hair, my smile impenetrable. It doesn't matter now that she's in my arms. Nothing else matters.

"You don't need to apologize, Cassie. You *are* right — it was him who made a move on you. You didn't do anything wrong."

"Except trust him. And decide that having a friendship with him was more important than making sure you were okay."

She throws my words from that night back at me, and I sigh, holding her tighter. "I know you didn't mean it that way, though."

"I didn't. But it doesn't change the fact that I hurt you."

I nod, falling quiet for a moment.

"You know, I love that your heart is so big. I love that you forgave him, even after what he did to you, that you wanted to have a friendship with him. I've *always* loved those things about you. If they weren't a part of you, you definitely wouldn't put up with my sorry ass."

She giggles, and the sound makes me want to throw my hands up and rejoice that she's still mine.

"I'm sorry I lost my shit and hit him. I just..." I shake my head, and then shake her gently. "I go *mad* when it comes to you. I can't lose you. I can't live without you."

Cassie peers up at me, her eyes big and soft. "You know, for once, it was me who messed up. You're supposed to let *me* apologize, but you're stealing all my thunder."

I laugh. "Okay. I'm listening."

She sits up and shimmies out of my embrace, facing me completely. "I'm so sorry I dug my heels in about being friends with him. I was holding onto something I shouldn't have. The truth is, I loved Grayson."

Bile hits my throat, but I swallow it down.

"*Did* being the keyword there. I guess there was a part of me that hoped I could have it all... a relationship with you *and* a friendship with him. But I was wrong. I should have known his intentions. And even if those intentions were pure, the fact that it hurt you for me to be with him should have mattered more than anything." She grabs my hands in hers, lifting my knuckles to her lips. "*You* matter more than anything to me. And I'm sorry I didn't prove that with my actions. But I will now. I will for as long as you'll have me."

At that, I bark out a laugh, shaking my head and pulling her into me. "You're crazy if you think I'd ever let you go."

She melts into my arms as I press my lips to hers, and the kiss is a seal of that promise, one I'll continue making over and over again, no matter what shit we go through.

Because if there's anything I know, it's that Cassie McBee is it for me. She always has been. She always will be.

And I'll weather any storm I have to to fight for our love.

"Has he..." I swallow. "Has Grayson talked to you since..."

Cassie scoffs. "Hell no. I mean, he tried reaching out, but I blocked his number and went to Professor Drumm to explain the situation. He told me I can finish out the semester on my own in lab. And Grayson can do the same."

"I'm sorry," I say with a sigh. "Are you going to be okay on your own?"

She arches a brow. "Please. Do you even know me? I'm a friggin' genius."

I laugh, kissing her nose. "Yes. Yes, you are." Tugging on the fabric of her sweatpants, I let the topic of Grayson fizzle out, focusing on the more pressing point, instead. "So, I take it we're not going to semi-formal?"

"Let's be honest — we don't have the best record at these things, anyway."

"Well, maybe we change that. Let's make a pact, right here and now."

Cassie sits up straight. "Okay. Hit me."

"No more fights. No more third parties. No more stupid drama or miscommunication or whatever other bullshit tends to wiggle its way between us." I hold out my pinky. "From now on, it's just me and you."

Cassie loops her pinky through mine. "Me and you."

"Forever."

"Are you proposing, Adam Brooks?"

"Not yet. But you can bet your ass I will someday."

She flushes, shaking her head as she watches me. "And you can bet *your* ass that I'll say yes."

My heart does a leap in my chest at the thought, and I pull her into me, pressing another kiss to her perfect lips.

"So," I say, still holding onto her. "We could lie here, order some greasy food and watch some movies. *Or*, we could crash semi-formal like a couple of bums."

Her eyes widen. "Dressed like *this*?"

"Mm-hmm. Just like this. What do you say?"

Cassie hums, eyes tracing the ceiling before she looks at me with a devilish grin.

And I know her answer before she can even speak.

Erin

IT'S MY LAST SEMI-FORMAL.

I don't know why it took so long to hit me, why all semester long I haven't taken the time to stop and really consider the fact that this is it.

This is my last semester of college.

This is my last month at Palm South University.

These are my last few weeks as president of Kappa Kappa Beta.

And after this, a completely new life starts.

"What planet are you on?"

I blink at the question, turning to find a grinning Gavin watching me, amused. His hair is styled for the first time since I've known him, and to my surprise, he showed up at the Kappa Kappa Beta house in a beige suit, one that brings out the blue in his eyes and highlights the dark olive of his skin.

"Hmm?"

"You were lost in space. Just wondering which planet you were on."

I smile, eyes trailing over the room. We rented out a gorgeous and historic hotel downtown for semi this year, and it almost feels like we've stepped back in time in the grand ballroom, the extravagant chandeliers casting a low-lit glow over my sisters and their dates as they dance. Gavin and I are alone at a cocktail table in the corner, and yet I feel so warm and full I could combust.

"The planet where I'm no longer in a sorority," I finally answer. "Where I'm no longer defined by the letters on my shirt or the title I hold."

"Sounds like an awesome planet to me."

I chuckle. "I'm sure it will be great in its own ways, but... I'm really going to miss this."

My heart squeezes the more I look around, and I can't help but smile when I see Cassie and Adam letting loose on the dance floor — both of them in sweat pants and standing out like two sore thumbs in the sea of suits and dresses. But they're laughing and spinning each other and having the time of their lives, and for the first time, I don't give a shit that they broke the rules. I don't care that they're out of dress code and mocking an event with history and purpose.

My smile climbs farther when I spot Jess and Kade making out behind the stage. The way the curtain is hung, no one else can see them, but our table just happens to have a perfect view. And again, I don't find a care in my soul about Jess being scandalous at a sorority event.

Because seriously, who the hell cares?

We're young. And limitless. And gloriously unbound.

It's magical.

And yet, with so much joy and love comes heartbreak in equal measure. Ashlei didn't even come tonight, to her last semi-formal, because she's heartbroken over her breakup with Brandon. And though Skyler is here, it's without Kip, and I know it kills her.

Little does she know that he's going to surprise her in a big way next week.

He called me right after she left California after Thanksgiving and asked me to help set it all up. He wants to surprise her the night she finds out she's president — because we *all* know she will get elected. So, he's flying in, and not just to see her.

But to lavalier her.

Getting a lavalier from your boyfriend is like one step away from an engagement ring, and about the most serious step you can take in college. It's a special ceremony for a silly little necklace that means everything to the two people exchanging it.

And I can't wait to be a part of it.

But tonight, she's solo — well, kind of. Kip might not be here, but just like always, she's got Bear by her side.

My stomach twists when I spot them at a cocktail table across the dance floor, and I tear my eyes away from them before Bear has the chance to lock his on me. We haven't spoken since he showed his ass at the Thanksgiving event he'd planned.

He'd tried calling me, but the truth was that I didn't want to talk to him. Not now. Not after the way he acted toward Gavin.

If anyone in my life knows what I've been through, it's Bear. And if anyone should know what a huge deal it is for me to open up to a guy, to let him in, to *date him* — it should be Bear.

He invited me there after denying my apology, after denying *me* all semester, and then he made me *and* my date feel like complete and total outcasts. It was like we were unwelcome, like we'd shown up despite him trying his best to avoid us.

I don't know what's going on with Bear, but I know one thing — I'm tired of putting in effort that he doesn't reciprocate.

I've tried apologizing.

I've tried explaining.

I've tried mending our friendship.

And he won't have any of it.

You can't force someone to care about you, and you can't always fix what's broken.

"So," Gavin says, wrapping me in his arms and pulling my attention away from the crowd. "What's next for Erin Xander?"

"Hmm... well," I say, lacing my hands behind his neck and looking up at the high ceiling. "Take the next few weeks off after graduation, try to relax I guess, and then sink or swim in law school." I pause. "I'm sure my *parents* are hoping for the former, while I'm praying for the latter."

"You're going to be the most kick ass lawyer to ever exist," he says matter of factly. "But I'm less interested in the school part, and more interested in what you're going to do with these few weeks of freedom you have in-between."

I shrug. "I told you. I'll go home for the holidays, maybe relax by the pool or something."

"Is that what you want to do?"

I tilt my head. "I mean... I want to do a lot of things."

"Like what?"

"I don't know what you mean."

"I mean, what if you didn't just go home and relax. What if you did something you really want to do, or something spontaneous and crazy before you commit yourself to law school?"

"Okay, I'm listening," I say warily. "What do you have in mind."

"What if we got out of here?"

"Like, took a trip?"

Gavin nods.

"You and me?"

Another nod, his smile climbing.

"Where would we go?"

"Anywhere," he answers easily. "In fact... what if we didn't make the decision."

I cock a brow, confused.

"What if we let strangers make it *for* us."

"Okay. You've lost me," I confess.

Gavin kisses my nose, and the notion makes my heart flutter. How is it that this strange, shadow of a man has somehow wiggled his way into my heart?

"Let's make a game of it. Pack a couple bags and just fucking *go*." He snaps his fingers. "I know. We'll go to the airport and pick two strangers. One of them gives us a terminal letter, the other gives us a number, and that's the gate we go to. That's the plane ticket we buy."

I laugh. "You're kidding, right?"

"I'm serious as a heart attack."

I shake my head, still laughing. "What if the flight is to another country?"

"Then we end up in another country," he says easily, on a shrug, nonetheless, as if it's no big deal. "You have a passport, right?"

"Well, yes, but..." I scramble for words, my mind reeling. "We wouldn't know what to pack."

"Pack the essentials. If it's somewhere freezing, we buy a heavier jacket. If it's somewhere warm, we buy a swimsuit."

"You make it sound so easy."

"It can be," he says, tipping my chin with his knuckles, his eyes searching mine. "If you trust me."

My heart surges in my chest, but this time, not from anxiety — but from pure, unadulterated excitement. I can feel the blood pumping through my veins, the unknown possibilities fluttering in my chest.

"This is insane."

"Aren't the best things in life?"

I chuckle, shaking my head again. "I'm scared," I admit.

"I've got you."

It's a promise he seals with a peppering of kisses on my neck, my chin, my jaw as I laugh and wriggle in his grasp. And when he captures my lips with his, I sigh into the kiss, leaning into everything that he is, everything he's brought into my life, everything still yet to come.

On the cusp of a new chapter in an already crazy life, I feel like I'm standing on the edge of a cliff, ready to jump, but terrified of the possible outcome all the same.

And maybe in this scenario, Gavin is the parachute.

All that's left to do now is take the leap and trust him not to let me fall.

Jess

"YOU OKAY, LEI?" I ask at our last KKB Chapter of the year — of our *lives*.

Ashlei sniffs, dabbing at the corner of her eyes so she doesn't mess up her makeup. "I'm trying to be."

"Is this about giving up your exec position and getting ready to graduate, or about Brandon?"

She visibly shrinks in size, as if just his name took the breath out of her lungs. And when she peeks a glance at me, it's the most pitiful I've ever seen. "Both," she whispers.

I squeeze her knee. "Hey, you two are going to work it out. Alright? Trust me."

She nods, but I know from our conversations over the past couple of weeks that she doesn't believe me. Brandon hasn't talked to her since the night she came clean about the intern. He's even been avoiding her at the office in her last two weeks there. And as of this weekend, she's a free woman.

Free from work.

Free from school.

Free from a relationship.

And though that could be seen as a fresh, new, and exciting step in life, I know right now all she can feel is heartbroken for everything she's losing.

Honestly, I can't blame her — especially when Kade and I are getting serious, and Erin is dating Gavin. I've been in that position before, when you try everything you can not to look around at everyone else's happiness and compare your lack thereof.

All I can do now is be there for her, and I nudge her to remind her of that just as Erin invites Skyler and the other presidential candidates back into the room.

We all sit and clap, Cassie yelling out *You got this, Big!* from her seat across the aisle. I give a hoot of approval, along with half the chapter, because we all know before Erin even announces it who will be the next Kappa Kappa Beta president.

It couldn't be anyone *but* Skyler Thorne.

It's not even because Erin is president now, and her big was before her, and her grand big before that, etc., etc. It's because no one cares about our sisters and this sorority more than Skyler does. No one else drops whatever they have going on in an instant to be there for their friends the way she does. And no one else could fill Erin's shoes — and maybe even do the job *better*.

"I've already given my sappy thank you speech," Erin says when the room has quieted, and I don't miss her tearing up just like Lei. "But I just have to say one more time that I am truly honored for the privilege you all bestowed upon me this time last year. I hope I made you proud, and I want you to know that I will never forget you — any of you — or this amazing sorority."

I start my favorite Kappa Kappa Beta chant, and sisters slowly chime in, until the whole room is full of laughter and yelling and crying and far too much emotion for me, personally, but damn it if I don't love it all the same.

Even I, Jess Vonnegut, am not immune to the sads that come with graduating college and leaving this part of my life behind.

"Okay okay, enough about me," Erin says, facing Skyler and the two other sisters who were brave enough to run against her for president. "This decision was incredibly tough for all of us. We had to ask ourselves who would be our best leader, who would fight for us, and most of all — who would represent everything we stand for?

"I have nothing but absolute faith that the person who you all chose to place your faith in will far exceed your expectations. This young woman is exciting, fresh, full of ideas and even more — spunk. She's everyone's best friend, confidant, and mentor. She's been through a lot in life, more than most of us will ever face, and she isn't afraid to own every part of her life that's made her who she is."

Erin smiles, and I nearly combust trying to hold in the cheer I know is coming.

"I am proud to announce that the new president of Kappa Kappa Beta is... should I let someone else say it?"

Erin pauses, and I huff, rolling my eyes. But before I can spout off a smart-ass remark, the back doors open, and all my sisters start cheering. I frown at first, standing and cheering along with them as the brothers of Alpha Sigma pour into the room. Half of them are wearing acoustic guitars around their chests, and when Kade slides by the front row and steals a kiss from me, I laugh and bat him away, still confused.

Until I see a familiar face that I haven't seen since last semester.

Well, I'll be damned.

Kip Jackson struts in like he owns the place, and I only look at him for a split second before I find Skyler, who covers her mouth with both hands and tears up immediately. The damn sight of it gets *me* choked up and Lei pokes my ribs, making fun of me as I swat her away like I did Kade.

Damn emotions.

Kip takes Skyler's hand in his, kissing it before thrusting it up into the air. "Ladies of Kappa Kappa Beta, your new president!"

We all clap and cheer and lose our shit, and then the brothers all start swaying — some of them playing guitar, some of them singing the lyrics to "My Girl." Before long, all my sisters join in, too, and when the song finishes, Kip calls our attention back to him long enough to present Skyler with the Alpha Sigma letters on a delicate gold chain.

A lavalier.

"Skyler Thorne, you mean everything to me. You are my world. When we met earlier this year, we were both playing a game that neither of us was prepared to lose. Tricks were played, hearts were broken, but in the end — we somehow made it out alive. Together. I promised to never gamble with your heart again, and this is me showing that promise to the world. Please, make me the happiest man in the world, Ella Mae. Wear my lavalier?"

God, it's just too fucking sweet!

I'm so annoyed that I'm all teary-eyed and gooey as the room cheers again and Kip puts the necklace around Skyler's neck. Kade's eyes find mine, and he winks, giving me a shit-eating grin that tells me he sees just how emotional I am over the whole night.

Damn it all.

"Alright, bitches!" I yell, standing up before I can cry. "Let's go party! Everyone to Ralph's!"

Ashlei laughs as the rest of the sorority cheers in agreement, and then Kade sneaks up behind me, squeezing my hips. I turn, and as much as the old Jess would have thumped him on the nose or shoved him away, it's the last thing I want to do. Instead, I throw my arms around his neck and kiss him for everyone to see, both loving and hating the butterflies in my chest.

This kid was just supposed to be a distraction, a free ride, a little fun in my last semester.

And then the asshole went and stole my heart.

"Someone is all in their feels tonight," he says, kissing my neck.

"Shut up."

"It's okay to be mushy sometimes, Jess. No one will judge you for having a pulse and emotions."

"*I* am judging me," I argue.

Kade chuckles, threading his hand through mine. "Come on, let's go get you drunk. That'll take your mind off your feels. Plus," he adds, sucking my earlobe between his teeth. "Then, I can take advantage of you."

"*Finally* on date 3," I muse.

"Finally."

"We could just skip Ralph's altogether."

"But it was your idea. You just told everyone to go there."

I huff dramatically. "*Fine.* But you're driving."

That earns me a kiss on the cheek, and I lean into Kade, wrapping my arm through his as we make our way to the back of the house and out to the parking lot before making our way down Greek Row to the Alpha Sig house.

"So, classes are over, graduation in just a few days... how are you feeling?"

I sigh. "Weird."

"Going to miss all this?"

"Of course. But, as much as I'm sad, I'm excited, too. I'll have a big girl job soon, and my own apartment, and who knows what else. College has been amazing, but... I'm ready for what's next."

"And what about me?"

I tap his nose. "What about you?"

"You going to miss me, too?"

All the joking is gone, and I see the vulnerability in Kade's eyes like I've never seen it before. I pull him to a stop on the sidewalk, frowning. "I don't have to miss you. I'll still be local. I thought... I mean, I thought we'd stay together."

He lets out a long breath. "You did?"

"Of course, I did, you dummy." I shove him playfully. "What, you think I'd spend all that time and effort morphing you into my perfect little sex god just to let some other girl reap the benefits? No way."

"Hey, I was a sex god *before* you got to me. You just made me better."

"Mm-hmm, whatever you say." I lean up on my tiptoes and press a kiss to his lips. "But seriously, I want to do this. I want to keep dating and see where this goes... that is, if *you* want to. I mean, you're a junior, you still have some time here, and I don't want to hold you back from enjoying it."

"You don't hold me back from anything," he says quickly, sincerely. "You make it *better*."

"That was borderline cheesy."

"You love my cheese."

I roll my eyes, but don't deny that he's right, and after another hot, longing kiss that has me wishing we were already done partying for the night and back in his bed, we continue our walk down Greek Row.

"I just have to run inside and grab my keys. Meet you at the car?" he says when we get to the A Sig house.

I nod, pulling out my phone to text the girls. My feet carry me on autopilot to Kade's parking spot, and it's not until I'm a few feet away from it that I look up.

When I do, I drop my phone.

I can't bend to retrieve it when the glass shatters on the ground. I can't even grasp that it fell at all. I can't do *anything* but stand there as if my feet are cemented to the parking lot, staring, unblinking, unbelieving at the sight in front of me.

My heart races in my ears, pulsing in my throat, consuming me with its erratic, suffocating rhythm. It's all I can focus on, and it's the only thing keeping me upright and alive, because every other organ slowly gives out.

"Jarrett?"

His name is a gasp of a whisper on my lips, and I blink over and over, trying to unsee him, to clear the vision of him leaned up against Kade's car. It *must* be a mirage. It *must* be a hallucination.

Jarrett's eyes are hard on me, brown and endless as ever, his smooth head and sprawling tattoos covering every inch of his arms a sight for sore eyes. I still don't believe he's real, even when he pushes off the car and tucks his hands into his pockets, crossing the small space between us and stopping with just a foot left to go.

His eyes search mine, and my stomach bottoms out.

He bites his lip, and my heart squeezes to a stop before kicking back to life painfully in my chest.

He lets out a breath that reaches my lips, and I inhale it shakily, swallowing it down, my entire body shaking with the familiar scent of it.

Kade's hand on my hip jolts me back to life, and I jump at the contact, breathing heavy and nearly fainting. The only thing that stops me from going down is Kade's arms around me, and he frowns, looking back and forth between me and Jarrett while I try not to pass out again.

"Are you okay?" he asks me, and I think I nod. I think I grip onto his arms to hold myself upright. I think I keep breathing.

What happens next, I only *wish* I could convince myself wasn't real.

Because Kade looks at Jarrett, and Jarrett appraises Kade, and then he says the last thing I ever could have expected.

"Hello, brother."

After that, everything goes dark.

Skyler

"SMILE, LADIES!"

Cassie holds out her Polaroid camera as far as she can with all of us piled into Erin's queen-size bed, taking a picture with a grunt. When she pulls the photo out and starts waving it around, she frowns.

"You cut off all our faces?" I tease.

"Surprisingly, no — but I look like I'm taking a poop."

"You do not," Erin argues, stealing the picture with a smile. "We all look perfect."

It's the night before graduation for Erin, Ashlei, and Jess, and with all their families coming into town and graduation parties and campus-wide celebrations, this will be our last chance to be all together, just the five of us.

Maybe for a very long time.

My heart twists, and I hug Cassie tight. "Welp, it's just going to be me and you now, Little."

"Hey! We're not dead," Ashlei argues.

"We're not even leaving the zip code," Erin adds.

"Still, it won't be the same without you *here* here," Cassie says with a pouty lip.

We all fall quiet at that, and I roll over to squeeze Jess. "You okay over here?"

"Yeah, I'm sorry," she says on a sigh, scrubbing her hands over her tired face. "I'm trying to be present, but I'd be lying if I said I wasn't all the way fucked up right now."

"I cannot *believe* Jarrett is here," Cassie says.

"*I* can't believe Jarrett and Kade are brothers," Ashlei chimes in.

Jess just groans, rolling until her face is buried in the covers. "Just kill me now."

"What are you going to do?" Erin asks.

"Move to Mexico?" Jess answers hopefully, popping her head up long enough to say the words before she face plants in the pillows again.

I chuckle, sweeping her hair back. "It'll be okay. You're with Kade now. Jarrett lost his chance, right?"

There's a long pause, and the girls and I exchange worried glances.

"Can we just talk about something else for now?" Jess begs.

"Sure. I can join in your misery and remind you again how I fucked up the best thing to ever happen to me," Ashlei offers.

"Lei," Erin says sadly.

"I was just trying to make a joke," Ashlei says, holding her hands up. "But, honestly? I'm doing okay. I think I'm starting to accept it... at least, a little bit. I wish he would talk to me, but I can't force him to." She shrugs. "There's nothing left to do, really, but to pick myself up and move on. Starting with a new job."

"Have you been putting in applications?" I ask, letting her avoid the fact that I *know* she's not okay. Ashlei is a lot like me in that regard — when she's hurting, she doesn't want to make a big show of it. She just wants to pretend like everything is fine and that she's moving on to bigger and better things.

But we'll be here when she needs to fall.

"I haven't had to. As soon as word got out that I was leaving *Okay, Cool,* my phone started ringing off the hook. I've got offers all over Miami *and* in other states, too."

Jess leans up and glares at Ashlei. "You're *not* allowed to leave. Not right now."

Ashlei chuckles. "I'm not going anywhere, Bossy Pants."

Jess face plants into the pillows with another grunt.

"You're going to be amazing, no matter where you end up," Cassie says to Lei. "And, I agree with Jess. I just want you *all* to stay here. Forever."

"Says the one who will leave for med school," I point out.

"Well, when that happens, you all have my permission to leave, also."

We laugh at that, and Erin catches my eyes from across the bed. "So, a little birdie told me that Kip is transferring here for the spring semester?"

I bite my lip, nodding. "That little birdie would be correct. *And*, he'll be here for the summer, too."

"How?" Cassie asks with a frown.

"He's going to be working on his show... about *us*."

"As in, how you two met?" she asks.

"As in everything — how we met, our crazy dating story, the tournament, all of it. His professors loved the concept and want him to bring it to life. He has through the end of the summer to shoot the pilot season, and then he'll submit it to compete for the chance to turn it into an online series hosted through the university."

"Holy shit!" Ashlei says on a grin. "That's a big deal."

"It is," I agree. "I'm so proud of him."

"So, do you get to help with casting?" Erin asks.

I laugh. "Oh, whether he knows it or not, I will be casting *director* — especially when it comes to who plays me."

"They'll never find anyone who comes close to the real thing," Ashlei says.

"What about you, Little? What are you doing for the holidays?" I ask Cassie.

"Adam and I are going to see our families... it'll be the first time for him meeting my parents and me meeting his aunt."

"Wow, big step," Erin says.

"It is... but we're ready. We've both decided this is it — no more games, no more letting other people get between us or standing in our own way. We just want to be together. Zero drama."

"Good luck with that," Jess says, her voice muffled by the comforter.

I pat her ass sympathetically.

"But there's something I wanted to tell you guys..." Cassie continues, biting her lip. "I'm going to graduate early."

Erin cocks a brow. "Really?"

"Yeah. I'm ahead in my classes. My GPA is killer, surely enough to apply to my med schools of choice. Adam graduates next semester, and Big," she says to me, smiling. "I think I want to graduate with you. Next fall."

I beam. "One last year together."

"One last year to raise some serious hell," she agrees.

"I'm proud of you." I wrap her in a hug, and then Erin takes her turn.

"Oh, and I was thinking... I know I'm a little late now, but... what if I *did* take a Little next fall? I'd only have one semester with her, but then she could start her own family, carry on our line."

At that, Erin sits upright, her eyes welling. "Wait. Are you serious? You really want to take a Little?"

Cassie nods. "I really, really do."

Something of a squeal comes from my Big, and then there's more hugging, and Jess makes a comment under her breath about us being entirely too mushy for her current depressed state.

She gets the next round of smushes.

For a long time, we just lie there in bed, cuddling and reminiscing on the past few years. Sometimes we laugh, other times we cry, and through it all, we hold onto each other and the memories we've made.

Everything is about to change.

It feels that way at the end of every semester, but this one is unlike any I've felt before. I'm officially the *president* of Kappa Kappa Beta — a responsibility I won't take lightly — and with Jess, Lei, and Erin graduating, it'll just be me and Cassie left.

The changing of the tides is cold and unfamiliar, and it leaves me wishing I could wrap myself up in what has always been and never let it go.

But this is the way life is. It's constantly ebbing and flowing, throwing us into new waters, testing our ability to float.

One thing I know for sure is that no matter where these girls end up in the world, we'll always have each other.

And as long as that's true, there's nothing we can't survive.

"Welp," Erin says when it's almost midnight, rolling out of bed. "As much as I'd love to just pass out right now, my bag isn't going to pack itself."

I frown. "Don't you mean your entire *room*?"

Erin shakes her head. "Nope. Mom and Dad are going to take care of packing up my room, actually. They're going to store everything at their house until I get back."

Jess sits up, blowing her hair out of her face. "Back? Back from where?"

"I don't know, actually," Erin says with a blush.

The girls and I exchange looks. "Okay..." I say after a minute. "You mind telling us what the hell you're talking about?"

Erin giggles — *giggles,* like a freaking kindergartner. "Gavin and I are going on a trip."

"What?!"

We all say it at once, and then it's a chaos of questions — *Where? For how long? Is this safe?* —before Erin holds out her hands to shush us all.

"We don't know where we're going," she says with a smile. "That's kind of the point."

Jess blinks. "I'm confused."

"We're going to let two strangers in the airport choose our gate, and then we're just going to buy a ticket and... go."

"Go," Ashlei repeats. "You're just going to get on a plane and fly wherever that plane is going with whatever you can fit in that bag." She points at the suitcase Erin has unfolded on the floor.

"Yep."

"Who are you and what have you done with our best friend?" Jess asks.

Erin laughs, jumping back into the bed with us. "I haven't been this excited in a long, long time, you guys. I trust Gavin. And I know it's out of character for me but... hell, I'm about to be in *law school*. There won't be any time for fun." She shrugs. "This is all I have for a while, and he wants to make the most of it."

"I like him," I say, definitively.

"Me, too," she whispers, her eyes meeting mine. "As much as it terrifies me, me too."

Cassie sighs, throwing her arms around all our necks. "I can't believe this is it. This is our last cuddle session in this bed."

"Hey, this bed is about to be *mine*," I remind her. "Consider it open for cuddle seshes."

Cassie holds out her pinky. "Let's make a promise. Anytime anyone needs us, all they have to do is say the word, and we're right here in this bed. No matter what."

We somehow manage to all loop our pinkies in one giant knot, and then we lean forward to kiss our knuckles, laughing when we bump heads.

And again, I'm reminded that no matter how things change, no matter what bumps lie ahead, I'm surrounded by the strongest, smartest, most badass girls to ever live.

The bonds of sisterhood don't just go away with graduation... and thank God for that.

Because something tells me we're going to need each other more than ever.

TO BE CONTINUED.

About the Author

KANDI STEINER is #1 Amazon Bestseller and whiskey connoisseur living in Tampa, FL. Best known for writing "emotional rollercoaster" stories, she loves bringing flawed characters to life and writing about real, raw romance — in all its forms. No two Kandi Steiner books are the same, and if you're a lover of angsty, emotional, and inspirational reads, she's your gal.

An alumna of the University of Central Florida, Kandi graduated with a double major in Creative Writing and Advertising/PR with a minor in Women's Studies. She started writing back in the 4th grade after reading the first Harry Potter installment. In 6th grade, she wrote and edited her own newspaper and distributed to her classmates. Eventually, the principal caught on and the newspaper was quickly halted, though Kandi tried fighting for her "freedom of press."

She took particular interest in writing romance after college, as she has always been a die hard hopeless romantic, and likes to highlight all the challenges of love as well as the triumphs.

When Kandi isn't writing, you can find her reading books of all kinds, planning her next adventure, or pole dancing (yes, you read that right). She enjoys live music, traveling, playing with her fur babies and soaking up the sweetness of life.

CONNECT WITH KANDI:
NEWSLETTER: kandisteiner.com/newsletter
FACEBOOK: facebook.com/kandisteiner
FACEBOOK READER GROUP (Kandiland):
facebook.com/groups/kandilandks
INSTAGRAM: Instagram.com/kandisteiner
TIKTOK: tiktok.com/@authorkandisteiner
TWITTER: twitter.com/kandisteiner
PINTEREST: pinterest.com/authorkandisteiner
WEBSITE: www.kandisteiner.com

Kandi Steiner may be coming to a city near you!
Check out her "events" tab to see all the
signings she's attending in the near future:
www.kandisteiner.com/events

More from Kandi Steiner

The Red Zone Rivals Series
Fair Catch
As if being the only girl on the college football team wasn't hard enough, Coach had to go and assign my brother's best friend — and *my* number one enemy — as my roommate.
Blind Side
The hottest college football safety in the nation just asked me to be his fake girlfriend.
And I just asked him to take my virginity.
Quarterback Sneak
Quarterback Holden Moore can have any girl he wants.
Except me: the coach's daughter.
Hail Mary
(AN AMAZON #1 BESTSELLER)
I used to love Leo Hernandez, but that was before I hated him. And now, I have no choice but to move in with him.

The Becker Brothers Series
On the Rocks (book 1)
Neat (book 2)
Manhattan (book 3)
Old Fashioned (book 4)
Four brothers finding love in a small Tennessee town that revolves around a whiskey distillery with a dark past — including the mysterious death of their father.

The Best Kept Secrets Series
(AN AMAZON TOP 10 BESTSELLER)
What He Doesn't Know (book 1)
What He Always Knew (book 2)
What He Never Knew (book 3)
Charlie's marriage is dying. She's perfectly content to go down in the flames, until her first love shows back up and reminds her the other way love can burn.

Close Quarters
A summer yachting the Mediterranean sounded like heaven to Jasmine after finishing her undergrad degree. But her boyfriend's billionaire boss always gets what he wants. And this time, he wants her.

Make Me Hate You
Jasmine has been avoiding her best friend's brother for years, but when they're both in the same house for a wedding, she can't resist him — no matter how she tries.

The Wrong Game
(AN AMAZON TOP 5 BESTSELLER)
Gemma's plan is simple: invite a new guy to each home game using her season tickets for the Chicago Bears. It's the perfect way to avoid getting emotionally attached and also get some action. But after Zach gets his chance to be her practice round, he decides one game just isn't enough. A sexy, fun sports romance.

The Right Player
She's avoiding love at all costs. He wants nothing more than to lock her down. Sexy, hilarious and swoon-worthy, The Right Player is the perfect read for sports romance lovers.

On the Way to You
It was only supposed to be a road trip, but when Cooper discovers the journal of the boy driving the getaway car, everything changes. An emotional, angsty road trip romance.

A Love Letter to Whiskey
(AN AMAZON TOP 10 BESTSELLER)
An angsty, emotional romance between two lovers fighting the curse of bad timing.
Read Love, Whiskey – Jamie's side of the story and an extended epilogue – in the new Fifth Anniversary Edition! (https://amzn.to/3FB1B7E)

Weightless
Young Natalie finds self-love and romance with her personal trainer, along with a slew of secrets that tie them together in ways she never thought possible.

Revelry
Recently divorced, Wren searches for clarity in a summer cabin outside of Seattle, where she makes an unforgettable connection with the broody, small town recluse next door.

Say Yes
Harley is studying art abroad in Florence, Italy. Trying to break free of her perfectionism, she steps outside one night determined to Say Yes to anything that comes her way. Of course, she didn't expect to run into Liam Benson...

Washed Up
Gregory Weston, the boy I once knew as my son's best friend, now a man I don't know at all. No, not just a man. A doctor. And he wants me...

The Christmas Blanket

Stuck in a cabin with my ex-husband waiting out a blizzard? Not exactly what I had pictured when I planned a surprise visit home for the holidays...

Black Number Four

A college, Greek-life romance of a hot young poker star and the boy sent to take her down.

The Palm South University Series

Rush (book 1) FREE if you sign up for my newsletter!
Anchor, PSU #2
Pledge, PSU #3
Legacy, PSU #4
Ritual, PSU #5
Hazed, PSU #6
Greek, PSU #7
#1 NYT Bestselling Author Rachel Van Dyken says, "If Gossip Girl and Riverdale had a love child, it would be PSU." This angsty college series will be your next guilty addiction.

Tag Chaser

She made a bet that she could stop chasing military men, which seemed easy — until her knight in shining armor and latest client at work showed up in Army ACUs.

Song Chaser

Tanner and Kellee are perfect for each other. They frequent the same bars, love the same music, and have the same desire to rip each other's clothes off. Only problem? Tanner is still in love with his best friend.

Acknowledgments

THANK YOU TO MY fantastic beta team. If it weren't for y'all, the Palm South University series would not be what it is today. Your feedback this round was absolutely crucial and I could never do this without you! Thank you Trish QUEEN MINTNESS, Sarah Green, Danielle Lagasse, Carly Wilson, and Kelle Fabre. I also want to give a shout out to two members of my ARC Team who offered to read Ritual early and provide additional feedback – Lindsey Barnett and Jan Cassi. Thank you!

My support system means everything when it comes to writing this series. I always refer to PSU affectionately as "my passion project" and it truly is a labor of love that wouldn't be possible without my team holding me up. Thank you Staci Brillhart for pushing me, Jack Hamm for loving me, Sasha Whittington for believing in this series as much as me, and Momma – for always loving and supporting me no matter what.

To the angel who makes everything easier – Tina Stokes. You are a shining beacon of light in my life and I'm so fortunate to call you my friend and to have you helping me in my career, too. Thank you for all that you do.

Thank you to Elaine York of Allusion Editing & Formatting. As always, you polished this book up to shine like a gem and worked with my crazy timeline. It's always so appreciated, and I couldn't do this without you.

I am so honored to be with the amazing team at Valentine PR. To Nina, Mary, Angie, Christine and the rest of the team, thank you for thinking outside the box on ways to promote this book and others. Your time and attention mean the world to me.

To the Palm South University Discussion Group and Kandiland on Facebook – YOU ARE MY HEART. You are my family. My best friends. My everything. Thank you for being there for this crazy ride and for loving my books and characters as much as I do.

And to you, the reader. Palm South University is so close to my heart, and it means everything to me that you picked up these books and gave them a shot. Thank you. Let's hang out and be friends on the interwebs, and maybe hug IRL at a book signing one day. ;-)